REVOL
AT
ZETA DORADUS

AN ISC FLEET NOVEL

ROCK WHITEHOUSE

DEDICATION

For Terry.

Somewhere, somehow, I hope you're enjoying this.

Thanks for being a fan.

AUTHOR'S NOTE

The war with the Preeminent is over but still there are those annoying loose ends to tie up, right? Like, Preeminent SLIP messages that don't exactly make sense.

So, David is headed out to see what's brewing there, while Carol is working hard at two jobs at once. That's difficult for anyone, but, in this time, especially hard for her.

Some of you have commented on the vast cast of characters I've used in the previous books, and I think you'll find that number much reduced here. I've still supplied a dramatis personae at the back of the book, just in case.

One note on formatting: I use dialog in italics to indicate that an alien is speaking in their own language when a human is present. The idea is to set that off in a way that lets you know what's going on, when the humans in the story can't understand what's being said. Someone asked me to explain it, so, there you are.

Send me your questions and/or feedback, especially the positive stuff, at rock@iscfleet.com. I'd be glad to hear from you.

Rock Whitehouse
North Ridgeville, Ohio
May 31, 2021

CHAPTER 1

ISC Fleet Covert Observation Post
Planet Zeta Doradus (b)
Thursday, February 29, 2080, 1215 UTC (Early Afternoon Local Time)

The white star felt uncomfortably hot on the back of his neck as Senior Lieutenant David Powell crawled to the crest of the small hill he was hiding behind. Perihelion was coming, and as it approached, the heat of the day, already warm, would grow gradually worse. In just the five sols they had been on the surface, David could feel the intensity of the star increasing. He slipped his wraparound system-specific sunglasses down his nose and carefully looked over the top of the little tree-covered knoll. As he did, he was reminded that it was his new wife Carol, now working in FleetPlans, who had made sure they had the right shades. She was good at the details.

Through the pungent, thorny underbrush he could see movement on the packed dirt road about fifty meters away. It seemed to David that there were a lot of walkers today, and only a few of the huge, six-wheeled cargo wagons he'd seen the last few sols. The smallish aliens walked easily in their dull, monochromatic clothes; long, straight trousers with a simple vest or tunic covering their torso. Their movement seemed very normal to David, unlike the ostrich-like strut of the bright purple Preeminents. David thought their faces were exaggerated, a heavy brow, deeper even than a Neanderthal, that wrapped around their eyes like a hood. There was no nose to speak of, but they had a mouth about where he would expect to find it. "I guess you need the food to enter where you also have binocular vision?" he had commented to his compatriots the previous evening.

He watched their movements, holding himself motionless for a minute, then made the adjustment to the small, cylindrical recon camera he'd originally come up there to do. He took one last look down the road and slid quietly back down to confirm the change on his NetComp.

"That's much better," Professor Gabrielle Este said quietly as she unconsciously glanced up at the top of the hill, almost as if she could see over it herself. David nodded and gave her a slight grin as he drew a water bottle from his backpack and laid back against the hill. Gabrielle was well accustomed to the heat, having spent much of her professional career on her hands and knees in the desert holding a trowel, a toothbrush, or sometimes a tiny paintbrush.

As David relaxed against the hill, listening to the muffled sound of the traffic in the distance, he considered his companions. Gabrielle Este, Ph.D., 'Gabe' to those close to her, had been a successful field archeologist at Ohio State until FleetIntel asked her to help unravel the genocide at Beta Hydri. Now, she was a full-time Fleet asset. David thought she looked a little strange, what with her small frame lost in her not-quite-small-enough field camouflage uniform, and her carefully camo-painted face that distorted her delicate features. David smiled slightly at that thought, knowing the Recon Marines had prepared his face as rigorously as hers. They had done a masterful job of disguising her. She was a very pretty woman, not that anyone could tell in her current condition.

But Gabrielle was there because she had a gift for understanding alien cultures. She had somehow transferred her ability to demystify ancient desert artifacts into an insight into societies completely unlike anything Earth had ever produced. Her life partner, Ph.D. linguist Greg Cordero, was likewise something of a savant when it came to languages. He'd broken down the 'Seekers' language at Beta Hydri to the point where he could stand on a beach and have a conversation with them. With placards and hand motions, mind you, but still, a conversation. That breakthrough had been a turning point in the War, and David was still amazed at how he did it.

David smiled a little as he recalled Carol's wildly humorous imitation of Greg writing and waving at the Seekers as they 'talked.' Touch your forehead for a question! Wave the left hand for 'yes,' the right for 'no!' Carol was great at it and Greg probably laughed harder than anyone else as she acted it out.

Gabrielle and David were accompanied by two Fleet Recon Marines, their short-stock 2K7X assault weapons at the ready, keeping their own watch for any intrusion on their position.

She pulled on David's arm, pointing at his NetComp with her other hand.

"The afternoon wagons are coming through."

David nodded and carefully shifted so he could see what she was pointing at, still worried about being seen or heard or otherwise found out. Sure enough, the screen showed a long train of cargo wagons, flatbeds loaded down with barrels full of a swimming ocean delicacy craved by the Preeminent population back at Alpha Mensae. Every afternoon since they had been watching the road, about twenty wagon loads had passed this point on their way to the Preeminent spaceport about five kilometers south.

David looked at his watch. "They're late."

The 'Zeds,' as Gabrielle and Greg had labeled them during their research back at Alpha Mensae, were usually punctual, the shipments passing their observation post the same time each day. Today, they were well behind schedule. The wagons were unlikely to arrive at the spaceport before nightfall.

Once the wagons were past, all appeared normal: just the typical comings and goings of a civilized society unaware they were being watched. As evening fell around them, Gabrielle looked at David and lifted her thumb as if to hitchhike. *Time to go,* she was saying. David crawled up the rise one more time, retrieved the camera, and then followed his escorts away from the hill. It was a three-plus kilometer walk back to the Recon Shuttle they'd ridden down from *Cobra,* through the thick meadows and around the spotty woods of planet Zeta Doradus (b). They walked in silence, the Recon Marines varying their exact course each day, trying not to leave a detectable trail.

He slid down a dry creek that had cut into the wall of the ravine where the shuttle was hidden. As he stepped through the hatch, David felt as if he had been teleported from the sixteenth century to the late twenty-first. Dirt roads lined by domed, stone-walled homes with small, crude glass windows suddenly gave way to stainless steel and polished aluminum frames around flashing LEDs and brilliant, large display screens. And, hot food.

And, hot showers.

After cleaning up, David and Gabrielle sat outside to compare notes with Greg and *Cobra's* Chief Intel Officer SLT Jack Ballard. They sat on the side of the shuttle away from the Zeds' village, but with the shuttle well concealed in a ravine, there was little chance of being seen. David looked around the small, dimly lit table, feeling a bit like a kid at a campfire. Every evening after returning from the observation post, they would finish their meals around the table and then chat for a while. They could not talk for long; the short days on Zeta Doradus (b) meant short nights, too.

"So, Gabe," Jack asked, "anything new today?"

"Other than their tardiness, no. But this is the first time they've been late with a shipment. I wonder if the PG will complain."

The team had been briefed about the local Preeminent Governor by Rmah Teo Segt, son of the new head of the Preeminent government. It was Rmah's job to oversee the divesture of the three worlds the previous leader, the 'Revered First,' had conquered and enslaved. Rmah expected this governor, a loyal disciple of the First, to resist his removal. David knew Rmah was probably right, but security prevented him from saying anything more about it. Rmah and his maleParent Glur Woe Segt didn't trust the PG, and David was pretty sure he knew why.

He picked up his NetComp, glanced at it, and quickly put it down again with a frown.

Gabrielle looked across at him as she picked up her cup of decaf tea. "So, what's up with you, mister Senior Lieutenant Powell? You've been unusually quiet the last couple of days."

"I just keep wondering about—"

He was interrupted by a sharp report followed by a low rumbling sound coming from the south. It rolled in like the echoes of an intense, far-off thunderstorm.

"What the hell was that?" Greg asked. They walked around the side of the shuttle and saw yellow light reflecting off the clouds to the south, somewhere near the Preeminent spaceport. David quickly moved back inside the shuttle, pulling up a detailed map of the area on one of the large display monitors. Recon Marine Sergeant Sabrina Herrera was right behind him. Without a word, together they began looking for a safe route south to get their eyes on whatever had just happened.

The phone on the console erupted with a loud buzz, announcing a laser call from *Cobra.*

"Powell."

On the other end was the New Zealand accent of *Cobra's* commanding officer. "Powell, what the bloody hell is going on down there?"

"Good evening, Commander Evans. We don't know, sir. We heard an explosion in the distance, and now we can see fire down south. Can you see it any clearer from *Cobra?*"

"No, the damned clouds are in the way. We saw a flash on IR, and now we can see the glow from the fire, but we can't get any detail."

David looked at Sergeant Herrera, whose dark brown eyes just looked back at him, waiting for him, the officer, to take the lead.

"We're looking at options to get a look at it."

Evans paused just a second before responding. "Don't forget, Powell, we're not here."

David could hear the frown in his voice. "Yes, sir, I know."

"So, being seen is not part of the plan, right?" Herrera, who could hear Evans clearly, nodded slightly.

"Of course, sir. Sergeant Herrera is looking at the map now. I'll go over it with her and we'll check back with you before we set out. OK, sir?"

"Yes, fine. But, Powell?"

"Yes, sir?"

"You can't be found out. If Sabrina thinks there's any chance you'll be detected — by anybody — just stay put, and we'll figure it out when we can."

"Yes, sir. Anything else?"

There was a pause on the line. "Seen any old people yet?"

David smiled to himself. "Well, sir, if you could describe for me what an old Zed would look like, I'd be happy to report that for you."

He could hear Evans laughing a little. "Oh, come on, Powell. Sagging jowls, sagging belly, stiff joints, canes, walkers, boring music — you know the drill!"

"Assuming they age like we do, sir, then, no, I haven't seen any old Zeds yet."

"Keep looking for them. Rmah said there weren't any and that just strikes me as very strange."

"Yes, Commander, we'll keep looking."

David hung up the phone and went back to studying the maps with Herrera as Jack Ballard joined in. There would be very little sleep for any of them tonight.

CHAPTER 2: EIGHT WEEKS EARLIER

Hansen/Powell Quarters
Ft. Eustis, VA
Wednesday, January 3, 2080, 0600 EST

She was beautiful. There was just no denying it. Even at six AM with her hair so far up in his face that it almost made him sneeze, she was amazing.

There were some details of married life that David hadn't anticipated. Like the morning he woke up early, and there was this hand hanging there in mid-air behind her. Try as he could, half-awake, he could not make that hand move. But there was just the two of them there in the bed, so, for sure, those slightly hairy fingers had to be his very own. As he moved to gently slide out of bed, she rolled away and the hand quickly announced its displeasure at his lack of attention to its circulatory needs with an excruciating restoration of blood flow.

But, wow, she was beautiful, even as she fell off the bed laughing at his temporary agony as he danced around the room moaning.

Carol's rank as a Lieutenant Commander rated them a small house on the far edge of the facility, but it was all they needed. Three small bedrooms and a bath-and-a-half was plenty for two still-young officers. Every day for them was a new day in the adventure. Peacetime was sweet, but there was still a shit-ton of work to do. Carol had a double assignment: from seven to eleven am, she attended the Deep Space Command School; from one to five pm, she was in Plans, working under the new Chief, Commander Catherine Miller.

Who, Carol was quite sure, hated her.

Miller had been the Weapons Officer on *Dunkirk* throughout the war, and while Dunkirk had seen plenty of action, some of it costly, she had not seen the kind of direct, in-person combat Carol had experienced. Miller began the war as a new Lieutenant Commander and was promoted just as she was assigned to command Plans, a section she had worked in when she was a young Lieutenant. Carol didn't know why Miller despised her so, but her weaponized vocabulary in her rich English accent left little doubt.

David's job was simpler, if no less challenging. He was assigned to FleetIntel, with a direction to understudy the tough, slightly mysterious Frances Wilson. Frances had come to FleetIntel from the US NSA years ago, which gave her an interesting air of mystery with just a touch of threat. How much did she, and by extension, they, really know?

Most mornings, David and Carol walked to Fleet Headquarters together. Sure, it was winter in Virginia, frequently cold and miserable, but still far less horrible than where they had both grown up in the Midwest. This morning as they stepped off their small front porch, David looked at his wife.

"We're going to have to talk about it eventually."

She looked at him with surprising annoyance. "It's nothing. You had some hard nights after *Sigma*, right? And I was there for you, right? Just be here for me and I'll be fine."

David let it go for a few houses as they made a good pace in the cool early morning light. "This is different. Yeah, I had two or three hard nights. You've been at it for weeks."

"I've got this, David. I do. Can we talk about something else?"

"Sure, we can. But don't think I'm going to just ignore what you're going through."

She slipped her arm in his, slowing their pace just a little. "I don't want you to ignore it. I want you to let me handle it."

"Don't ask me to just watch you struggle with this."

"I'm not, really, I'm not."

David let the topic of her sleepless and restless nights drop, and the conversation moved on to Carol's work in the Command School, which was going well, and her frustration with her new boss in Plans, which was not. Carol thought it plain that David's new boss, Admiral Fiona Collins, who was the previous head of FleetPlans, was a far superior leader.

She squeezed his hand tightly just before they split in front of the HQ building. Then Carol headed for the Command School next door, and David into the main HQ building and downstairs to FleetIntel.

Despite the early hour, Frances Wilson was already at her desk, reviewing the last 24 hours of SLIP intercepts and locations. The ability to detect and locate the Preeminent's FTL SLIP communications had been a major break in the war. Looking back, Frances thought that breakthrough alone might have decided the conflict. Since the end of the war, she suspected that not all the Preeminent forces were accounted for, and to her, that left open the possibility of some kind of follow-on attack, either on the Fleet or the new leaders at Alpha Mensae. New admiral Fiona Collins doubted that there was much of a threat. Still, she trusted Frances' instincts enough to keep her watching for more evidence. Frances took her assignment as David's mentor seriously, and the search for any residual threat from the Preeminent seemed like the perfect training ground for her student.

David flopped into the aged leather chair in the corner of her office. "Good morning, Mrs. Wilson."

Frances looked skeptically at David, then at the chronometer by her door. "You're early again."

David nodded. "Yes, ma'am. Carol's classes start at seven, so I just walk down with her."

"I see. Well, try to remember, Mister Powell, that you are young and a newlywed. Don't waste it."

Her deadpan delivery only added to the surprise twist in her message. Frances was all work at work, but clearly, she remembered what it was like to be twenty-five.

"Yes, ma'am. I will try to keep that in mind."

"Meantime, I have a project for you."

Frances had previously laid out for David her suspicions about the Preeminent. Today she sent him a large batch of SLIP intercepts beginning a few weeks before the end of the war. He now had location, time, and duration of about five thousand messages. Frances' instructions were to find the pattern, if there was one, and see if any of it was unexpected.

After the requisite detour to the commissary for an extra-large dark roast, David retired to his small office next to Frances' and started sorting through the messages. This task would be both tedious and vital, and therefore typical of intelligence work.

FleetIntel Plans Division
Ft. Eustis, VA
Monday, January 8, 2080, 1330 EST

Chief of Plans Commander Catherine Miller looked across her desk at Carol, skepticism clear on her face. "Just how old are you, Hansen?"

"Twenty-six, ma'am."

"Somewhat young for a Lieutenant Commander, don't you think?"

Carol's defenses were immediately up, but she answered in a neutral enough tone. "Perhaps, yes, but these things happen in war."

Miller shook her head slightly. "It may please CINC to create you comets, but it makes a mockery of those of us who've been here for a decade."

"Comets, ma'am?"

"That's what the rest of us call you bright little fast movers. You, and Smith, and a few others. Melville, perhaps. All Yanks, for whatever that means."

Carol paused, wondering how, or if, she should respond to the insult. For the first time, she looked carefully at the woman seated across the desk from her. She was probably thirty-three years old, at most. Her full blond hair was cut relatively short and brushed back, which Carol had to admit was good for her angular features and bright blue eyes. But what anyone noticed most about Miller was the accent, the full-throated I-went-to-Oxford-and-you-didn't English accent.

Finally, Carol said, "With respect, ma'am, we didn't make these decisions. CINC and FleetPers determined our promotions."

"Yes, yes, I know," she said dismissively. "I just hope you're up to it."

Miller shifted in her chair, then picked up her NetComp. "We've just finished a conflict in the southern sky that, in my opinion, took too long because we had not carefully examined the habitable stars in that region." Miller looked up, waiting for a response from Carol. When none came, she continued. "The miners have done better in the northern sky, but I am still not satisfied."

Carol nodded her understanding. "Yes, ma'am."

"I want a list of potentially habitable stars with declinations greater than, say, minus fifteen degrees, that the miners have not yet examined. You'll need to consult with RussMine, Galactic, and Systemwide to get their latest data."

"Yes, ma'am. Did you have a distance in mind?"

"Fifty light-years should cover it, I should think."

"Yes, Commander. Anything else?"

"That will do for now. Dismissed."

Carol rose and returned to her workstation. The star search was simple: just position, distance, age, and spectral type. From there, pleasing Miller would be a far more difficult task.

Near the Preeminent Spaceport
Zeta Doradus (b)
Saturday, January 6, 2080, 0030 UTC (Late Afternoon Local Time)

Riaghe Kutah crept forward carefully through the undergrowth that bordered the Violets' enormous landing field. He'd been coming there every two suns for a long time, spying on the hated invaders just as the sun set behind him. Kutah despised everything about them: their bright purple plumage, their deadly weapons, even their odd backwards-knee walk. But he especially hated their arrogance and casual brutality. *They shouldn't be here,* he thought. *Someday, we will be rid of them.*

Today, there was no massive silver ship on the field. There had not been one for many suns. Until just before the first snows of the previous winter, the shiny metal giants had landed on one sun, loaded the latest batch of the swimming deleelinosh from their massive storage tanks the next, and departed on the third sun. There would be two or three suns with no activity, then another behemoth would arrive and the process would repeat.

So strange, Kutah thought to himself. *What has happened to them?*

He focused his telescope to see what the Violets were doing, but there was no one around. That, too, was unusual. Even on off days with no ship, they would be working around the storage facility or patrolling the outside of the field. They'd almost caught him twice, but he'd managed to slip far enough back under the thick cover and escape.

This time he easily slipped away; his small frame perfect for slinking under the low thorny bushes that covered the last fifty meters of the forest floor. Once clear of the Violets' perimeter, he walked quickly back to his village, where the Elder was waiting impatiently for his report.

Elder Riaghe Wocos had resisted the Violets when they first arrived about fifty snows ago. But their ability to kill efficiently from a distance quickly overcame any resistance, and the Guild had reluctantly submitted to the demands of their rule. Wocos had no idea where the Violets had come from or how they had traveled to his home planet. Nor did he care. His only interest was keeping them happy and thereby keeping as many of his clan alive until something could be done to remove them. Wocos and the other clan Elders gave the Violets what they wanted, feigning the respect and obedience they demanded, but never actually believing them to be anything but alien invaders.

Kutah trotted breathless into the village hall, anxious to make his report. "There is still no ship on the field!"

Wocos frowned. "Twenty suns with no cargo ship! What are they doing with the deleelinosh?"

"I could not tell. There were no Violets in sight, which is very unusual. There were none working on the field or walking the border."

"Something happened before last winter, something that weakened them and they have not recovered themselves." Wocos said, thoughtfully, looking absentmindedly towards the Violets' enormous field several kilometers away.

Kutah clenched his fist in agreement. "Yes, I believe that is true."

Wocos turned back to Kutah, a decision clear on his face. "I will take this to our GuildMember, Kutah. Thank you."

"Do you think this means the time is near?"

Wocos raised his three fingers to discourage his young spy. "Patience, Kutah. Only the Guild can decide what we may do."

"It has already taken them too long." Kutah took a deep breath, blowing out his anger. It wasn't Wocos' fault the Violets were still here. "Shall I continue to observe?"

Wocos ignored his young spy's impertinence. "Yes. Do you think you can safely watch them every sun? You must not be caught."

Kutah waved off the Elder's concerns. "I have a safe route in and a different route back out. Yes, I can go every sun."

"Then do so, and bring me your report as soon as you can."

After Wocos turned away to begin his walk north to see the GuildMember, Kutah made his way to his family's home clutch, a small group of houses a few rows off the central courtyard of his Riaghe clan village. As he stood on the rise just behind his home, he could see the Kouhti and Niocli villages to the north and fires of the Saolki to the east.

The sun was setting behind the small tree-topped hill just to the west, and as it did, Kutah heard his friend Riaghe Tefin approaching. It was always good to see Tefin, but far better to see his sister, Udoro. "Tefin! What have you to say for yourself this sun?"

Tefin smiled at his oldest friend. For many snows they had been almost inseparable companions. "I have worked at my job, Kutah, while you have been off on your adventure!"

Kutah laughed. "It's not such a great adventure, Tefin, if it can get me killed."

Tefin dropped next to his friend on the crest of the small hill. The sun was just disappearing below the long horizon, the sky golden above it.

"You keep disappearing like that, Kutah-boy, and when repro time comes no one will remember you!"

Kutah's shoulders fell slightly. "I might get invited, or I might not. It doesn't matter." Kutah said nothing more as he stared at the point where the star had just disappeared.

"Udoro?"

"Yes, as you well know, I would give up repro altogether to spend all my snows with your sister."

"I do know. But I also know you cannot repro with her."

"Yes, I don't need to be reminded."

"What will you do if she gets a license? She'll have to—"

"Shut up, Tefin. I know what will happen. I just don't want to think about that right now." Kutah immediately regretted snapping at his old pal, but he was tired, a little afraid, and it just came out.

Tefin touched his friend gently, expressing his sympathy. "So, tell me what you saw today."

Kutah told him about the empty field, the lack of activity, but not much more. He'd already told the Elder everything, and now the story felt old and stale. The thought of Udoro leaving for repro had taken hold of his mind, and he couldn't focus on anything else.

FleetIntel Plans Division
Ft. Eustis, VA
Monday, January 8, 2080, 0930 EST

Carol presented Commander Miller her list of stars, explaining where each was and why it was a reasonable candidate.

"There are fifty stars in the region you specified that meet current Fleet astrometric criteria as suspects. The nearest twenty-nine have been visited or examined remotely by the miners well enough to rule them out. That leaves twenty-one, beginning at right around forty light-years, for us to examine." Carol took a breath. "We're still sketchy on detecting habitable planets at that distance, so I have no further data that I can use to eliminate them."

"Fine, twenty-one it is, then. Now, how long will it take to check these out?"

"I don't know. That was not part of your assignment to me."

Miller dropped the NetComp in frustration. "What do we call this division, again, Hansen?"

"Fleet Plans."

"Good, correct. And what is it that we do here?

"Mission Planning."

"Excellent answer!" she exclaimed sarcastically. "Did you notice it is not Fleet *Research*?"

Carol, stung by Miller's attitude, didn't respond.

"What I expected, Lieutenant Commander Hansen," Miller's tone made her rank seem an insult, "was for you to bring me a set of options for how we could examine these suspect systems."

Carol paused just a second before answering. "That was not clear to me from our previous conversation, ma'am."

"Well, it should be clear enough now, don't you think? Get back to your desk, Hansen, and get me a proposal to recon these systems."

Carol thought for a moment as Miller looked out the window to the courtyard outside.

"Yes, ma'am. What constraints did you have in mind, Commander?"

Millers' eyes snapped back to Carol. "Constraints?"

"Yes, ma'am. Am I to assume a single ship tour, or one ship per star, or something in-between? Are you looking for the fastest resolution or the most efficient?"

"I suspect both extremes are undesirable. Apply some reasonable number of ships and see where the tradeoffs lie."

"Yes, ma'am. I will need a few days."

"Fine. Be ready to present your options to me by Friday." Miller leaned forward in her chair. "Are we clear on this assignment now, Hansen?"

"Yes, ma'am. If I have any other questions, I will check back with you."

"Just get it done. You have all you need. That will be all, Hansen."

Carol returned to her desk angry, hurt, and frustrated. She dropped into her chair with an audible sigh and a thud that attracted the notice of the officers on either side of her. "Oh, sorry," she said quietly.

The ensign to her right asked quietly, "Are you all right, Commander?"

The lieutenant to her left responded without looking up. "She'll be fine. She's just been Millered for the first time."

Despite her frustration, Carol had to smile at that.

The ensign just replied, "Oh, yeah? Ouch."

Carol began working on her list, looking for stars that might make logical groupings by position and distance. If she could break the job up into four or five lesser tasks, the AI trip planner might be able to find an efficient route.

Or, she thought, she could just dump in the whole list and see what it spat out. There would be a certain evil satisfaction about that, just letting the supposedly omniscient planner plan. But that wasn't Carol's way, so she went back to work. If there was a route, she'd find it.

Somehow.

ISC Fleet HQ, FleetIntel Division
Ft. Eustis, VA
Tuesday, January 9, 2080, 1430 EST

David had spent several days staring at the spreadsheet on his workstation. He'd mined and sliced and diced the SLIP intercept data until he felt his eyes would bleed.

Then, all at once, he saw something new; something so shocking that he didn't believe himself at first.

"If that's right...then...they must have..." he mumbled to himself as he rearranged the messages, adding new columns for time and distance. He resorted it several times, each time getting closer to proving his hunch. He leaned hard on what he had learned about SLIP from Lloyd, the oddball Forstmann Propulsion Inc. engineer who had helped invent it. There was no noise in SLIP, Lloyd had said. Any signal in a SLIP channel was non-natural. *Anything.*

Yes, his hunch was paying off. The data looked right. So now, he could begin to look for what Frances sent him after.

It took another day, but finally, David saw a pattern that worried him. And, excited him.

He sent the worksheet to Frances Wilson and headed for her office next door.

"I think I see something," he said as she opened the document.

"OK, see what?"

"Well, two things, actually."

"OK?"

"First, almost half the messages we've copied from them are short, a second or less."

"Yes, I know that."

"I don't think those are messages, exactly."

Frances looked hard at him. "So, what are they, exactly?"

David smiled. "Acknowledgements."

Shock covered Frances' face. "What?"

"Acks, Frances. Return messages confirming receipt."

Frances kept her eyes on him, unblinking. "Explain."

"We can associate certain SLIP channels with Preeminent locations."

"Yes."

"But from what I see here, when a SLIP message goes from, say, a ship on channel 20 to a place on channel 76, there is a short response on the receiver's channel."

"76 in your example."

"Right. So, since we know the time and location of every message, we can calculate the time an acknowledgment would be sent from any potential receiver."

"And if you can associate the ack with the message, you can infer who the receiver was?"

"Yes. It helps that we know the channels for their static locations. I mean, after all, there aren't that many. So, we can calculate when that receiver should have responded and see if there is such a message."

"So, David, am I to understand that we can now determine not just the source but also the destination of a Preeminent message?'

"In most cases, yes. Not all messages seem to have received an acknowledgment. I don't know what that means."

"You said two things."

"Well, now that I can tell who's talking to whom, there's an unusual pattern of messages from a single deep-space location, on several channels, to and from one other transmitter. I don't see anything like it anywhere else."

Frances looked up from the spreadsheet. "Don't keep me in suspense, Powell."

"Zeta Doradus."

She shrugged and looked back at his list. "And why is this not routine traffic?"

David smiled, the small smile of a sleuth who's found the critical clue. "Overall, there are very few messages from either location back to Alpha Mensae, and none to that way-station that Carol wiped out. They're communicating among themselves, not to Armada headquarters, or anyone else." David took a moment to think. He didn't want to leave anything out. "Also, it's ongoing. Most Preeminent traffic stopped at the end of the war. These guys are still talking."

Frances set the NetComp down on her desk without taking her eyes off David's analysis. "How did we miss this, again?"

"Well, there isn't *that* much traffic between them. Given the overall volume of Armada messages we've intercepted, it's not obvious until you start to filter out exactly who's talking to who, and especially who they're *not* talking to, and when."

Frances flipped through the document. "And, discover that you can tell who the recipient of a message is."

"Yes, that's true."

Frances looked at David for a moment, realizing that she had acquired an asset far more valuable than she had previously imagined. She set down the NetComp. "So, where is this place?"

"The deep-space location is down past Alpha Mensae, about three light-years from Zeta Doradus."

"How many ships?"

"Six, that I could identify. There could be more, I suppose."

Frances switched screens, looking back at the analysis David and Rich Evans had made of the Preeminent's enslaved systems. "Zeta Doradus is listed as a stable situation. We're not planning to go there for some time."

"I'd have to say that assessment is no longer operative. Something is brewing there, something secret that has to do with at least six ships that are unaccounted for."

"Yes, I agree." Frances looked off into the distance for a few seconds.

"So, what now?" David asked.

"Now, we go see Collins." Frances stood and walked down the hall to Fiona's office, with David close behind. The door was open, and the discussion was pretty brief. What she heard forced Fiona to call a meeting of the entire staff for later that afternoon.

Fiona watched with interest and amusement as her staff gathered around 'The Table.' No one seemed to know just how long it had been here in the Intel conference room, but it proudly displayed its years of service with numerous dents and nicks and not a few beverage stains. Some said it had been secretly pilfered from the Library of Congress, others that it was found on the street, destined for a landfill, or maybe a bonfire. Whatever its true heritage, it was now as much a part of Intel culture as the people, almost another character in their collective story: solid, unmoving, always there when needed.

David Powell's discovery of a suspicious communications pattern worried Fiona enough to 'gather the troops' for a review of his findings. She admired her staff; both those who had been there since before the war, and the others who had transferred in more recently. Their morning status updates at 'The Table' were a long-standing ritual, but this late-afternoon assembly was unusual.

As the Chief of FleetIntel, Fiona's place was at the 'head' of the table, with her Deputy Chief Senior Lieutenant Ann Cooper on her right and Frances on her left. David, the most junior member, would be at the foot of the table, opposite Fiona.

"OK, Lieutenant Powell," Fiona said, smiling and leaning back in her chair. "Make your case."

David started by describing the task Frances had given him, then presented his discovery of the acknowledgment messages.

There was a gasp in the room.

"Holy hell, how did we miss that?" Ann said quietly.

"Well, Lieutenant," David answered, "our SLIP systems don't do that. I mean, it's a really bad idea, right? It reveals location and hints at message content, both of which we know are dangerous. But that just seems to be how their system is designed."

David then went directly to the fifty messages that he had fished out of the thousands of intercepts the Fleet had obtained.

Gentle, motherly Ann Cooper started the inquisition from her seat next to Fiona. "So, what makes these fifty so different than any others? I mean, I love that you found the acks, but I'm not seeing that these messages are such a big deal."

"As I said, they're talking among themselves, not to headquarters, and still talking well after the war is over."

"You saw that in no other set of messages?" another analyst asked.

"I did not."

"Did you look?" she challenged.

"Yes, I did." David was beginning to wonder if he was really ready for this discussion. "Just to be clear, there was no bias on my part towards Zeta Doradus. I was tasked to look for unusual patterns in the intercepts, and this is what I found."

"Yeah, right," Lieutenant Weeks, replied. Weeks was a more recent addition to FleetIntel. "But even assuming these are as you say, they could just be old shipmates whining about how they got their asses kicked, right? It doesn't have to be some dark conspiracy."

David paused before responding. Craig Weeks was a competent, tough officer, and he had a point. He'd been hard on David before. Weeks still seemed to have a chip on his shoulder from being transferred off *Intrepid* by Joanne Henderson in favor of Ben Price early in the war. The fact that the transfer might have saved his life apparently didn't register with him.

"That is possible, yes. But, if that was a common practice in the Preeminent Armada, I would expect to see it with other groups of ships. We don't see that at all."

"Back to how unique these are," Ann responded. "I mean, we copied so many messages; how sure can we really be that these are so unusual? I'm just wondering if you really have the data set you think you do."

David forced himself to not look to Frances for help. She had yet to speak up, which David took to mean it was up to him to convince his peers that his conclusions were correct. She was not going to bail him out. *So much the better,* he thought.

"I started with the subset Frances gave me, but I applied the same algorithm to the full dataset of intercepted messages, so there was no selectivity there. I had everything there is to have. Again, I looked for patterns of messages that don't look like others and don't make sense as regular command-and-control comms."

David took a breath, then pushed on.

"There is a general suspicion around here that not all Preeminent ships are accounted for. I think these messages to and from Zeta Doradus are exactly what we might expect to find if there really was some kind of resistance still out there."

"That is not a universal opinion, Lieutenant," Ann Cooper said. "Many of us are skeptical that anything is actually missing."

"Yes, Lieutenant, I know. I share a bit of that skepticism, but I am much less skeptical with the discovery of these messages. I know it's not hard evidence. I know. But it is evidence that something odd is going on, and we know at least six Preeminent ships and one major ground facility are involved. I think that deserves investigation."

There was a silence after David's response. Fiona looked around the Table. "Any other questions?"

After a moment, Weeks leaned forward. "Solid work, Powell. It's suspicious as hell."

"I should say so!" Ann added. Turning to Fiona, she said, "We should get this in front of CINC as soon as we can."

"I'll get us on his calendar." Fiona looked around the Table once more. "OK, that's all. Thanks, everyone."

David remained in his chair at the bottom of the Table as the others filed out. Frances waited with him from her seat, one removed from Fiona. Once everyone else was gone, he looked at Frances. "That was harder than I expected it to be."

Frances didn't smile. "The challenge, David, is how to adequately question what we think we know. We argue to find the truth, to test our assumptions, and scrub out our biases. Whatever small doubts we have must be brought out in the open, examined carefully, and then either confirmed or disposed of."

David spread his arms wide. "Weeks all but called me stupid."

"No, he gave you a hard kick in the assumptions to see if they were solid. They were."

"Is this, like, some rite of passage? I mean, I know I'm the new kid."

Frances shook her head. "You will find over time that any important research report is going to get the same treatment. Yours, mine, even the Chief's status reports to CINC are sometimes reviewed if she thinks she needs it."

They got up and left the conference room. David was surprised to find Craig Weeks waiting in the rickety extra chair in David's small office. Weeks had pushed him hard in the review.

Weeks grinned. "Nothing personal, Powell. OK?"

"Yeah, that was tough."

"Think of it like a test drive. We need to be sure all the options work, the windows open and close, and the autopilot works."

David had to smile a little at that. "I'm just glad I got through it."

"You did great. It's a guess, I know, but it's a pretty solid guess." Weeks leaned forward, the old chair creaking as he did. "You're still new here, David. I know the feeling myself. But you belong here. Don't wonder about that like I did. Just do your thing, and you'll be fine."

"Thanks, Craig. I appreciate the support."

Weeks stood to leave. "No sweat. Lunch tomorrow?"

"Sure, I can do that."

David closed his door after Weeks was gone and slumped in his chair. He felt drained, more so than he could ever recall. He could feel perspiration cooling down the back of his neck. But it had ultimately worked out.

Next, he'll only have to convince CINC, OPS, Plans, and who the hell knows who else.

No sweat.

Kutah's Observation Post
Zeta Doradus (b)
Tuesday, January 9, 2080, 1800 UTC (Late Afternoon Local Time)

Riaghe Kutah had a thorn in his side. Well, it was more in his back, actually. But wherever, it was stuck in there pretty hard and the pain made him wince. Kutah's larger problem was that he had another twenty meters to crawl to get to his observation post, and if he pushed forward any harder, he might get a deep wound and make a lot more noise. He was annoyed with himself that he had been careless enough to get hung up on one of the large spikes that stuck out below the shrubs. He'd been here dozens of times before without getting himself impaled. Why now?

He had to be very quiet. The Violets seemed to be patrolling more carefully than they had in the last few six-days. So, he squirmed backward far enough to dislodge the small spear from his skin, then adjusted himself slightly and made the last distance to the edge of the undergrowth. He pulled out his small telescope as the stinging pain in his back began to subside.

He had been able to see the Violet ship through the trees for the last kilometer, but now that he was on the edge of the landing field, its actual dimensions became clear. Their shiny silver ships were impossible: taller and longer than anything anyone had ever seen before. It was clearly made of some kind of metal, but nothing that he or his people knew about. Nothing that came out of the iron forges up north ever looked like that.

The Violets' weapons were likewise beyond understanding, firing hot bolts of something that could easily kill on contact. Even a near-miss could result in a severe burn. They could kill from a distance of perhaps fifty meters, but beyond that, their weapons were less accurate and less lethal. There were wild rumors among the clans that thinkers and metalworkers and chemists were working on something to counter their power. But, as yet, Kutah had not heard of anything new.

He stopped thinking about all this as he heard Violet footsteps nearby. He shrank back as they strutted along the edge of the field, holding his breath as their strange, backward-bending legs went by. He froze as they stopped a few paces past him, their heads suddenly raised.

"I smell something, 52845. It wasn't here on our last round."

Kutah heard them talking, an alien noise filled with guttural grunts and whistles, a sound unlike anything on his home planet. He began carefully pulling back from the edge as they hesitated.

"Yes, I smell it, too. Blood."

"What is it?"

"Native, I think. Smells like when we swatted them for being lazy."

"Enticing. Have we tried any native meat?"

"The Governor forbids it. He thinks they might be poisonous."

Kutah breathed very slowly, controlling his heart rate best he could as the Violets continued to talk.

"I don't smell it anymore. The wind has changed. Let's see what's back there."

As the Violets turned back towards him, Kutah panicked, scrambling quickly back from his post, deeper into the forest underbrush. As he did, he re-snagged the thorn he'd just removed, pulling the low shrub sideways and making a loud noise as it snapped back. He heard raised voices from behind just before the tree beside him exploded in flame. He dove to the ground and crawled sideways for a few meters, then got back up and ran down his backup path, hot bolts striking all around him. After about sixty meters, there were enough trees that the Violets could not see him anymore. He could hear them trying to pursue him through the undergrowth, but their size and the sharp undergrowth worked against them, and he was able to get clear.

After a hundred meters, he stopped to catch his breath and listen. The Violets were still coming, but slowly. If he kept moving, he'd be safe. He got back to his usual path and headed for his home village.

The Elder was waiting for him. Kutah told him the whole story, from thorn to hasty escape. All Riaghe Wocos seemed to care about was the ship. Disappointed, Kutah headed home, only to be met by Riaghe Udoro.

She looked at him intently. "You're hurt! What happened?"

Only now did Kutah see the blood staining the side of his shirt. "Just a thorn. I'll be fine."

"Come with me!" she ordered as she seized his hand and pulled him towards her home. Once inside, she took a cloth and cleaned the wound, a long gash just under his shoulder. She smiled as she worked in the healing herbs, much to Kutah's displeasure. "I hate to see anything mar your beauty, Kutah. You must be more careful."

Kutah heard the real meaning of her comment. "We all show the price of our snows, Udoro. You and I will be no different than the rest." She ran her arms around him, pulling him close to her.

"We will always be different than the rest, Kutah."

He held her arms in his for a few seconds, then pulled them away as he stood and redressed. "I should go. Tefin will want a full report."

"Yes, my little brother thrives on your adventures. Perhaps I should go with you next time?"

"I don't know. I am safe, or, I *was* safe, but I am not sure I should take a female there."

"As if I cannot walk so far? You think I cannot be quiet enough?"

Kutah waved off her anger. "That is not the question. You are taller and wider than either Tefin or me. I'm worried that you would become entangled in some of the small areas I crawl through."

Udoro was silent for a moment. "I would see them for myself, Kutah. I would see the Violets' giant vessels."

"And the Violets themselves?"

"Those I have seen. But, yes, I have never seen them up close, either."

Kutah was unmoved. "And are you ready to trade all your snows for that one glimpse?"

"You will protect me, brave Kutah. I will always be safe with you."

He looked at her for a long moment, then turned to leave. At the door, he looked back at her.

"Next sun, I will see whether it is safe. If so, perhaps you can go with me after that."

She rushed to the door to embrace him, touching him gently on the back of his neck. He felt her touch go through to his innermost self, an almost irresistible craving surging in him. But he turned to her and said,

"Not now, Udoro. I need rest, and Tefin won't let me sleep until he has his report."

She gently let go and stepped back. "As you say. I am here, Kutah. I will always be here."

Kutah looked at her for a second, then turned, closing the heavy wooden door behind him. *If only it were true,* he thought as he walked to the little hill where Tefin certainly waited.

Office of the Fleet Commander
Ft. Eustis, VA
Wednesday, January 10, 2080, 0900 EST

After reading Fiona Collins' assessment of the SLIP intercept data David and Frances had found, CINC Connor Davenport called in his operational brain trust to decide what to do about it. *Intrepid* was in orbit, back a week ago from a diplomatic trip to Inor, so he called Joanne Henderson down to join her old boss Fiona Collins and the others. CINC knew Joanne's experience at Beta Hydri and Alpha Mensae would be valuable. The truth was, if he had to send a cruiser out there right away, he'd prefer it was *Intrepid.*

David found a chair along the wall, behind and slightly to the right of Frances. She would be the one really leading the discussion, with Fiona there in support. Carol's new boss in Plans, CDR Catherine Miller, and FleetOps Admiral Patricia Cook rounded out the group. After his customary greetings and small talk, CINC moved on to the subject of the meeting.

"I've read the analysis from Fiona's group and I believe there is no question but we must act on it. If there is some kind of secret resistance group based at Zeta Doradus, it could be dangerous for us."

Fiona shifted in her chair. "And for the new government at Alpha Mensae. We need to get some direct intelligence on this, sir. We should get *Cobra* there as soon as we can, map the populated area and get the overall lay of the land."

"And check out the way station," Frances added immediately.

"Yes," Fiona responded, "exactly. David, what can you tell us about that?"

David unconsciously sat up straighter in his chair, taking a second to formulate his thoughts as he addressed himself to CINC. "Well, sir, it's clear from the SLIP traffic that there are at least six transmitters located somewhere about three light-years from Zeta Doradus. There's nothing there, astronomically speaking, so we've designated the position as Deep Space X, or DSX for short. We think DSX is something like Enemy Station: just somewhere to congregate and get food and gas."

CINC smiled. "I see. Where is *Cobra* now and how soon can Evans get to DSX?"

Fiona looked at her NetComp. "I did some quick calculations, but Plans will need to give you the exact numbers. Anyhow, Evans is currently at the enslaved planet at Zeta-1 Reticuli. It will take nearly two and half days to get a message to him. Then, six days or so to DSX, figure a day or two there, then two and half more to Zeta Doradus." Fiona took a breath, "All up, I think Evans can be at Zeta

Doradus somewhere around the end of January, maybe a day or two into February, depending."

"Very well. What then?"

Fiona took a second to look out the large windows of CINC's office at the snow accumulating on the sash.

"Gabrielle Este and Greg Cordero are still at Alpha Mensae, researching the conquered systems." She turned back to CINC. "If we're going to Doradus now, we will need their expertise. They must make it a priority to get whatever information Asoon and Rmah have on the culture there."

"And," Fiona said, "I will need to send someone from FleetIntel to lead."

CINC nodded. "You have someone in mind?"

"Yes. They will need to be on the initial recon team, too."

Operations Admiral Cook spoke up. "So, someone will need to take your asset out to Alpha Mensae, get the academics, and then move on to Doradus, correct?"

Joanne smiled. "I think, Admiral, that's where I come in."

Cook laughed. "Yes, Captain, I suppose it is."

CINC looked up at his senior officers. "What do we say to Segt about this abrupt decision to relieve Zeta Doradus? He's going to wonder what's behind it."

"Nothing," Miller answered coldly.

CINC looked at her skeptically. "Go ahead, Commander."

"Segt is obligated to cooperate with the liberation of all enslaved worlds, sir. We decide what the priority is, he doesn't."

"So," Fiona asked, "we just tell him that we've suddenly decided to start liberations now instead of later and leave it at that?"

"Yes. Tell Segt it's an area we've previously planned to explore, tell him it's just more convenient. Whatever." Joanne and Fiona exchanged a surprised look that was not lost on CINC. Miller never noticed.

"In this case, Commander," Joanne began in her best didactic tone, "we must have a plausible explanation, or the Preeminent will be alerted." She pointed at Fiona. "Intel's analysis indicates there may be some remnant of the Armada willing to resist us. It's quite likely they have agents or contacts back on Alpha Mensae. We can't tip our hand that we're on to this new station or whatever role the facility at Zeta Doradus plays."

Miller looked surprised. "Yes, Captain, I see."

FleetOps Admiral Cook took over. "Very well. We need *Cobra* to map Zeta Doradus. We need to get our academics at Alpha Mensae to prepare to liberate the Zeta Doradus culture. We also need to examine this unknown facility close by." She turned to Miller. "Commander Miller, I need a plan for *Cobra* and *Intrepid* to complete these tasks, as we've described, with logistic requirements and a timeline. Let's have that by close of business tomorrow. We won't be able to get the logistics in motion before then, anyhow."

"Yes, ma'am."

Cook turned to Henderson. "Captain Henderson, I want you to begin preparations for a long trip. Figure Alpha Mensae, then significant time at Zeta Doradus, then home."

"Yes, Admiral. I should be able to make a reasonable estimate from that." She turned back to Miller. "Send me your proposed plan as soon as it's drafted. I want to review it before it's finalized."

Miller looked at her a moment before answering. "Really, Captain, with all respect, I am FleetPlans now, not you, and I will issue the plan to OPS and CINC when we have completed it."

CINC broke the uncomfortable silence that followed. "Commander, submit the plan to Captain Henderson as she has requested. Copy Admiral Collins as well. Please."

Miller nodded stiffly, saying nothing.

The meeting broke up quickly after that, and David walked back to FleetIntel with Fiona and Frances. As they entered their section, Fiona motioned them to join her in her office.

"What the hell was that?" she asked.

"Prickly much?" David answered.

"Yeah, I'd say so," Fiona responded.

"Well, don't forget she was outnumbered, and very new in her job," Frances said. "The previous head of FleetPlans, and her deputy, who is now a ship commander, were questioning her opinions. She had to feel a little defensive."

"Yes, I suppose so," Fiona said. "I'll call her."

David shook his head. "I suggest you *not* do that, ma'am. It might just make the situation worse."

Fiona paused, her phone in her hand. "Fine, we'll leave it alone."

About this same time, Catherine Miller was in her own office, fuming. *Henderson should stick to her own job and leave me the hell alone!*

She looked again at the task CINC had given her, deciding that it would be a chance to see what Hansen could do on short notice. Carol came in immediately after Miller's call.

"I have a new job for you." She handed over her NetComp with the trip requirements.

"Yes, ma'am. I'll start on it right away."

"I want it by noon tomorrow, so get the AI on it and then bring me the three best options."

"Yes, ma'am."

"Don't forget the supporting details, Hansen. Logistics, weapons, whatever they may need."

"Yes, Commander, I understand."

"OK, get on it."

Carol understood a dismissal when she heard one, so she stood and returned to her own workstation. She reviewed the rough requirements, breaking them down into discreet, ordered steps for the AI trip planner to crunch. Before long, she saw a problem and returned to the Commander's office.

"What is it, Hansen?"

"The requirements are incomplete, Commander."

"How, exactly?"

"Well, *Intrepid* is taking an Intel asset to Alpha Mensae to pick up Gabrielle and Greg, then go on to Zeta Doradus. But Collins wants that asset on the initial covert recon team."

"Go on."

"So, *Intrepid* will need to arrive at Doradus secretly and much earlier than announced. We'll need some kind of cover story for why they are taking longer than necessary to get there after they pick up Gabe and Greg. Also, how long does *Cobra* need to map Zeta Doradus (b) before *Intrepid* arrives? And, how long do they all plan to be there after that? I'm also concerned about the time for *Cobra* to check out this new DSX. Like ES, it's out in the middle of nowhere. It might not be easy to spot, and we only have a rough approximation, about a tenth of a light-year, of where it is. None of that is spelled out in the requirements."

Miller paused, realizing that Hansen was right in her concerns. "Anything else?"

"Yes. They'll need the F-star wrap-around sunglasses for those going to the surface. Zeta Doradus A, which is really the star we're talking about — Zeta Doradus B is a much fainter orange dwarf — is hotter than the Sun, and brighter, too."

"Sunglasses? Really?"

"Yes, ma'am. I can tell you from experience the Inor-specific version was vital during the time I was there. I believe the situation would be even worse on a planet orbiting Zeta Doradus A."

Miller tapped her stylus nervously on her desk. "You seem to know these people pretty well, first names and all."

"Yes, I know them well. *Antares* took the second trip to Beta Hydri with the academics. We spent a lot of time together walking the Seekers' towns."

"And, of course, Powell."

"Yes, ma'am, him I know really well."

Miller leaned back in her chair, seemingly reluctant to make the decision she was about to make.

"OK, fine. Go over to FleetIntel and see if they can clarify what's missing.

We need this on time, Hansen."

"Yes, ma'am."

Hansen/Powell Quarters
Ft. Eustis, VA
Wednesday, January 17, 2080, 0455 EST

David woke up from a nasty dream about the descent to the Revered First's chambers, a dream where the confrontation ends with him frozen in fear as the First slaughters Carol and everyone else in the room while he watches. He shook his head and looked across at the clock: 4:55. *Too early*, he thought.

In the dim light from the window, he realized that Carol was not there. He felt the mattress on her side. Cold.

Fully awake now, he heard the shower running in the bathroom just down the hall. He got up and knocked gently on the door. She didn't answer. He thought about it for a few seconds, then opened the door.

Carol was curled up in the corner of the shower, shivering. She looked up at him without recognition.

"Carol!"

She blinked, then held up a partially dissolved bar of soap, the soft leftovers squeezing through her clenched fingers.

"She won't come off! I can't get her off!"

David grabbed her towel and turned off the water. "Who, Carol? Who won't come off?"

Carol wailed, "Michael! I can't get her blood off me! It won't come off!"

He wrapped her in the towel and knelt down next to her. "Wake up, Carol, you really need to wake up!"

She was no less disoriented as she repeated, "Can't... get...her…off...."

David picked her up and carried her back to the bedroom, where he finished drying her off and put her in the bed to warm up. He sat next to her, stroking her damp hair, and calling her name. When she seemed to go back to sleep, David went to the kitchen and made coffee.

He was halfway through his first cup and staring out the window at the fading darkness when her sudden appearance made him jump.

"How, exactly, Mister Powell, am I wet and naked in bed?"

David didn't answer at first. He turned to her, offering her favorite mug filled with her favorite brew.

"What do you remember?"

She took the mug without releasing her lock on his eyes. "Remember? If I remembered anything, I wouldn't need to ask."

"Sit down, please, just sit down." Carol sank into a chair at the small kitchen table, self-consciously pulling the blankets she had yanked off the bed tighter around herself. David leaned against the counter next to the coffee brewer. "I found you in the shower about forty-five minutes ago. The hot water was all gone, and you were curled up on the floor, shivering."

"Bullshit."

David ignored the challenge. "I have no idea how long you were there, but the bed was cold when I woke up."

"Double bullshit."

David knew how hard-headed she was. "OK, fine. Call me a liar, but somehow I don't see how you wind up, uh, as you, uh, are, without your knowledge."

She looked at him for a long time, then seemed to surrender to her need to talk. "I had a really awful dream — "

"About Terri Michael?"

Carol looked at him in surprise. "Yes. How — "

"You were saying in the shower that you could not wash her blood off."

"It was just a dream," she said, as if willing herself to believe it.

David knelt on the floor and held her hands in his, feeling her let go a little as he did.

"I guess I sleep-walked," she said quietly.

"Oh, I think it was something more than that. I love you; you know that. But something is going on here we need to deal with." She stiffened under his arms as he hugged her.

"I just sleep-walked. It's not a crime."

David didn't answer but just held her a while longer. "We'll talk later, OK? Can you make it to work today?"

"I'm fine." She twisted out of his arms and stood. "I need to get dressed."

David watched her as she disappeared down the hall. For the first time since he met her on the first day of freshman year at Fleet University, he was worried about her mental and emotional well-being. This wasn't like her at all, and she didn't seem to realize what was happening to her.

ISC Fleet HQ
Ft. Eustis, VA
Wednesday, January 17, 2080, 0945 EST

As Fiona stepped out of the Intel Section, Carol Hansen was walking towards her, headed for Plans.

"Good morning, Admiral," Hansen said flatly.

"Good morning, Hansen. How are you doing in Plans?"

Carol stopped, turned to Fiona, and paused before speaking. "Fine, ma'am."

25

Something in her tone told Fiona that things in Plans were anything but 'fine.'
"Really?"

"Yes, ma'am. I enjoy the work and the staff very much."

"Well, they're mostly my old staff, so I get that. Still, I have to say I am not convinced."

Carol was silent for a few seconds. "Any issues I might have with my assignment should be addressed within my chain of command, ma'am," she said, quoting the manual almost verbatim. "Respectfully, Admiral, I should not discuss them with you."

"Granted, yes, that's correct." Fiona looked at the younger officer for a long moment before taking a half step closer and looking around to make sure they were alone in the hallway. "But if there are issues, Commander Hansen, I suggest you do address them. Letting things just fester isn't helpful."

Carol nodded. "Yes, ma'am, I will think about it."

Fiona paused one more count before she turned and headed for the commissary for coffee. As she returned to the Intel section, her voice rang through the offices. "POWELL!"

David looked up in surprise from his SLIP intercept analysis and walked cautiously to the Chief's office.

"You called, Admiral?"

"Damn right. Sit. Close the door." David suppressed his instinct to make a joke of the order of her instructions, closed the door, and sat down. Fiona looked down at her desk, face in a stiff frown, her elbows hard on the desktop. After a few seconds, she looked up. Having no idea what this meeting was about, David waited patiently but nervously for her to speak.

"I ran into Carol just now."

David relaxed slightly. This wasn't about him.

"Yes?"

"What's going on over there?"

David thought for a second. This was not a topic he'd anticipated. "I'm sorry, Admiral, but I'm gonna plead the fifth pretty hard on that question."

Fiona was undeterred. "Clearly, she's having problems. What's going on?"

David leaned back in the chair, drawing his best verbal shield. "I could also plead marital privilege, too, I suppose."

Fiona's face broke its frown, allowing a small smile to escape. "Very funny, David, but clearly bullshit. Talk."

"I'm really uncomfortable with this, Admiral. Carol and I are pretty open with each other, and I'm not about to go chatting around what she says to me in private." David took a breath before continuing. "You wouldn't want Commander Miller pumping her for my feelings about you, right?"

Fiona's posture softened. "No, I would not."

"So?"

Fiona sat up a little straighter, taking her elbows off her desk. "Just tell her that she has friends here — people who know what she's done. People who care about her. And, remind her that FleetPers can help her deal with any problems she might be having."

"FleetPers? Yes, ma'am."

"I'm not kidding about FleetPers." She leaned back in her chair; arms crossed. "In most organizations, the personnel office is there to protect the company from the employees. It's not like that here. She can talk to them, in confidence."

David thought about that for a moment. "If the opportunity arises, ma'am, I will suggest it to her. That's the best I can do."

"Fair enough, I'll take that."

"Are we done here, ma'am?"

"Not quite. I have news for you, and, I guess, for Carol, too."

"Yes?"

"Your analysis is pretty convincing, David. I need you to go confirm it."

"Go?"

"Alpha Mensae, then Zeta Doradus, then, well, who knows? *Cobra* will do an initial recon and then meet you on *Intrepid* at Zeta Doradus. I'd expect it to be about three months."

David held back his reaction best he could, but the disappointment was plain on his face.

"All in all, ma'am, I'd rather not. I feel I need to be here right now for Carol."

Fiona leaned forward on her desk, looking down at her folded hands. "I know this is hard, David. I have such admiration for you both, but you are the one person I can count on to get this done and done right."

David's shoulders sank as he considered what she was suggesting. "I really don't need another mile of broken glass to cross barefoot, Admiral."

Fiona cocked her head just slightly, smiling. "Oh, David, don't I know it," she said softly. "But I have to ask you this once more."

David looked up from his gaze at her small, beautiful hands, meeting her eye. "Somehow, Admiral Collins, I suspect there will always be another 'this once more' just over the horizon."

She nodded sadly. "Could be, yes. But I promise to keep you off them best I can."

David looked away from her, then right back. "If I may be candid, ma'am, that's a promise you can't make. CINC or OPS or whoever else will pick up the phone, and then I'll be headed back out to wherever the trouble is."

Fiona, recognizing the truth when she heard it, nodded. "Yes, you will."

"I'm supposed to be Frances' understudy. How is that supposed to happen now?" He swallowed his anger. "Three months. Shit."

"I understand."

"For the record, Admiral, and do feel free to write this down, I hate the whole idea of this."

"Understood. Will you go?"

David looked around as if there was someone else he could draft in his place. There wasn't. "Yes."

As he rose to leave, she looked up and smiled. "So, you have feelings about me?"

David looked back from the doorway. "The fifth, ma'am, I really do plead the fifth."

Fiona laughed as her door swung shut behind Powell. *He's a good kid,* she thought. *No wonder Hansen latched onto him.*

ISC Fleet HQ, Plans Division
Ft. Eustis, VA
Thursday, January 11, 2080, 1130 EST

By midday Thursday, Carol had completed the planning and made her presentation to Miller.

"It's a long mission, ma'am. A little over three months from start to end."

As Miller studied the plan, she said, "Well, we've seen longer. Zeta Doradus is a long way off."

"Yes, ma'am, that plays a major part, along with the time to covertly examine the planet and DSX."

Miller looked up from her NetComp. "You only have one option?"

"The AI only generated one. I shifted some of the requirements to get different options, but this is the only one that meets all of Intel's needs."

"Fine. Send it to me, and copy Collins and Henderson."

"Yes, Commander, right away."

Carol returned to her desk, did a quick final edit on the overview, and sent it. She had no illusions about who the 'Intel asset' would be. David had done the research. He knew Asoon and Rmah well and had worked for Evans aboard *Cobra* towards the end of the war. He had been the one to confront The First at the very end, and she and David had put two of the five slugs into The First that ended his reign. He was the obvious choice. If they accepted her plan, she was pretty sure that in just a few days, David would be gone until mid-April, at least. Possibly longer. She'd queued up consumables for 120 days for *Intrepid*. Henderson would also be taking along a 45-day resupply for *Cobra*, which would be getting close to Fleet minimums by the end of the mission. *Intrepid* had plenty of space, and *Cobra* had already been out sixty days. They could use the refresh.

Once the plan was sent and out of her control, the reality of a hundred days without David gave her a nervous dread. Things had been hard for her lately, and his ever-present support was part of what was holding her together.

Hansen/Powell Quarters
Ft. Eustis, VA
Thursday, January 11, 2080, 1815 EST

Carol, feeling very much herself for once, served up dinner and carried it out to David in their small dining room. Despite the pleasant aroma flowing out of the kitchen, he set down his bowl and turned to her.

"Collins called me in today."

Carol nodded. "You're going to Zeta Doradus for three months."

David looked at her in surprise.

"I did the plan," she said, smiling slightly. "They told us they were sending an 'Intel asset,' but there's only one person in FleetIntel that makes any sense."

David shook his head, "I'm worried about the time away. I don't want to leave you alone that long."

Carol poked at her dinner for a moment without picking anything up. "I'll be fine, really."

"Let's be honest, OK? You're still processing what happened during the war. I should be here with you. I *want* to be here with you. Let them send Jackson, or Weeks...anybody but me."

Carol shook her head, replying between small bites, "I'll be fine. I have my job. You have yours. Go."

David remained unconvinced. "I can talk to Collins again. I can get her to send someone else."

Carol sent her silverware clattering as she set it down. "I will be fine. Yeah, maybe Collins can send someone else but that someone would not be David Powell. She's sending you because she needs *you* to go."

David rolled his eyes as he said, "I'm not that special. There are others — "

"No!" Carol interrupted. "She needs *you*. You know the Preeminent. You understand the intel as well as anyone. I mean, what the hell? You *generated* the damn intel in the first place, right? We've been apart before, and then we didn't know if we'd ever see each other again. "

"It's not the same. There was a war on then, and now there isn't. I'm worried about you."

"You have to stop that. I am fine. Yeah, I'm having some dreams or whatever, but I can function just fine."

David picked up his bowl, smelling the pork and spice chili that Carol had prepared. He started to eat but then put it down again.

"I just feel like I'm walking out when you need me the most." His shoulders fell in resignation as he lifted his spoon and resumed eating. "Wow, Carol, this is really good."

Carol raised an eyebrow as she smiled. "Should be. It's Mom's favorite." She watched David carefully as he took a few more bites. "You're not *leaving* me. You have an assignment. Go do it and come back to me, OK? That's all I need."

"Still — "

"No," she cut him off. "Case closed. You're going."

David sat up straight, a reluctant smile appearing on his face. "Yes, Commander, ma'am, as you wish."

Carol smiled. "Very well, Lieutenant. Carry on."

"Oh, yes, ma'am, carrying on would be fun..."

"Later, hot shot. Later."

As they settled down for the night, Carol drew herself close to him, pulling his arms around her.

"We are always together, you and I," she whispered. "We are never really apart."

David's only response was to hold her a little tighter, relaxing as the clock on her dresser began to dictate their need for sleep. In only a little while, he could hear that she was sleeping, her soft breath brushing his arm. He was still wide awake, necessary thoughts rampaging through his head.

Tomorrow, he would need to begin packing his NetComp with the data he'd need for Alpha Mensae and Zeta Doradus. He'd also need to clean and prep his great-grandfather's .45 caliber M1911 pistol. You just never knew when that hand cannon might save your ass.

Tomorrow, he'd see Ann and Kathy Stewart and Admiral Collins for a final briefing on what Gabrielle and Greg had reported from Alpha Mensae. Carol always raved about them, and if there was an upside to this assignment, it was the chance to work more closely with the Fleet's best pair of academics.

Tomorrow, he'd begin the transition from his comfortable HQ assignment with Carol next to him every night to another long stretch of solo nights in a cold cabin. From together to alone; warm to cold; from near, to far.

David finally drifted off, the gentle smell of her hair filling his head, the soft, warm breeze of her breath on his arm a lullaby for his unsettled soul.

Kutah's Observation Post
Zeta Doradus (b)
Saturday, January 13, 2080, 0825 (Late Afternoon Local Time)

Four suns after Udoro asked to accompany Kutah, they carefully made their way to the Violets' landing field. The Violets had leveled three villages to create it, killing any who tried to stop them. Over the last three suns, Kutah had found a new route through the forest, one a female could follow and which also gave him a better view of what the Violets were doing on the other side of the enormous field.

As they hunkered down just off the empty field, there was a spark of light in the sky to the east. Kutah touched Udoro on the shoulder and pointed to where the ship was descending. He was surprised at their good fortune; only one other time had Kutah actually seen a Violet ship land. It grew in size as it slowly descended, finally settling softly on the ground.

Udoro could not take her eyes off the metallic monster that had just materialized before her. It was as long as a town and taller than any tree she had ever seen. As she watched, a huge section of the side opened, and as it swung wide, more Violets came out.

"They will take all night to load the deleelinosh," he whispered to her.

"Why so long?"

"They gather them from perhaps twelve clans. They must keep them in clean water or they will die. It takes time to move so many from the storage tanks over there," he pointed to some low silver domes on the other side of the field, "into the ship."

"What do they do with them?" she asked, a little too loud.

"Quiet, please! I suppose they eat them, same as us."

"I hate deleelinosh. It's so bitter."

"As do I. But, let's not tell the Violets!"

"Oh, no—" She stopped as Kutah gently placed his hand over her mouth. Taking it away, he pointed off to his right. Turning slightly, Udoro saw four Violets walking the edge of the field, coming in their direction. She instinctively drew closer to the ground, trying to make herself less visible to the invaders. Kutah likewise carefully crawled back a meter to conceal himself. They controlled their breathing, keeping as silent as possible.

They were relieved when the ugly foursome moved on by, looking out into the forest but not down at the undergrowth where Kutah and Udoro lay motionless. As soon as the Violets were out of sight, they moved quietly away from the landing field and began the long walk back to their home village. Udoro went to find Tefin while Kutah reported the new arrival to Elder Wocos.

"They are still at half their previous rate," Wocos commented.

31

Kutah looked off in the distance, towards his home. "I should think the deleelinosh are quite unpleasant by the time they are delivered! They can't live very long without food and fresh water."

"That is not our problem, Kutah. But the fact that they don't punish us for it says something I don't yet understand."

"Yes, it is not like them to forgive any shortfall."

"I will be away for several suns, Kutah. You may skip the next two suns. Spend your time with Udoro while you can."

Kutah left Wocos and walked towards his mother's small house, a house that had been in her line for thousands of snows. He was almost there when Wocos' cryptic comment about Udoro struck him. *What did Wocos know that he did not?*

He dismissed the thought for the moment. After his evening meal, he mounted the small hill nearby where his oldest friend, and his one true love, waited for him.

CHAPTER 3

ISC Fleet HQ, FleetPers Division
Ft. Eustis, VA
Friday, January 19, 2080, 1100 EST

Carol spent several nights thinking about what Fiona had said. Focusing more on her current work problems seemed to help her nightmares, but her unpleasant bed companions still tormented her most nights. David had gone up to *Intrepid* almost a week ago, and she already felt his absence.

Commander Miller seemed determined to make her fail. Even the unquestioned result of her plan for the Zeta Doradus mission did not quench Miller's zeal for criticism. Carol wondered where that intensity had come from. After all, Miller had been a Weapons Officer on *Dunkirk*. She'd had her share of action, and her performance in that action had certainly accelerated her promotion to full Commander. Carol just didn't understand why she was so focused on young officers like Dan Smith and herself. They had done what was asked, what was necessary at the time. They did their duty, no more, no less.

She finally decided she'd take Fiona's advice and seek some help. Walking to her appointment in FleetPers, she tried to gather her thoughts about Miller. What, exactly, had Miller said and why did Carol think it inappropriate? It was a complex question, one she had to approach with clarity and some degree of fairness to Miller.

All her careful preparation evaporated in a split-second as she entered FleetPers.

"Wow, if it isn't the hero-chick herself!" Rick Court snarked at her from behind a desk. "Come looking for some help, little hero chick?"

Carol's face went stone cold. "Stand up, Lieutenant."

"Oh, relax, Carol. Just havin—"

She didn't blink, but her head was roaring with emotion. "Stand up, Lieutenant," she repeated.

Court stared back at her, defiant. Their exchange gathered uncomfortable looks from the other workers in the outer office. "Make me. You used to make some parts of me—"

"On your feet, Lieutenant, at attention, or I will gladly make you."

Court smirked at his coworkers as he slowly drew himself up. "Better, sweetie?"

Carol moved very close to him. her eyes furious. "You will address me as Commander, Lieutenant. You will speak to me, your superior officer, with respect. I don't give a damn what you think you are, or *were*, but here and now you are several ranks below me, and you would do well to remember that."

His smirk barely faded. He stood casually as if challenging her to forcibly change his posture.

A door opened behind him, and a senior lieutenant emerged. He looked at the two officers standing at Court's desk, the rest of the office staring at them staring at one another.

"Commander Hansen, ma'am, I'm ready for you."

Her eyes didn't leave Court's as she replied. "Very well." She held him there for another second before breaking off and following the lieutenant into his office.

She sat without being invited, her face now red with anger and her body shaking with emotion. She focused on the nameplate on the desk: *SLT Darin Perez, MS, LPCC.* Perez poured her a glass of water, placed it on his desk across from her, and sat back down without speaking. He opened his NetComp and read for a few seconds, waiting.

When Carol set down the glass and looked up at him, he was ready. "Shall we talk about what just happened?"

"Bastard."

"Succinct is always good, Commander, but somehow I think there's more about this than his parentage."

"It's more his character, or maybe his soul, or, his lack of one, than his family history, Lieutenant."

"Please, in here, Darin. May I call you Carol?"

"Yes, that would be fine." Carol thought for a few seconds. "Funny, I have never been prickly about rank, you know? We all have jobs, and all the military formality can get in the way sometimes. People don't always feel free to speak their minds."

"But not with my Lieutenant Court?"

Carol shook her head. "No." She took another sip of water. "I thought he was out of the Fleet after Henderson fired him."

Perez nodded. "He very nearly was. He pleaded his case with my predecessor, did some counseling, and promised to do his job."

"And?"

Perez leaned back. "And, until today, he's been unremarkable, but problem-free."

"We were a couple at the U, Court and I. Worst mistake I ever made. Cost me four years with someone who actually loved me."

"Powell," Perez stated.

"Yes. I see you've done your homework."

"Oh, the Ballad of Carol and David is all but a country-and-western song around here. From Inoria to putting a bullet in the Revered First, we all know the story."

She stiffened in her chair. "Well, then, I'll just have to go get me a hunting dog and a pickup."

"Don't be offended, Commander. People admire that you've done amazing things under difficult circumstances, both of you, and the fact that the media has publicized most of it doesn't change anything."

"I suppose."

"But, one questionable lieutenant is not what brought you here today."

"No."

Perez picked up his stylus. "So, tell me about Commander Miller."

Carol described the incidents that bothered her the most, from being called a 'comet' to being constantly questioned and criticized. Perez agreed that some of Miller's behaviors seemed right on the edge of being unprofessional. He agreed to talk to his superior and get back to Carol in a few days.

She felt relieved as she returned to FleetPlans, taking up the northern star recon that Miller had interrupted for the Zeta Doradus trip. It was slow work, and Miller's daily queries just added to her stress. Her Command class was not going well, either, as incomplete assignments piled up in her in-box.

As she left Fleet HQ that evening, Court was waiting.

"What the hell was that?" he yelled at her.

"Listen, Lieutenant—"

"And you can shove that rank shit up your ass, Carol. Perez chewed me out for an hour! After, of course, he interrogated everyone else in the office."

"You had it coming. Now, get away from me!"

"Oh, sweetie, your boy is away. Don't you want me to drop over and—"

"I said leave me alone, Lieutenant."

"You only came there to see me! Admit it, Hansen, you want me back!"

"Don't make me puke, Rick."

He reached out to grab her arm. She let him, then grabbed his arm to pull him off-balance. A heel to his foot and a knee in his groin, and he was on his knees, looking up at her cross-eyed as she gripped his hair. She thought hard about a fist to the throat to finish him off but held back. Instead, she lowered him to the ground as Fleet Security gathered around them.

"Get lost, Court," she hissed at him through clenched teeth. "Leave me, and mine, alone, or next time I will finish this little fight."

Carol looked up to see Lead Security Tech Orr standing next to her. "Is there a problem here, ma'am?"

She released Court and stood up straight. "No, Mister Orr. I think we're done."

Court scrambled unsteadily to his feet, then sank back to his knees as his groin screamed. "You heard it! She threatened me!"

"I am sorry, Lieutenant Court, but I heard no such thing." Orr looked at his two assistants, "None of us did."

"She struck a junior officer! Ask her!"

"Well, about that, Lieutenant, we *did* see you assault her, and so it is no surprise that she would defend herself."

Court tried to respond, but the pain sank him all the way down to the pavement, his breathing labored.

Orr leaned over him. "Really, Lieutenant, if I were you, I would follow the Commander's advice. It would be best for your health." He stood up straight and turned to Carol. "How do you want to handle this, ma'am?"

"Handle what, Mister Orr?"

"Very well, ma'am, as you say, we have nothing to report. Would you like a lift home?"

Carol looked down at Court, "Yes, that would be fine."

Orr pointed to one of his junior techs, who left to fetch the duty Jeep.

It was a three-shot night.

After the confrontation with Court, she'd taken a long shower, trying to rid herself of feeling his hard, coarse hands on her again. She was exhausted by nine but unable to sleep. She knew the Balvenie was trouble, but without sleep, she'd be even worse off.

Or, so she thought.

It was Jimmy Cornell again tonight, walking towards her with that ghastly crater in his chest.

"But Miss Carol, you asked me to follow you!"

She stared back at him.

"So, I did. I trusted you. You promised! You promised not to get me killed!"

She felt the same pain in the pit of her gut she had that day on Beta Hydri.

"I didn't know, Jimmy. I'm sorry, I just didn't know!"

Another familiar but unpleasant voice came from close by. A tiny Rick Court was standing on her shoulder.

"You know he's right, hero chick, you never knew shit about what you were doing! You were just making it up! What a worthless joke you are! You and that wimp-ass Powell."

Jon Swenson wandered past, confused, trying to understand where he was, blood flowing freely from his chest. When she turned away, it was the Revered First, his ugly mouth wide, the dripping saliva cascading off as he moved to grab her. She turned to run, only to find her feet stuck in coagulated blood a foot thick. She pulled at her feet as the monster's teeth sank into her.

Carol sat upright on the bed, drenched in sweat, tears running down her face. She screamed in frustration, the sound echoing through the empty house. As a part of her asked what more she could have done, another part yelled, "Something! *Something!*" She tried to shake the memory of the nightmare as she got out of bed and headed for the bathroom.

She stared at the woman in the mirror for several minutes, studying the face as if she was looking at a portrait and wondering what the artist was trying to say. The woman looked old to Carol, tired and spent. She looked thinner than Carol remembered, too. She thought about the Scotch but decided that after 4 AM was not the time to medicate herself that way. Caffeine was the prescription now, so she walked back to the bedroom, pulled on one of David's uniform shirts for warmth, and headed for the kitchen.

As the coffee maker hissed and grumbled, she could still see Cornell, both the dead-but-alive version in her nightmare and the real version: the one so young and frightened that first day on Inor, and the grown-up, brave one running her message down to Swenson, who was dead, too. A dead tech taking a dead message to a dead officer. What—the hell—was the point?

Eaagher came unbidden into her mind, Ullnii next to him. Carol wondered for a second if maybe she was still dreaming.

"*We* were the point," he said in perfect English, then nodded to his grandchild. "*She* was the point, Carol."

"Maybe," Carol said out loud, answering him. "Maybe. But the cost was so high."

"Do not let it be your soul," she heard Ullnii answer in her head.

Carol left the coffee in its cup and climbed back in bed. David's absence was a hard pain in her chest, a nagging emptiness she could not fill or ignore. In times like this it was David who was her refuge, her recharge. She remembered those few hours they had spent on Beta Hydri after she landed *Antares,* and the strength and confidence he restored in her. She could still hear his words as she drifted off to sleep.

Cobra
Orbiting Zeta-1 Reticuli (a)
Friday, January 19, 2080, 2255 UTC

It was late in the evening when Elaine DeLeon was called to the Bridge by her Comms techs. Double-duty as XO and Communications Officer kept *Cobra's* crew count down, which was good, but it also meant extra calls at inconvenient times, which was, well, less good. The tech showed her the dispatch from Fleet.

```
PRIORITY 20801171200UTC
TO: COBRA
FROM: CINC
```

SUBJECT: DISPATCH ORDER

1) RECENT INTEL INDICATES POSSIBLE SECOND PREEMINENT DEEP
SPACE WAYSTATION NEAR ZETA DORADUS AT X 2.25 Y 6.00 Z -9.10.
2) SAME INTEL IMPLIES THIS MAY BE A PREEMINENT RESISTANCE
FORCE ORGANIZED BY THE GOVERNOR AT ZD.
3) DECISION HAS BEEN MADE TO LIBERATE NATIVES AT ZD ASAP TO
CONFIRM/DENY EXISTENCE OF A RESISTANCE FACTION AND POSSIBLY
DRAW THEM OUT.
4) INTREPID DEPARTING 20800117 WITH POWELL FOR ALPHA MENSAE
TO EMBARK ESTE AND CORDERO.
5) COBRA WILL WRAP UP WORK AT ZR ASAP AND PROCEED TO RECON
WAYSTATION. INTEL INDICATES SIX PREEMINENT SHIPS ARE PRESENT.
6) COBRA WILL THEN PROCEED ZETA DORADUS (B) ARRIVING O/A
20800130 TO COVERTLY MAP SURFACE AND ASSESS PREEMINENT FORCES.
7) INTREPID WILL ARRIVE ZD COVERTLY O/A 20800222.
8) EVANS/HENDERSON/ESTE/CORDERO/POWELL TO DETERMINE NEXT
STEPS TO UNDERSTAND ZD CULTURE AND HOW BEST TO LIBERATE THEM.
LOCAL GOVERNOR WILL BE TOLD YOU WILL ARRIVE O/A 20800304.
9) INTREPID CARRYING ADDITIONAL 45 DAYS OF CONSUMABLES FOR
TRANSFER TO COBRA.
10) REPORT ONLY AFTER INVESTIGATION OF WAYSTATION
OR IF UNABLE TO PROCEED AS DIRECTED.

DAVENPORT

END

"That may just be the longest SLIP I've ever seen," Elaine said to herself. *Cobra*'s captain, Commander Rich Evans, had also been alerted by Comms techs and arrived on the bridge just a minute later.

"CINC is worried," Evans said quietly. "He's never this verbose."

Elaine looked up at Evans. "OK, so, what is 'ASAP' in your mind?"

Evans' answer was to turn and walk aft to the Operations Center, where Jack Ballard and his crew were observing their target planet at Zeta-1 Reticuli. DeLeon was right behind him. The small terrestrial planet was on the list Rmah Teo Segt had given David of the races that the Preeminent had conquered. Their extensive use of radio gave the techs in the Ops Center plenty of work to do, and they were just beginning to understand the myriad of signals, their possible sources, and uses. The race there did not yet have space travel, but based on their technological level, Jack thought they would have soon achieved that but for the arrival of the Preeminent.

"I thought Zeta Doradus was stable, and we'd get to them later," Jack said after reading the dispatch from CINC.

"It was, or, is, I guess," Evans answered. "But the discovery of this station nearby, with some connection to the Governor there, changes the calculus. Intel suspects something else is going on."

Jack nodded. "Well, we can wrap up anytime, sir. We've got enough recorded intercepts to keep us busy for a while."

"Anything new?"

"Yeah...we're beginning to think these weird sounds down in the HF band are actually music stations. The planet is Earth-like enough that they would see an ionospheric bounce at those frequencies, just like we do back home. The VHF stuff is still a mystery. I'm not sure it's encrypted, exactly, but we haven't figured out what the modulation is, either. I think it's FM, but there is something more to it we that haven't resolved yet."

Evans nodded. "Fine. Have we seen any Preeminent ships yet? As of a couple days ago, there hadn't been any."

"And there still haven't been, but last time we checked, the open-pit mine and refinery are still working."

"OK, let's get one more good set of images of the spaceport and the mine. Record whatever radio traffic you can collect while we're doing that, and then we'll bug out for this new station FleetIntel found."

"Any chance we could get those images up close, sir?"

Evans looked at the ship status display in Center Console. He was ten-thousand kilometers above the surface, getting around the planet every five-and-three-quarters hours. That was fine for this kind of reconnaissance work. But if he really wanted good pictures, low was the way to go. He turned back to Jack.

"How's the weather?"

"Clear, for the moment. There's a front moving in later tonight."

"What time is it at the mine?"

Jack looked at a different readout. "Late morning. Still an hour to noon."

"OK, we'll go down to two hundred, get some nice close-ups, and then we're out of here."

"That's great, sir."

Evans called his navigator and got the ship moving lower. After the captain was gone, one of the techs walked over to Center Console. "Two hundred, sir?"

Jack smiled. "Yeah. I'd have been happy with a thousand. Let's set the AI to scan the RF bands and free up a couple people to work the cameras. I don't want to miss anything." Jack had been about to call it a night, but this new priority changed all that. Jack shook his head slightly. He'd sleep once they got into FTL. For now, it was time for a side-trip to the wardroom for the midnight meal and more coffee.

It took *Cobra* two hours to get down and in the right plane. They did two low passes over the mining operation, getting imagery in visual, infra-red, and ultra-violet that they hoped would help them identify what the Preeminent were pulling out of the planet. Or, more precisely, what the slaves were pulling out for them.

That done, Navigator Lena Rice pointed her ship towards DSX and pushed the pedal to the floor. Shortly thereafter, Jack Ballard was snoring quietly in his bunk.

Kutah's Observation Post
Zeta Doradus (b)
Sunday, January 21, 2080, 16:55 UTC (Mid-Afternoon Local Time)

Udoro was beginning to enjoy her daily treks with Kutah to spy on the Violets. She had always been a careful female, knowing her prominent role in society placed limits on her options. Her mother, second-mother, and third-mother took great care with her education so that when her time arrived, she would be prepared.

But once Kutah entered her life, she found she cared less about her position and more about spending time with him. They were of the same generation, and they had seen just twenty snows when her brother Tefin brought him home from school. Udoro thought he was the most beautiful thing she had ever seen, and before long, she was spending her afternoons with them both and her nights with Kutah.

She thought of those first nights now as they slowly crawled under the forest floor's sharp shrubs to his new observation post. They were on a small tree-covered knoll off one corner of the Violets' landing field, and from here, they could easily see all the way to the other side. As they burrowed down into the low depression Kutah had made, there was one thing they could not miss.

The smell.

It assaulted their senses, nearly watering their eyes. The deleelinosh were dying and rotting in the storage tanks. Udoro had never experienced anything so distasteful, so aggressively unpleasant.

Kutah leaned towards her, speaking quietly. "I worked in the pens before Wocos made me a spy. They die easily, and when one dies and is not removed, many more follow. Then, even more after that. It can transform a normal creche into a grisly morass overnight."

Kutah focused his telescope on the storage tanks. Many Violets were working around them. The circular covers on the top were up, and they were working on an access door on the side. As it opened, an ugly sludge spilled out. He was amused as the Violets sprang back, apparently repulsed by the sight and scent pouring out.

"So, you've smelled this before?" Udoro asked.

"Yes, several times." He put down the telescope. "They're emptying the tanks, draining them back into the sea. The whole shipment looks like it may be dead."

Udoro looked up into the trees above them. "I wish the wind would change."

"That would help the stench, yes, but this time of day, the breeze blows towards the forest. That's good for us."

"Good? How?"

"The Violets have a very acute sense of smell. The day they almost killed me was the day I was caught on the thorn. I think they smelled my blood. Other spies have been killed when the Violets discovered them, even when they knew how to be silent."

It had been another six-sun since they had seen a Violet ship. Kutah had been there every day, checking. They were now arriving on an irregular schedule; if there was a pattern to it, neither Kutah nor Wocos could discern what it was.

As the sun drew near the western horizon, Udoro and Kutah crept back from the landing field and began the walk home. They talked sporadically, Udoro seeming preoccupied, responding only briefly to Kutah's prompting. The last few kilometers, they walked in silence, in step, brushing arms and hands from time to time.

Wocos was surprised at their report. "I have not heard of any reprisals, Kutah. You're sure what you saw?"

Udoro stood over the old male. "There is no question what we smelled, Elder Wocos. The air reeked of waste and death."

"It is not our fault that the Violets can't get the deleelinosh transported," Kutah declared.

Wocos turned to him. "They have not been so reasonable in the past, young Kutah. They haven't cared before about facts or what is fair in our eyes."

Kutah replied more quietly. "Yes, Elder, I understand. But I can only report what I see."

Wocos placed his hand on Kutah's arm. "And you do so very well. I will take this information to the GuildMember, and we will see what he says."

"Do that, Elder Wocos," Udoro said, "and spend less time questioning those who have seen with their own eyes."

Wocos looked at the young female for a moment, then turned and began his walk to see the GuildMember.

Home of Riaghe Kutah
Zeta Doradus (b)
Tuesday, January 23, 2080, 1424 UTC (Just After Sunrise)

Kutah woke to the sound of Elder Wocos pounding on his door. The star was just up, and as usual, Udoro had already gone home. He pushed aside warm thoughts of the night just past and opened the door.

"Come, Kutah, come! I have new instructions for you."

"It is early, Elder Wocos."

"No, Kutah, is it late, and we must move quickly. The Guild has new orders

41

for you."

Kutah wearily returned inside his home, dressed quickly for the forest, and came back out. "As you say. Elder Wocos. What is it you require of me?"

Wocos stepped close to Kutah, who had never seen the Elder so animated. "Tefin has said you have a new observation post."

"Yes, yes, I do. Udoro and I have been going there each day, just before dusk."

"Can you see from this new place where the delivery wagons are taken once they pass through the Violets' gate?"

Kutah thought about that for a few seconds. "I believe so. What is it you want?"

"You are to observe what they do with the delivery wagons. How do they empty the casks into their storage tanks?"

Kutah looked at the Elder with disgust. "Elder Wocos, I respect the Guild's wishes, of course, but I fail to see what good such information would do us."

Wocos replied simply, "It is the order of the Guild. You can refuse, of course, and go back to the pens."

Kutah needed no time to consider that option. "No, Elder, I will go. The wagons begin to pass through the gate about midday. I will be ready."

Kutah quickly ate his morning meal, then walked to Tefin and Udoro's home. Tefin was up and about, but Udoro was still asleep.

"It's just as well," Kutah said quietly, "I think you and I should go without her."

"She will be angry with you!"

"Fine. She will be alive to be so. Let's go."

Tefin looked at his friend with surprise. "But it is still early."

"Not anymore. The Guild orders me to observe the deliveries. I must leave soon, or I will not be there in time."

"You would prefer to go alone?"

"I would prefer to not go at all, Tefin, but I must. Since I must, I would prefer your company and assistance. But if you choose to remain, I must still go."

Tefin was surprised at Kutah's intensity. Not in twenty snows had he seen such anger from him. "No, Kutah, I will go with you. But I confess you frighten me."

"Good. In that we are united. Let's get moving."

Nothing was routine in their journey to the landing field. At this earlier time of day, there were many more travelers on the roads and from many different clans. He and Tefin received surprised looks from others along the road. Some appeared suspicious, and Kutah only hoped that word of his presence would not somehow get back to the Violets. At the entry point, they paused until no one was in sight and then disappeared into the forest.

They arrived at their hiding place just as the first wagons were being brought in. Through his telescope, Kutah watched as the Violets struggled with the large draft animals, apparently uncomfortable or uninformed in how they should be handled. It took a surprising amount of time for them to get a wagon stopped next to a tank, lift the casks, and load the splashing deleelinosh in. It was awkward, Kutah thought, crude for such an advanced race. He had expected some kind of mechanized process, not mere brute strength. He noticed that they emptied every wagon in the same way, back to front, letting the empty casks lie on the ground until the wagon was empty. They would then replace the casks on the wagon and move on to the next.

Kutah and Tefin were twice alarmed by Violets patrolling the perimeter of the landing field, but each time they passed by, apparently in conversation, without breaking stride. Kutah and Tefin remained there until it was almost dusk. As they left their observation post, Kutah wondered if the Violets knew how close they had come to catching them. *If they just patrolled in silence,* he thought, *we might have been discovered.* He reminded himself to be more careful. Just a few moments of inattention could mean a painful death.

Wocos was excited by their report, more so than Kutah would have thought, and he wondered what this was really all about. It was a simple but awkward procedure, far less sophisticated than he had expected it would be. Wocos ordered him to do the same again next sun.

Kutah decided that this new task was safe enough, so for the next few suns, both Udoro and Tefin came along. The threesome still endured some strange stares from the usual travelers, but, by the third day they seemed to blend in to the rest of the traffic and didn't feel so conspicuous.

Each day, the Violets wrestled the draft animals into place and manually unloaded the delivery wagons. It took a long time, Kutah thought, much longer than necessary.

This information seemed to please Elder Wocos far more than Kutah understood.

Riaghe Village
Zeta Doradus (b)
Thursday, January 25, 2080, 1535 UTC (Early Evening Local Time)

Tefin waited patiently on the hill. Kutah would be along soon, right after his evening meal. Udoro was staying in tonight, huddled with her mothers. The scattered clouds in the west, back-lit by the sun, spoiled the sunset for Tefin, who preferred clear, unblemished sunsets. Udoro told him it was because he was too rigid, too much a purist in his thinking. He just thought he liked his sunsets his way. Others? Well, for Tefin, they could like whatever they liked.

Tefin took a long drink from his mug of grog. The hard ceramic container kept the mixture of fermented fruit and other spices warm. And even as the days hurtled on towards the hot season, he enjoyed the rich flavor of his clan's particular version of the drink.

Kutah arrived just after the sun slipped below the horizon, the sky still darkening above.

"So," Tefin asked, "what does the Elder Wocos have to say?"

"Very little. He listens to my report, and then he stands up and heads off to see the GuildMember. I am not sure yet that even he knows why they have asked for this information."

"Yes, but it seems very important, does it not?"

"It does."

"What do *you* think it is?"

Kutah didn't answer right away. He looked up from the fading sunset to the stars above, then back over his head to the Night Glow rising in the east. After a moment, he turned back to his friend.

"I don't know, but I believe they are planning some kind of attack on the Violets. I can't imagine what else it would be."

Tefin waved his agreement, and they were silent for a while. Finally, Tefin could wait no longer.

"Udoro got a license."

Kutah's heart raced as his body stiffened. He took some time to control his reactions, then asked, "When?"

"She didn't tell you? Three suns ago."

Kutah was crushed that Udoro had been alone with him for most of two suns and had said nothing. But that wasn't what he really needed to know.

"No, Tefin, when does she leave?"

"On the next six-sun."

Kutah didn't look at his friend. Instead, he stared out at the darkness, clenching and releasing the three fingers on his right hand, all four knuckles in sequence: in, out, in, out. His head was a shambles, a disastrous riot of feelings and thoughts, counter-feelings and counter-thoughts, all screaming for his attention, each one insisting they were his truth. He felt like a solitary raindrop caught in the whirlwind of a perihelion thunderstorm, storms so violent they threatened to push over their stone houses and drown them in their keeps. *You knew it might happen, probably would happen,* a part of him said. *You knew. What did you expect when you fell in love with her?*

In that instant he hated the clan system he lived in, even his own Riaghe clan, hated Wocos and, in a way, Udoro, too. But he could not hate her for long, and the realization grew in him that whatever his feelings, or hers, she would be leaving for repro. Such was her duty.

Tefin sat by his friend without speaking, allowing Kutah to absorb the news he had delivered. Like Kutah, he knew this could happen. Repro licenses were strictly controlled, and once received could not be declined by the female. The orders from the Shepherds of ancient times demanded that once a license was issued, they must find partners outside their own clan. Tefin let his friend think for a while before speaking again.

"She wasn't happy, Kutah. She did not seek this."

"A female can't seek it, as you well know."

"She is terrified you will be dissatisfied with her — that you will reject her."

Kutah looked at his friend. The pain of a moment ago was fading as he thought of how Udoro must be feeling. She would not want to leave him, but she must.

"That I could never do."

He side-stepped down the hill and began the short walk to Udoro's home.

She was waiting at the door, sadness covering her face. They began to walk, first around the narrow paths of their village, then onto the wider packed-dirt road that led to the next village. It was empty at this hour, the darkness cloaking their faces.

Udoro finally spoke. "When I saw the Elder coming, I knew he had a license. I hoped it was for mother or second-mother, but no, it was for me."

"We have been together for fifty snows. We know the rules. We knew one of us might be called. I guess I just hoped it wouldn't happen."

"Please don't question me. Please don't think I am happy about this."

"I don't. We can never repro together. Never. Not in the same clan."

"I still feel the same about you," she said quietly. "Nothing can ever change that."

"I know."

They walked in silence for a while. "I have to select a partner and then raise the children."

Kutah stopped walking and turned to her. "Children?"

"Yes, the license is for three." She reached out to him, but he didn't respond. "But, after that, I will return to you. I could never stay with anyone else."

They began walking again, turning back towards home. "It will take a long time to bear and raise three. I see many cold nights in my future."

"Yes, there is no denying that. But afterward, we will be together, and there will be hundreds of snows, thousands probably, that we will abide together."

"I will look forward to that."

"You may yet see an invitation."

"Yes, it is possible, I guess. I don't see it myself."

The dim lights ahead told them they were approaching their home village.

"I will not see you again, Udoro, until you return to me."

She looked at him hopefully. "You would not have one last night? Or, two?"

"The time has come for me to be alone. I will begin that time now and not drag out the moment of separation any longer than necessary."

They held each other briefly, Kutah refusing Udoro's gentle encouragements and turning for his home. He hated what was about to happen, but this was the way of his society, and he had no choice but to accept it. Still, the fire in his heart would not cool for a very long time.

Cobra
Zeta Doradus (b)
Tuesday, January 30, 2080, 1400 UTC

Commander Rich Evans looked at the chronometer on his duty cabin wall. They'd been at Zeta Doradus for three hours already, and nothing from Ballard. He pulled up the results of their visit to DSX, a disappointing encounter. As he reported to CINC, there was really nothing there but the six ships he'd been told to expect. There was no space station, no resupply depot. There were just six fat targets loosely floating around together.

Frustrated by the delay, he got up and headed for the Operations Center. SLT Jack Ballard had been running the op since they'd arrived. Jack looked over at his boss and shook his head.

"It took us a while to find the planet, sir. It's in an elliptical orbit; looks like it's heading back towards perihelion, but we haven't worked out all the details yet."

"OK, so what about it, now that we're here?"

"Nothing definite yet, sir, but based on what I see on IR and the info we got from *Resnick,* the star should be up soon where the inhabitants live." With a few touches and swipes of his controls he put the IR feed up on the large display monitor that covered the aft wall of the Operations Center. On it, Evans could see a large landmass about to move through the terminator and into the light of the star. Jack pointed to a shadowy dark area on the screen. "They supposedly live in this wide bay on the eastern edge of the smaller continent. We can see a few hot spots…here…and…here, that are probably villages or small towns. I'll know more once the star is up and we can get some visuals."

"Anything in orbit?"

"Nothing artificial, sir, at least, not yet, but we're still watching for those. There are two small moons, say, Phobos-ish, in fairly high orbits. They're not a factor for us."

Evans nodded. "OK, Jack, stay on it and I'll be back in an hour. If you need a maneuver, call Nav and they'll accommodate you."

"Sir, yes, sir."

As Evans left to return to the bridge, Jack settled back into the mission controller's position in Center Console. The room was busy, but quiet, as his techs worked their cameras, receivers, and sensors to learn as much as they could as fast as they could. There could be danger here, and Jack knew his first priority was to understand the ground they might be fighting on, even if there was no actual ground involved.

As the star rose over the populated area, Jack could not miss the massive open field with modern buildings and storage tanks on one side. It was a flat open scar in the otherwise natural, partially wooded landscape. That had to be the Preeminent spaceport, with a headquarters and barracks for the Combatants. They'd also been told the commodity here was a specific species of fish, so the storage tanks were no surprise.

They were high above the planet, orbiting at fifty thousand kilometers. At this altitude, the planet would rotate beneath them twice in the time they would orbit once. Jack was happy with that for now, but once he had the overall picture, he'd ask Evans to put them in synchronous orbit over the inhabited area. It was right on the equator, which struck Jack as odd, but it did make his job a little easier.

From there, they could get very detailed data in visual and IR. Within days, Jack thought, they would know far more about the inhabitants' movements and habits.

And, the Preeminents' as well.

Hansen/Powell Quarters
Ft. Eustis, VA
Saturday, February 10, 2080, 0830 EST

Carol was trying to wake up, pouring her second cup of coffee as she sat in her empty kitchen when her phone signaled a message from Denise Long. Denise had been a rookie Warrant Officer in Inoria, paralyzed with terror as death fell all around her during the Preeminent attack. But she quickly grew past that as Reactor Officer on *Antares*, and again on *Sigma* when Carol took command. By then, she was well seasoned, the timidness replaced with both technical competence and a strong measure of courage. Denise was coming down from *Sigma* with some of Carol's former shipmates. They were headed out for an evening on the town up in DC, and they wanted Carol to join them. It took Carol until lunch to respond, but she decided to say no.

She had work to do, she told Long, that she could not put off. That was a lie. Well, that she had work to do was not a lie. That she planned to do any of it, was.

Late in the afternoon, Denise showed up at Carol's door anyway, hoping to jawbone her out with the group. When Carol answered, Denise was shocked at what she saw. Thinner, paler, with dark circles forming around her eyes, Carol was a shadow of the vital, energetic commander of *Antares* and *Sigma*.

Denise made no pretense of rank. "Carol Hansen, what the hell is going on with you?"

"What? I'm fine."

"No, you're not. How long has Powell been gone?"

"Oh, a little over three weeks, I guess. Not that long."

By now, Denise had pushed her way into the living room, Carol retreating before her.

She decided to make conversation while she tried to figure out what was happening with her old commander. "So, tell me about command school."

As Carol talked, Denise saw flashes of Carol's old self through whatever veil of haze was over her. She looked to Denise like a TV with the intensity turned down to where you could just barely see the picture. It was terrible.

"Come on out with us, Hansen, really. Please come. We'll have a couple glasses of wine, a few pizzas, and some laughs. Come with us."

Carol shook her head. "Can't. Too tired tonight, and I need to work in the morning."

Denise cocked her head and put her hands on her hips. "In the morning? In the morning, it'll be Sunday."

"I know. Still, I have stuff I need to do. Miller gave me this enormous project, and it's way behind schedule."

Denise looked cautiously at her former commander, unsure if she should ask what was on her mind — what had been haunting her since the attack on Inoria two years before.

"Can I ask you something? You were with Marty?"

Carol looked at her with surprise. "I try not to think about that much, but, yes, I was with him. It wasn't pretty."

"But he knew you were there? He wasn't alone?"

Carol fought back against the softball-sized lump that instantly jammed her throat. She was suddenly back on that street in Inoria, the grit of the street digging into her knee, the taste of fear in her mouth, and Marty bleeding out in front of her, his bright eyes quickly fading. "I was with him all the way, Denise. I was with him…until he wasn't there anymore."

Denise looked down, then away, then back to Carol. "He was so kind. I was just getting to know him when it happened. I thought maybe…"

Carol managed a small smile. "Well, for what it's worth, I think he had the same idea."

Denise shook her head to toss away the vision of Marty Baker's face. "Please come, Commander. Please? For Marty, if no other reason?"

"No, I can't."

Denise's shoulders sagged with resignation. Carol Hansen wasn't going to relent. "OK, well, I guess I should get going. The others are waiting for me."

As they walked to the door, Denise turned back and hugged Carol tightly. "Thank you," she said quietly.

"Thank you? For what?" Carol asked wearily.

"For saving our collective asses and getting all of us home in one piece. Don't think we don't know why we're all still alive."

Carol stiffened and looked off into the distance. "I didn't get all of us home."

Denise let her go only to stand very close to her, looking up at the taller woman. "I know, and I can see how that might be hard. But without you, none of us would be here."

"I suppose."

Denise looked at her for one last moment. "So, final answer? Not coming?"

Carol shook her head. Denise went out the door and down the four steps to the sidewalk. She looked at the closed door for a few seconds before turning to her ASV.

She was lying, Denise knew, but she wasn't sure what to do about it. After all, Hansen was a lieutenant commander, and there was only so far Denise could push her. If Alex Williams was here, she thought, he might be able to coax her out, or at least get her to talk about whatever was eating at her. But Alex was still aboard *Sigma*, demoted from temporary XO to Navigation officer. Not that he minded. And, he had the watch tonight and wasn't coming along, either. So, he was unavailable.

Long's evening with her friends was fine, pleasant even, but the glow was off, and she didn't enjoy it nearly as much as she had expected. She was worried, and she wasn't sure what to do about it.

Science Directorate Headquarters
Alpha Mensae (c)
Monday, February 12, 2080, 1200 UTC

Ateah Gi Seba was a good Speaker. She knew it. Her teachers knew it. But now, Ateah was suddenly less sure about what her expertise might mean. Rather, she was less sure about the implications of what assignment it might bring her than the expertise itself. She went over all this slowly in her mind as she sat next to Vermin Speaker Asoon Too Lini. Across the table from them sat the repugnant Vermin representatives, who seemed bent on dragging her off to talk to the actual aliens whose language she had struggled to learn.

David Powell, freshly down from *Intrepid* with Captain Joanne Henderson, looked across the table at the second speaker that Asoon had brought in. He was no authority on Preeminent body language, but he sensed a resistance, perhaps a reluctance, on the part of this female.

He let Gabrielle lead off the discussion.

"We have decided to start the liberation of enslaved cultures at Zeta Doradus, what you know as System 952." She waited for Asoon to translate, and there was a small exchange between them.

Asoon nodded slightly. David noticed she was beginning to adopt a few human gestures. "Yes, Ateah understands."

"You understand, this means we will be working to remove them from Preeminent rule. Do you, or Ateah, have any reservations about this task? Can you commit your full talents to it?"

"I can, yes," Asoon answered as she turned to Ateah, speaking as directly and frankly as she could.

"The goal is to liberate the aliens at System 952. They will be left alone, and we will abandon our control of the planet. The humans ask if you are willing to participate. Your talents will be critical to this task."

"The Vermin are too presumptuous, Asoon. Do you not see it? How dare they dictate to us?"

"Ateah, refer to them as human, not Vermin. You have been assigned because you are the most adept at the 952 language. The Science Directorate has taught you this, and now it needs your services."

David glanced at Gabrielle as the Preeminents conversed. She let go just a hint of an eyebrow to express her concern over this extended discussion. It was a simple question, after all.

"So, what will they do if I refuse?"

Asoon looked at Ateah for a micRot, then turned to the humans.

"She asks what will happen to her if she refuses."

"Nothing," Gabrielle answered immediately.

"No harm will come to you, Ateah."

"This one," she said, pointing to David, *"killed the Revered First, did he not? You saw this, did you not? Why would he not do the same to me if I should displease him."*

"He killed the First when he had no choice. Had the human not killed him, I would be dead, and so would many others both Preeminent and human."

Ateah raised her hands in defiance. *"It's a lie. He was murdered."*

Asoon kept her voice calm but firm. *"He was not, Ateah. But it doesn't matter now. The humans defeated us in the war, and we are now required to free the cultures we conquered."*

"Humiliating to even be in the presence of such inferior creatures."

"What's going on, Asoon?" David asked, his impatience slipping through.

"We are having a discussion, David. Please give me a short while to reason with her."

David nodded, then looked away, hoping to take the pressure off Asoon.

"What did he say?"

"He asked what the delay was about. The humans are honest, Ateah. They don't kill without need or alternative. I have seen this myself."

"Perhaps. But for me what you say is as difficult to accept as the defeat itself."

Asoon fought against the growing irritation she was feeling towards this Speaker. There was a job to be done. No more explanation was needed. *"The Science Directorate provided you with the training in the 952 language. Did you not think that it would be needed at some point?"*

"Not in this way, no."

"The aliens there must be freed. The SD requires it. We, you and I, need to know no more than that."

Ateah folded her hands across her chest. *"I am Preeminent. I will comply."*

"That is not enough, Ateah. You must participate fully in this. You and I are the only way the humans can talk to the Governor and the natives. We must be ready to use all our talents objectively and accurately."

"Yes, I see, I agree."

"Good."

"Now, maybe he won't shoot me."

Asoon looked at Ateah for a long moment before turning back to the humans across the table. "Ateah agrees to participate. I must tell you that she retains some measure of loyalty to the Revered First, something not unusual in our society at the moment. It will fade in time. But she has committed to full and honest translation for you."

"We're betting our lives on her, Asoon. She understands that?" David didn't wait for an answer. "And, many Preeminent lives, too. This is important."

"She understands. She is also thrilled you're not planning to shoot her."

David looked at her. "Asoon, is that a joke?"

"I think the vernacular response is 'I wish.' She is willing to cooperate, but only because the SD has ordered it."

Greg, who had been listening to the exchange, leaned into the conversation. "I'm not sure that's enough. Are there any other options?"

"There are none as expert as Ateah. The local Speaker would be equally qualified, of course, but Rmah is suspicious of the Governor, and therefore the Governor's Speaker."

David looked up, wondering how to explore this without appearing to explore it, to be interested, just not *too* interested. "Suspicious?"

"Rmah has had several communications with the Governor, and he believes there is a strong inference of disrespect in his responses. It is almost, but not quite, outright disobedience."

"I see. Perhaps the Governor just likes his position and is loath to surrender it?"

"Yes, that is possible."

David worked extra hard not to toss a knowing look at Gabrielle or Joanne Henderson. Time to let this drop and move on. He turned to Gabrielle and Greg.

"OK, what's the verdict? Is she in or not?"

Ateah spoke to Asoon. *"What are they saying?"*

"They are deciding whether or not to trust you. They asked if there were any other Speakers available, and I told them there were none as expert as you. They are also discussing the Governor. Rmah Segt is suspicious of his intentions."

"He should obey his commanders."

"Yes, Ateah, he should. The humans are not confident that he will. Neither am I."

Greg shrugged. "She's the best available, right? So, I guess we take her."

Asoon turned to Ateah. *"They have decided to accept your services. My life may depend on your skills, too, Ateah. Do not disappoint me."*

Gabrielle picked up her NetComp. "I've made a summary of what we've learned about the Zeds — "

"Zeds?" David interrupted.

Gabrielle smiled. "At some point, David, you get tired of saying 'Zeta Doradus culture.' So, yes, *Zeds*."

"I see. Go on."

"As I was about to say, before the Preeminent arrived the Zeds were a peaceful, hard-working species. They hunted small animals, fished in the rivers and ocean nearby, and grew crops that, based on the descriptions we've been given, appear to be similar to beans and wheat."

"Seems pretty normal," Joanne commented.

"Yes, surprisingly so," Gabrielle agreed, "They're bipedal, warm-blooded, in their general form not that different from humans. Three fingers on each hand, so, six in total. Their society is organized by family, eighteen major groups."

Joanne looked at David. "They sound a lot like the Seekers. Didn't they also have six fingers?"

David nodded. "Yes, but six on each hand."

Gabrielle went back to her summary. "The Preeminent can offer nothing about their mating habits or societal norms. The Preeminent overcame their resistance easily — they don't seem to have much military technology — and since then, the natives have not been a security problem. The only complaint from the PG is that sometimes they did not produce the required quota of 'deleelinosh,' a swimming food animal much desired by the Preeminents here at

Alpha Mensae."

"Um, PG?" David asked.

"Preeminent Governor. Same logic as 'Zed.'"

"Got it. Just what is their level of tech?"

"Their homes are mostly stone, with some glass and primitive steel and iron components. Think, like, Europe in the middle ages or something. Wooden wheeled vehicles, large domesticated work animals, that kind of thing."

"So, Asoon," David asked, "is the inference here that they are lazy, or resisting somehow, or are their production failures due to some natural process?"

"There is no conclusion regarding that. The natives claim natural reasons like disease, or heat, or cold, or some similar reason."

"I see, thanks."

Gabrielle cleared her throat before going on. "There is one more item that is very curious."

"Oh?"

"There do not seem to be any *old* Zeds. The Preeminent reports indicate that they all seem to be in early adulthood: fit, hard-working, strong."

David looked up from his note-taking. "No elderly? No grandparents?"

Asoon spoke up. "I should point out, just for clarity, that there is no such concept in Preeminent society. I, for example, have had no contact with my maleParent or Egg-layer since I walked up the steps to the Pairing Facility to meet Scad. This is just our way. So, what you describe is not something we look for in an alien society."

"Still, no old people? No one slower, possibly bent-over, with other physical changes due to aging?"

"No."

David glanced at Greg, who gave him a slight shrug. "What is your conclusion?"

"Well, my best guess is that they are culling the old somehow. Upon reaching some predetermined age, they are removed."

Joanne spoke, her curiosity aroused. "Any chance they're just moving them away, keeping you from seeing them?"

Asoon turned to look at her. "We think not. We have examined the entire culture in detail from orbit. If there were other settlements, we would know."

"Anything else?" David asked.

"No."

There was an uneasy silence which Joanne thankfully broke. "*Intrepid* has another assignment we must fulfill before we go to Zeta Doradus."

"When do you expect to arrive?"

Joanne checked her NetComp. "Current estimate is that we will be there about 4 March."

Asoon checked her own notes. "Yes, I will let Rmah know. He will inform the Governor. Why so long? It isn't far."

"We have a scientific task we must complete before we will proceed to Zeta Doradus."

"I see."

David thought he caught a hint of skepticism in Asoon's voice, but her intonations were not quite human, and it would be easy to misinterpret her. He'd ask Gabrielle and Greg about it later.

"Ateah and I will be there to meet you."

Their discussion completed, they rose and walked down the long corridors of the SD Headquarters building to the landing field where David had first landed in the pre-dawn darkness to meet Asoon and Scad Nee Wok. As they emerged into the bright light of Alpha Mensae, Joanne looked at David, her face twisted unpleasantly.

"Does it always smell like this?"

David just smiled as they strapped themselves into the *Intrepid* shuttle's cockpit and Joanne prepared to fly them back to the ship.

"Oh, yeah. Always."

Office of Rmah Teo Segt
Core City, Alpha Mensae (c)
Monday, February 12, 2080, 1330 UTC

Rmah Teo Segt thanked and dismissed Asoon, her report of the meeting with the humans complete. He left his small office and walked up several flights of stairs to the spacious, window-lined office of his maleParent, Glur Woe Segt, Principal Scientist and de facto leader of the society.

"They're gone," he reported.

"And what did they say about System 952?"

"Nothing significant. Powell and Henderson say that it is merely the system where they have chosen to begin."

"Do you believe them?"

"No. I'm quite sure they're lying, but I don't know why. You and I have our own suspicions about the governor there."

Glur Woe Segt stood and looked out his window at the city a hundred meters below. "Yes."

"It can't be by chance that the humans are starting there. They said nothing about starting liberations at all until a decirev ago. Then, all at once they're asking about 952? It's very suspicious."

"Yes, I agree. And this supposed scientific task they claim *Intrepid* must attend to is another transparent lie."

54

"I thought so as well. Asoon feels the same."

"They don't lie casually, Rmah, and they don't always lie to deceive."

"Why else would one lie, except to deceive?"

Glue turned to his maleChild. "To protect. By not telling us the real reason they're going to 952, we can't interfere with their plan, whatever it is, even by accident."

"Are they protecting themselves or us?"

"Possibly both." Glur returned to the large armchair that was the province of the Principal Scientist. "The Governor there is a rogue. I can feel it in my teeth. I know it. But beyond his attitude, I lack any kind of proof."

"Somehow, I doubt the humans are worried about his loyalty to you."

"You may be right, but remember, they spent blood and treasure to dislodge the First and by doing so place me here. They would not want that investment threatened. Stability here is ultimately in their interests, too."

Glur thought for a moment, moving slightly left and right in his chair.

"Still, I agree that would not be their first concern. They know something, Rmah, something important, something they don't believe they can share with us."

"Something that they see as a threat."

Glur stopped moving. "Yes."

"When will we know?"

"When they're ready. Possibly never."

"We have trusted them, maleParent, but I remain uncomfortable with them. Their power..."

"Remains a threat to us, I know. For now, we are at peace, and we shall remain so. I believe in Powell. I do not think he would betray us."

"So, we wait?" Rmah responded impatiently.

"Yes, for now, we wait. And, we watch."

Rmah rose and made his way back to his own workspace. The humans *had* shown integrity so far, even to the point of combat to remove the Revered First when the SD could not do it. But Rmah knew very well that every culture must defend itself first, and if something threatened the humans, they would defend themselves. If that act also protected the Preeminent, that would be a secondary consideration.

Trust did not come easily to his species, but he saw no reason to break with the humans despite his suspicions. He could not conceive *how* his culture could break with them, having just lost an expensive war with them. He would have to wait, however uncomfortably, and see what develops.

Hansen/Powell Quarters
Ft. Eustis, VA
Monday, February 12, 2080, 2100 EST

There had already been two SLIPs from David. She had read them but not replied. If she didn't respond soon, she knew he would do something dramatic to rescue her because he wasn't here to rescue her himself. She loved that part of him, the protector who didn't protect too closely but was there when she needed him.

It had been a long day, and she felt drained by the effort each day took, but she set down her drink on the nightstand and picked up her NetComp to send him a message. He wouldn't see it for almost sixty hours, but if she didn't send something soon, he'd just worry that much more.

```
SLIP PERSONAL 208002130100UTC

TO: INTREPID/SLT DAVID POWELL
FROM: FLEETPLANS/LDCR CAROL HANSEN

DEAR DAVID -

GOT YOUR MESSAGES BUT BUSY WITH WORK AND SCHOOL.
I WAS BEHIND AT COMMAND SCHOOL BUT NOW BACK UP TO SPEED.
ALL WELL THERE NOW.

MILLER STILL SAME PITA AS BEFORE.
WISH I KNEW WHICH ONE OF US PISSED HER OFF.

I'M TIRED BUT OTHERWISE OK. DON'T WORRY SO MUCH.
YOU'LL BE HOME SOON.

LOVE, CAROL

END
```

The fact was, the AI Planner had made an incomprehensible furball out of her proposal for the northern recon project. Carol looked at the complex routing and bewildering pattern of ship assignments and wondered if she couldn't have done better with a corkboard, index cards, and string.

Miller was not impressed with her assessment of the AI's performance. Very much not impressed. So, Carol returned to revising the goals and constraints to get the software to cough up something more palatable.

And no, she wasn't up to speed at the Command School. Truth was, she was behind, and the distance between her and her classmates was growing daily.

Intrepid
En Route Zeta Doradus
Wednesday, February 14, 2080, 0645 UTC

Another day's review of the Preeminent data on the Zeds lay ahead, but David hadn't left his cabin. He was pleased to be bunked with his old buddy and classmate Larry Covington, and they spent several evenings in the wardroom catching up on everything that had happened since they'd been apart. A lot of it was just 'guy-talk,' but it was really good guy-talk.

This morning, though, David's mind was fixed on Carol. He'd been worried about her before he left for Alpha Mensae, and nothing had happened since to alleviate that. His two previous messages had gone unanswered, and he was at a loss of what to do next. *One more message,* he decided, *I'll try once more.*

```
SLIP PERSONAL 208002140700UTC
TO: FLEETPLANS/LCDR CAROL HANSEN
FROM: INTREPID/SLT DAVID POWELL

STILL HOPING TO HEAR FROM YOU SOON.

DAVID

END
```

After it was sent, he wondered again if it had been enough, if he'd really chosen the right words. Was it too little? By the end of the day, he decided he'd done enough worrying. He had to get more help. Carol wasn't one to just ignore his messages.

Something was up.

```
SLIP PERSONAL 208002141500UTC
TO: SFU/LDCR NATALIE HAYDEN
FROM: INTREPID/SLT DAVID POWELL

LCDR HAYDEN:

I AM WORRIED ABOUT CAROL. SHE WAS HAVING NIGHTMARES AND
OTHER SLEEP ISSUES, ETC. SINCE BEFORE I LEFT.
NOW SHE IS NOT RESPONDING TO MESSAGES.
ANY CHANCE YOU COULD MAKE A SHORT TRIP TO HQ AND SEE HER?
I AM THINKING AN IN-PERSON VISIT BY SOMEONE SHE RESPECTS
WOULD BE HELPFUL.

MANY THANKS.
POWELL

END
```

It was a considerable risk, but David felt he was running out of options to help Carol. Natalie Hayden would go, he was sure, but how Carol would take it was another question. He considered a separate message to her folks in Ohio but decided against it. They would be alarmed and come rushing in like good parents do, but that was not what he believed she needed.

Space Fleet University
US Campus
Friday, February 16, 2080, 1230 EST (1730 UTC)

Natalie's eyes widened as she read the SLIP message from David Powell. She remembered him, of course, having been at their wedding back in September. She'd danced with Carol's father Ols, a gentle, funny old farmer who'd made her laugh for the first time in recent memory. Her first impression of David was of the nondescript, sandy-haired lieutenant who had gone face-to-face with the Revered First and fired the first shot into him. She'd learned of his relationship with Carol only as they started up the long, bloody spiral ramp from the First's inner sanctum.

She more vividly remembered Hansen as the enormously brave and competent officer she'd first met just after she'd done the impossible: landing a Mercury-Soyuz class destroyer on the Beta Hydri planet they called 'Big Blue.' Then, of course, there was the Battle of Seeker Woods, where she, Carol, and Marine Lieutenant Liwanu Harry had teamed up with the Seekers to defeat two shuttles full of Preeminent Combatants. The bright red tunic she'd ripped off a Preeminent officer's corpse, just before the Seekers dragged it into the ocean for disposal, had been thoroughly cleaned and was even now secure in her personal footlocker back home. She smiled slightly at the memory of her exchange with Carol, who had shot the officer as Natalie was lining him up in her sights.

The idea that Hansen might be suffering emotionally from her war experiences surprised Natalie. She seemed so level-headed, so, well, skilled at managing stress, Natalie just would never have expected her to be susceptible to PTSD, or whatever it was she was experiencing.

In later, more casual conversations, David didn't strike her as the hysterical type, someone given to overreaction. That he would call on her, a good six hundred kilometers away, spoke to his level of concern about his wife. She booked a room for Friday night at the Ft. Eustis BOQ and took a late afternoon subcar to Virginia.

Saturday morning, she stopped in the HQ commissary for coffee and bakery and arrived at Carol's door just before 8 AM. When the door opened, Natalie could scarcely believe it was her.

"Natalie? What the hell are you doing here?" she asked in a hoarse voice. Her hair was shoved to one side, her eyes bloodshot and rimmed with red. There was a drawn, drained look to her face that Natalie didn't like at all. Clearly, Powell had known what he was talking about. Natalie knew there was no time to waste, and she was not about to exercise much subtlety.

"Saving your ass, that's what," she said as she pushed past Carol into the house.

"What?"

Natalie took her by the arm. "Come with me." She pulled her down the hall into the bathroom, standing her in front of the mirror. "See *her*? *See* her? Where's that girl I fought with in the woods, Carol? Where's the commander who landed a freaking destroyer and saved the entire crew?"

"Natalie, I — "

"Where is she, Carol?" Natalie stepped back and looked hard at her friend. "Jesus, Carol, how much weight have you lost?"

"I don't know, I just haven't — " Natalie pulled her onto the scale.

"One fifteen, Hansen. You've lost at least twenty."

Carol just looked down. "I guess. Maybe twenty-five."

"Yeah, getting married is kinda like freshman year, right?"

"I lost ten freshman year."

Natalie rolled her eyes. "Of course you did." Natalie led her back to the kitchen, never letting go of her arm. She set her down in a chair and put the coffee and bakery in front of her. "There. Drink. Eat."

Carol took a cautious sip of coffee but just stared at the gigantic cinnamon swirl donuts.

"You went to the commissary."

"No shit. Eat."

She took a careful bite. "There, satisfied?"

"Not really, no." Natalie sat down next to Carol. "Tell me what's going on."

Carol looked up, suspicious. "David sent you?"

"Does that matter, I mean, really? I'm here. Talk."

"I'm fine. I'm doing OK."

"Yeah, bullshit. Tell the truth, Hansen."

Carol worked her way through half the donut in silence. After another sip of coffee, she looked up at Natalie. "They won't leave me alone."

Natalie paused, taking a sip of her own coffee to buy herself a few seconds to think. When she spoke, the confrontation was gone from her voice. "Who won't leave you alone?"

"The ones I got killed. Michael, Swenson, Cornell, all of them."

Natalie pushed the chair aside and put her arms around Carol, who didn't resist. In a few moments, Natalie could feel her sobs and let up just a little.

As she did, it all came pouring out. "Oh, god, don't you *see*? Can't you see I was just faking it? *All* of it? I had no idea what I was doing. They promoted me and put me in charge, and I just had to pretend I knew what I was doing...and I got them all killed, Natalie, it's ALL my fault!"

Natalie let her talk, not wanting to interrupt her now that the emotional gates were open.

"They always talk about me in Inoria...Leon was the genius in Inoria, not me...and I got him killed, too. He protected all of us...and Beta Hydri...I just got lucky that Jack was there so I could follow his lead.... then Captain Michael...and Marcia, dammit, Marcia..."

She cried again, hard, then said, "Oh, god, I think..." Natalie got her to the bathroom just in time, then held her hair back as she retched out the pain and grief. As the spasms faded, Carol slid to the floor, leaning back against the tub, and looked up as if to see Natalie for the first time as she handed her a glass of water.

"What *are* you doing here?"

"Like I said, saving your ass." She shrugged. "Someone has to. Might as well be me."

Carol laid her head back, eyes closed. "I'm not sure it's worth the effort."

"I'll be the judge of that. Feeling better?"

Carol covered her eyes with her hands. "So tired. Abs hurt."

"Yeah, barfing your guts out can do that to you. How about you get a little more sleep? I'll hang around and we'll get out later."

Carol reached out and Natalie helped her to her feet. "I'm still pissed David sent you."

"Did I say that? I don't recall saying that."

"Jeez, you're a crappy liar. Worse than David."

Natalie walked to the bedroom with her, pretending to help but really making sure there was nothing there she could take or drink. There wasn't. Carol shed the sweatshirt and baggy sweatpants she'd pulled on when Natalie was at the door and climbed back into bed, pulling the covers up to her neck.

"OK, Hansen. Sleep a couple hours, and then we'll take a walk or something, OK?"

"Whatever." Carol closed her eyes, and in a minute or two Natalie could tell she was asleep.

Natalie went back to the kitchen to think. She finished off her own donut and most of her coffee as she considered what to do next: where to go and who to call. She was at a loss until she thought to check on ship dispositions to see who was in orbit.

Sigma.

Of course. Carol's old ship was here. Her second command, a ship full of people who adored her. She opened her phone. "*Sigma*, XO."

There was a delay of several seconds before the line connected. "Commander *White*."

"Peg, it's Nat Hayden."

"Hello, Nat. Long time."

"Yeah. Beta Hydri, I guess. Listen, I have a problem and I need your help."

"Oh? What's the problem?"

"Hansen."

Denise Long was at Carol's door by 1300, with Lori Rodgers at her side. Alex Williams, Carol's XO while she was in command, wanted to come too, but Lori and Denise insisted this must be a women-only intervention.

"There will be too much stuff we'd need to explain to you that we won't have time to explain." was all Lori would tell him. He was left alone in the hangar, still trying to parse that sentence as the doors of the ShuttleLock closed behind them.

Carol had just awoken when they arrived and was both surprised and wary of her new visitors. But she was happy to see their smiles. Natalie pushed her into taking a shower, and then Lori spent a good twenty minutes on her makeup. That was more time than Carol would usually spend in a whole week, but she looked much more herself when it was done.

They piled into Natalie's rented ASV and headed north across the York River to a restaurant up in Stingray Point that Ben had introduced to her. The food was excellent, and the atmosphere was different from anything in Newport News. Carol needed a change in scenery, and she sure needed a decent meal. Here, she got both.

Intrepid
En Route Zeta Doradus
Tuesday, February 20, 2080, 0700 UTC

David was just finishing breakfast when his phone buzzed with a message.

```
SLIP PERSONAL 208002171700UTC
TO: INTREPID/SLT DAVID POWELL
FROM: SFU/LCDR NATALIE HAYDEN

YOUR CONCERNS ARE WELL FOUNDED. I ARRIVED THIS MORNING AND
TALKED TO HER FOR A LONG TIME. CLEARLY NOT SLEEPING AND I
THINK SELF-MEDICATING WITH ALCOHOL WHICH AS YOU KNOW IS
NO HELP.

SIGMA IS HERE. LORI RODGERS AND DENISE LONG ARE ON THEIR
WAY DOWN TO JOIN US. I AM PLANNING TO GET HER OUT OF THE
```

```
HOUSE WITH US FOR A WHILE.

I WILL UPDATE YOU LATER AS NECESSARY. I ARRANGED FOR A FEW
DAYS OFF FROM SFU.

HAVE FAITH. SHE IS STRONG UNDERNEATH IT ALL AND YOU MADE
THE RIGHT CALL TO GET HER HELP.

NAT

END
```

Gabrielle could not miss the pained look on his face. "David?"

He shrugged. "Carol is having a hard time with what happened during the war. I think she just lost too many people she cared about."

Gabrielle shook her head. "She did so well. I would never have thought..."

"Yes, she did great. But it's all coming back to her now, and she's just not so sure she did all the right things."

"But. she did, right?"

"I think so, yes. So does everyone else I know. But, that's not what she thinks, and that's the problem."

"You'll tell me if there is anything I can do? I so admired her work at Beta Hydri."

"You and I are too far away at the moment to do much good. But I will let you know if there is something that would help."

"You do that."

David got up and left the wardroom, headed for his cabin. He thought about sending Natalie a response, but her message was already two days old, and whatever she, Lori, and Denise had been able to do for Carol had already been done. The best choice for him was to sit tight and wait for more information from Natalie.

He set down his phone and picked up his NetComp, dutifully studying again the information Gabrielle and Greg had collected from the Preeminent about the Zeds. It wasn't easy to concentrate, but it was his job, and he knew Carol would be sorely disappointed in him if he let worrying about her get in the way of his duties.

No old Zeds. That tidbit kept coming back to him, and he just could not let it go. There had to be a rational explanation, but he had no idea what it might be. Ritual slaughter at some arbitrary birthday just didn't seem very plausible to him.

Two days later, he received Natalie's second message. The women had stayed with Carol for two more days, and by the end, she was ready to admit her pain was more than she could handle on her own. Natalie took her to FleetPers where Darin Perez spent several hours with her.

A day after that, Carol's message came:

```
SLIP PERSONAL 208002201030UTC
TO: INTREPID/SLT DAVID POWELL
FROM: FLEETPLANS/LDCR CAROL HANSEN

HAVE I MENTIONED LATELY HOW MUCH I LOVE YOU?

THANKS FOR THE RESCUE PARTY EVEN THOUGH I DIDN'T WANT IT.

I WILL SAY MORE LATER AFTER I'VE HAD SOME TIME WITH THE COUNSELOR.
NATALIE RATTED ME OUT TO CINC SO HE PUT ME ON INVOLUNTARY
MEDICAL LEAVE FOR THE DURATION. SHE IS THE BEST.

BUT I THINK MILLER'S HEAD MAY SPIN OFF ITS AXIS.

THREE TIMES.
CAROL

END
```

He smiled at 'three times,' an ongoing reference to a moment just after they were first together as a couple. David was just back on Earth after being thought dead on *Sigma*. Carol told him 'I love you' three times, emphasizing a different word each time. That had made it finally sink in for both of them, and it had been something of a touchstone for them ever since.

He laughed at the reference to her new boss, Commander Miller, who had been giving her a rough time. Some time away from that stressor would be a welcome change.

As he re-read the message, he realized it sounded like her; the bright, quick, courageous young woman he had fallen hopelessly in love with years before. He had not seen that person for several months, and he was glad she was back.

CHAPTER 4

Cobra
Zeta Doradus (e)
Friday, February 22, 2080, 1300 UTC

Rich Evans brought *Cobra* out of FTL near the fifth planet in the Zeta Doradus system, a gas planet well out from the star, listed in the catalog as Zeta Doradus(e). *Intrepid* was already there, and laser communications were quickly established between the two vessels. Henderson packed her passengers and herself into a shuttle and headed over to *Cobra*. This briefing would be best done there.

Gabrielle began with a review of what the Preeminent had told them about the Zeds. The lack of old people surprised them, but David, as usual, tempered that.

"Let's remember, everyone, that we're assuming Zeds age like we do — weakness, sagging muscles and connective tissue, that kind of thing. We don't know that is true for the Zeds."

Jack Ballard pulled up a display of the settled part of the planet. The Preeminent spaceport was in the center of the culture, four large roads radiating out. "The main roads then split into smaller roads that eventually lead to these pens in the shallows of the ocean." He pointed to a large area of constructions just a short distance off the beach. "There are hundreds of these six-sided objects we've assessed as fish hatcheries."

David pointed to the pens as he looked across at Evans. "That tracks with Asoon's information, sir. They export some kind of fish as a delicacy back to Alpha Mensae."

"Good, that makes sense. Now, these roads — " Ballard indicated the large roads leading from the spaceport, " — are new. We assume the Preeminent carved those out to get the product in more efficiently." He then shifted the picture slightly and changed to an IR image. "But these paths, here almost under the tree cover, are old." The IR image revealed a different network, leading away from the spaceport to the north and south.

"Clearly," Rich Evans said, taking the reins from Ballard, "the spaceport split this old path, which seems to be the original main line of communication among the Zeds." He looked back at his audience to see that they were following.

"So," Joanne asked, "what is that area up north at the end of the old road?"

Evans smiled. "Very good question, Captain. We don't know."

"Traffic?" David asked.

"Yes," Ballard replied. "Foot and cargo traffic every day until dark. After that, there is some minor foot traffic, but once we start to get towards midnight, it stops until after sunrise."

"Cargo?" David asked. "Oh, and how do they carry stuff around, anyway?"

"Carts. Shadows make them look six-wheeled, and something like four meters long. There is some cargo traffic on the old path, but most of it is on the Preeminent roads, serving their ships from the shoreline."

"What about the people?" Gabrielle asked.

"That's interesting, too. There are two distinct populations. The workers in the pens and most of those on the wagons are shorter, maybe a meter and a half, give or take. The second population is taller, at least a meter and three-quarters. They stay closer to home, it would seem."

"Males and females?" Joanne asked.

Evans shrugged. "Maybe. Workers and thinkers? Who knows?"

Gabrielle looked again at the information she had gathered at Alpha Mensae. "No mention of gender or body size in the info from the Preeminent."

"They probably didn't care," Joanne said.

Jack smiled. "One more thing: the planet rotates in twenty hours, twelve minutes."

David sank back down into his chair. "Gonna be some short nights, folks."

"Yeah, and the orbit is way more eccentric than any inhabited planet we've seen before. The planet has only a slight inclination, five degrees or less, but they must have seasons because of the variation in distance from the star."

"Where are they right now?"

"They're about two-thirds back towards perihelion, so it's getting warmer. Their year is 494 days, which correlates to 587 sols."

"But, sir," David asked, "what the hell are they doing here?"

"What do you mean?"

"The Zeta Doradus system is less than a billion years old. It's far too young for higher forms like this — I mean, come on! Trees? Grasses? Fish? People? Really? It makes no sense."

"Well, Lieutenant Powell, maybe we can ask them just how they got there."

David looked at his old boss and frowned. Evans just looked back.

It was time to regroup and split; David and the academics remained on *Cobra*, destined for an in-person, close-up ground examination of the Zeds. Joanne and her officers headed back to *Intrepid*, which would remain away from the planet, ready to back up *Cobra* if needed, then 'arrive' on schedule after Asoon and Ateah.

A few hours later, *Cobra* slipped back into high orbit at Zeta Doradus (b). After several hours of searching, Evans was satisfied that there was nothing new above the planet. There was, in fact, nothing in orbit; not a single artificial satellite to be found. That made sense given the technological level of the Zeds, but Evans was surprised the Preem, as those on *Cobra* had come to call the Preeminent, didn't have some kind of presence overhead. Another example of their conceit? Maybe.

David and Jack Ballard spent the next day reviewing the imagery *Cobra* had obtained over the previous week. They generated a 3-D rendering of the landscape just north of the landing site and studied it with the Recon Marine lead, Gunnery Sergeant Sabrina Herrera, looking for the right place to spy on the Zeds. They finally settled on a small hill near a town, one village removed from the Preeminent landing field.

Sabrina pointed to a feature off to the west. "Here, see, is a little ravine, maybe thirty meters wide. There's a small stream at the bottom, but see how it's all off to one side? There's a flat ... here… that we can put the recon shuttle down on."

Evans looked over her shoulder at the display. "Looks like someone would have to be almost at the edge of the ravine to see the shuttle in that location."

Herrera nodded. "Yes, sir, that's my analysis, too."

David, standing on the opposite side of the worktable, asked, "How far is the walk?"

"Three kilometers as the bird flies, maybe three and a half on foot."

Gabrielle looked at the location, moving the display down to see the full 3-D effect. "I can handle that. Gravity is a little less, right?"

"Not that much," Jack answered, "about eighty-five percent. But the star is brighter than Sol, and the days shorter."

David looked at the display again. "Any evidence that the natives venture out into this area? Any paths or trails?"

Ballard shook his head. "None that we can detect in visual or IR. It seems to be a bit of wilderness that they more or less ignore."

"Kinda close to the town to call it a wilderness," David commented.

Evans crossed his arms and looked at David. "Come on, Powell, how many times have you ridden down a highway and seen a forest or woods that's overgrown, complete with fallen trees and rotting stumps? No one has been in those places for years, while thousands have passed by a few dozen meters away."

"Respectfully, sir, you don't know that, but I do understand what you're saying. I agree it's a good location, as good as we're likely to find, but it is not a location without risk."

"'No risk' is not part of our business, David."

"Yes, sir, true."

"OK then, it's decided. You'll go down after the next local midnight."

"That's 1150 tomorrow, sir," Jack offered.

"Fine. Five days on the surface. I want heartbeat messages by laser every four hours." He turned to his lead marine. "Herrera?"

"Yes, sir. I'll take three RM's with me. I don't see that we need any more than that."

"Just so we're clear, Sergeant, you may fire only if fired upon, and even then, only if you feel that fire is a real threat."

"Are we talking Zeds or Preem?"

"Preem. If the Zeds fire on you — which I strongly doubt is even possible — you can shoot in the air or whatever to scare them off, but don't fire on them directly."

"Very well, sir."

"With Ballard and Powell, there's eight of you. That maxes out the recon shuttle. The days are short, so make sure you're planning your trips and returns accordingly."

"David and I have already talked, sir," Jack said. "We'll split the day-trips between us, alternating teams with the RMs and Gabe and Greg."

"Good. Powell, you're nominally in charge down there. But you all know how to work together, and I expect you to do that."

"Yes, Commander," Jack replied, "it won't be a problem."

Just before 1100 the next day, David and Jack flipped a coin for the left seat, and David 'won' the right. That is, he lost. As they slipped out of *Cobra*'s ShuttleLock, he felt the familiar apprehension of a mission about to begin, one that carried some danger but one he had also prepared for about as well as he could. He was reminded of the wreck at GL 876, entering through a shattered window in an EVA suit and winding through sharp, broken metal to find the first bits of Preeminent remains. Then, he was truly scared.

David watched the planet grow in the windscreen, a dark disk that became punctuated with the dim light of torches and home fires only as they passed through a thousand meters on the descent. Looking up, directly overhead, he could clearly see the reddish glow of the dust ring that lay about five AU from the star. This was the first star system he had visited with such a distinct dust feature, but this was also easily the youngest star they had visited. Those facts were not coincidental in David's mind. He was pretty sure only a young system like this one would have such a significant ring.

Jack landed the shuttle quietly in the ravine, next to the creek, aided by his night-vision glasses and the 3-D rendering of the location in the heads-up display. They cut the red-mode interior lights before they opened the starboard hatch, and Herrera and her RM's stepped out. After a few minutes, David heard 'all clear' in his headset and stepped out himself.

The first thing he heard was the familiar sound of water flowing just a few meters away, dropping over rocks, splitting and rejoining in small sub-streams.

The air was calm and cool, and he caught a hint of smoke in it as well. The planet suddenly seemed less alien, but right behind that feeling was David's internal danger alarm: *never get too comfortable*. He kept up his guard as he explored around the ship.

Jack finished his post-flight checklist, then came out to inspect the shuttle's position and verify that they were on a solid footing. He flipped his communications to the ship channel.

"Shuttle One down and secure." He received a quick, one-word acknowledgment from *Cobra*.

While David and Jack were checking the shuttle, Herrera and her RM's were climbing the east wall of the ravine, using a dry creek bed they'd seen in the imagery as a ramp. At the top, they spread out and lay prone, watching for any movement in the direction of the villages.

After a half-hour, they came back to report there was nothing to report.

A good start, David thought.

Well before dawn, David, Gabrielle, and two RM's began the long walk to the hill they had selected for an observation post. It was just west of a decent-sized village, far enough that the Zeds would be unlikely to see them but close enough to watch their activities. The star was just beginning to light the sky in the east as they set up on the west side of the hill. David placed the recon camera, a tube a few centimeters in diameter and a quarter meter long, beneath the underbrush at the crest. The planet had forests much like Terran forests, but near the edges there were low shrubs: prickly, densely convoluted things about a meter tall, with a wide gap underneath that gave them easy vision to the road about fifty meters away. As David looked through the opening, he realized the shrubs were actually enormous structures. They had trunks not dissimilar to what he might see under a bush back home, but they were at least ten meters apart.

The camera placed, he moved back to the foot of the hill and pulled up the video on his NetComp. The recon camera also contained a laser range-finder and a sensitive, highly directional microphone. Greg would no doubt enjoy listening to the new language, and the range-finder would help them better quantify dimensions they had only been able to estimate from orbit.

The first day passed without incident. David observed many Zeds walking the road, some carrying what looked like large backpacks. Not long after solar noon, a parade of a dozen cargo wagons moved past, twelve large round barrels on each six-wheeled flatbed, moving south towards the Preeminent's spaceport pulled by large work animals that looked a lot like oxen to David.

After he shared this with her, Gabrielle looked at him and said, "Different planet, same task, same solution? Could this just be natural selection making similar choices in similar circumstances?" David had to agree it seemed plausible.

But it also seemed decidedly weird.

Everything was normal for four Zed sols. David and Gabrielle swapped duty with Jack and Greg each sol, the duty team staying at the observation post from before sunrise to after sunset. Once back at the shuttle, they would sleep well into the next sol while the other team worked.

Greg was getting plenty of audio, which he compared to what he had learned of the Zed language back on Alpha Mensae. The language reminded him of some Asian languages on Earth, with complex tonalities and lifts and drops he didn't yet understand. It was far more familiar than the Preeminents' bird-like language or the guttural complexities of the Inori. Greg thought if the Preeminent could speak it with their somewhat underdeveloped vocal system, he ought to be able to master it. Eventually.

Everything was normal until the fifth sol. When, as David and Gabrielle watched, the Zeds sent an extra wagon, and sent it late. They had no idea what that might mean until well after dark.

Then came the rolling sound of multiple detonations from the south.

Pouring over the overhead imagery after the explosion, David and Sergeant Herrera found what they thought was a safe route south. The spaceport was about six klicks to the south, a half-klick east of the ravine at that point. They could walk almost all of the way in the ravine, hidden from the village they would pass, then make their way across a meadow to a small forest that bordered the landing field on the west.

Jack Ballard and the academics would remain at the shuttle, with the vehicle powered up and ready to pull David and Sabrina out of trouble if necessary. The other three RM's would stay with the shuttle in case the Preeminent discovered them.

David and Sabrina set out before midnight, with just five hours before the star would be coming back over the horizon. As they worked their way quickly to the south, trying to both keep their feet dry and not trip over the numerous rocks and boulders that populated the floor of the ravine, they watched the yellow light dancing off the clouds.

"It's fading," she said, just above a whisper.

"Yeah, no question," David replied. "Whatever is on fire is burning out."

They hit their departure point from the ravine ahead of schedule, an hour before sunrise, and moved quickly across the open meadow to the relative safety of the forest. Sabrina knelt down behind the ubiquitous low shrubs and dropped her backpack on the ground. Quickly unzipping it, she drew out the padded plastic container holding the small recon drone. She assembled it in less than a minute, attaching the battery pack, then holding down the master switch until it came to life. As it did, it rose a foot off the ground and deployed the sensor apparatus on the bottom. David smiled as he selected an IR camera and snapped it in place.

"OK, are we ready?" he asked.

"Yes. I've set auto-return for this location, just in case."

"Right, the shuttle would be out of range. Let's fly."

Sabrina set the drone's altitude for a hundred meters, and it rose rapidly above them. As the picture steadied on the controller's screen, she rotated it to face the burning landing field, then moved it forward across the tops of the trees. It was silent, black, and theoretically invisible to anyone not specifically looking for it. Evans had agreed to let them use the new 'toy' since presumably the Preeminent would be preoccupied with the fire. And, it would still be night.

As the picture got clearer, they could see the wreckage of dozens of cargo wagons, their 'oxen' either dead or dying in their yokes. There were a few dozen Preeminent Combatants lying about, apparently dead, and thousands of small objects, likely the fish that were supposed to be in the barrels.

There were also several Preeminent standing at a distance, watching. The heat plume on the IR was fading, but David and Sabrina could clearly see the burnt-out remnants of some wagons, the open hatch on the storage tank, and the Preeminent wandering around.

"What are they doing?" Sabrina asked.

"Well," David answered, "if they're Combatants, as I expect they are, they're not all that smart. They wouldn't know to fight a fire."

"Or have the tools to do it?"

"Right. I doubt there's a fire hydrant anywhere around."

Sabrina stifled a laugh as she pointed to the storage tanks. "Are those holes?"

David looked carefully, zooming in as close as the IR optics on the little drone allowed. There were indeed randomly spaced, round spots on the side of the storage tank facing the explosion. There were none on the other side.

"Shrapnel?" she asked, surprised.

David nodded. "Can't think what else it would be. Rocks, maybe? Hunks of iron?"

"Whatever they used, it worked."

"Yeah, and maybe too well. This PG is a hard case, a follower of the Revered First. I would not want to be a Zed come sunrise."

"Anything we can do about that?" she asked hopefully.

"Nope. We're not here, remember?"

"Even if — " she stopped herself. "Never mind. What happens, happens. We're not here."

"Sergeant Herrera, you are beginning to understand intelligence work. Boring, frightening, sometimes infuriating."

She nodded grimly. "I'll recover the drone. It will be light before long, and we need to be back in the ravine before that."

They made it back to the ravine in darkness. The walk back north to the shuttle took over an hour, as they hustled as fast as they dared. No one saw them.

Once back in the shuttle, David dumped the drone's images into the shuttle database and uploaded them to *Cobra*.

Weiknu Village
Zeta Doradus (b)
Friday, March 1, 2080, 0220 UTC (local sunrise)

Udoro arose early, before sunrise, as was her habit. Even when she spent the night with Kutah, she was rarely still next to him when the sky became light in the east. The Weiknu village was close to the ocean, much closer than her own, and she had seen several striking, unusual sunrises since she arrived a few suns before.

She found that her chosen repro partner, Weiknu Tisok, was a decent male, a supervisor in the Weiknu ocean pens. He promised to be a good match for Udoro, kind and dependable, but he could never be like Kutah to her. She had made this plain to him from the first, and he had understood her easily, as there was a Weiknu female waiting for his return, too. Still, they found they liked each other well enough, and it seemed their repro time would be pleasant and productive.

As she stood outside his family home admiring the morphing colors in the sky, there was a cry of alarm from the north. Tisok rushed out of the rough-hewn hardwood door, the iron hinges squealing in protest. He took her firmly by the arm and pushed her back into the house, into the arms of his third-mother.

The star was just above the horizon when the Violets came strutting down the village's main street, where the most influential members of the village lived. They moved systematically from house to house, silently pulling males and females out of their homes and executing them. They dragged the bodies to the town's grassy center green, a pleasant space where the townspeople might gather to talk or celebrate, and stacked them there, blood flowing down and between and out of the remains. The screams and shouts of the natives were ignored until the body count got to twenty. At that point, they finished stacking the bodies and stood back.

A gray alien, what Udoro and her society call a 'Gray Liar,' since it was one like the Violets but smaller and dull in color, came into the square and announced that the deaths were in response to the attack on the Violets the previous night. Nothing more like that must happen again, it said, or many more would die.

The Gray Liar turned on its heel and walked back to the landing field, escorted by the killers.

Riaghe Udoro had hidden in a small room at the rear of her partner's home with his third-mother. The Violets didn't find them or, more accurately, didn't need to find them. They had killed their quota.

As the screaming outside subsided, Udoro emerged into an ugly, bloody scene of death and outrage. Looking for Tisok, Udoro followed the cries of anger and pain, only to see that Tisok had not been so fortunate.

There would be no happy homecoming for Tisok's Weiknu Enote. Her beloved male lay dead in the dark red mud in the center of the village. Udoro stared at Tisok's corpse for a full minute, the random, unthinking cruelty sinking deep into her as she listened to Enote's wails. She suddenly saw Kutah's face on his and felt for a split-second the bottomless loss of a thousand shared snows. She felt his now-cold body next to her own. Her knees failed her, and she found herself next to Enote, feeling real grief for perhaps the first time in her young life.

She hated it.

Cobra
Zeta Doradus (b)
Friday, March 1, 2080, 1330 UTC

Commander Rich Evans paced *Cobra*'s Operations Center, taking multiple laps around Center Console as he considered his options. The clouds that had concealed the fires at the Preeminent landing site had mainly cleared overnight, and he could now see the damage the Zeds had done to the Preeminent Combatants and storage tanks. Powell had just uploaded the drone imagery, too, and it was as dramatic as it was graphic. The whole scene was an ugly mess.

But the visuals from the first town to the northeast were far worse. They had seen Combatants move into the town, then lost coverage as a few inconvenient clouds moved past. An hour later, the clouds cleared, and they could see the Zeds removing bodies from the town circle that was a feature of every Zed town and village.

Evans knew what that meant, and he'd been expecting it since the first flash the night before. The unlucky, fickle weather had kept him from understanding the full scope of the Preem retaliation, but his techs had counted at least a dozen bodies being carried away.

The PG had extracted his pound of flesh.

Ballard asked for instructions shortly after dawn, as Powell was still working his way back. Evans ordered them to hold their position until he had a clearer picture of what was happening. Henderson had seen the data, too, and her platoon of Marines under Lieutenant Liwanu Harry was ready to suit up and teach the Preeminent 'a lesson they won't soon forget!' Evans knew Liwanu as a good leader, proven in combat with the Preeminent on at least three occasions, but this was not the time for an invasion. Evans counseled patience and adherence to the plan, and Henderson agreed.

Not long after David uploaded the drone images to Cobra, Evans had made up his mind.

"Comms...get me Powell."

David jumped as the communications console in the Recon Shuttle buzzed. "Powell."

"David, it's Evans."

"Yes, Commander." David flipped on the speaker so all could hear.

"The situation down there is no longer stable. This strike by the Zeds and retaliation by the PG has changed the dynamic."

"Retaliation, sir?" Jack Ballard asked.

"PG sent a squad into that first village to the southeast. Body count is at least a dozen, probably more."

The swear words ricocheted around the inside of the Recon Shuttle. Evans let it die down before continuing.

"I understand how you feel, believe me. The Marines up here are ready to put an end to this once and for all. But we can't do that. I want you to sit tight today. Get some sleep if you can. After dark, get back up here and we'll discuss what to do."

David hit the mute on the comms station. "Thoughts?"

"Shit," Greg commented.

David smiled slightly as he un-muted the comms. "Yes, Commander. We'll wait until, uh, maybe halfway to midnight. There'll be less traffic on the roads by then."

"That will be fine." There was a pause as Evans considered what else to say. "Listen, Jack and David, no adventures, understand? No little side-trips because it's your last chance to satisfy your curiosity. Stay right there and come back tonight."

"Understood, Commander. Wouldn't dream of wandering off."

"Very well." Evans hung up the phone without waiting for an answer.

Ballard heard the laser line drop and turned to his compatriots. "I've been with Evans for a while now. He means it. We stay right here and head back to *Cobra* after dark. OK?"

"Fine with me," Gabrielle commented. "I don't have to look like vegetation today."

Greg smiled. "But, my dear Gabrielle, you look so good as vegetation."

They laughed a little, then broke up to get some rest. Herrera maintained a two-hour watch rotation at the edge of the ravine, two RMs with field glasses at the top of the dry creek.

The warm, sunny day went by slowly. They spent it mostly outside under the clump of trees on the far side of the ravine. The calm and quiet of the day felt strange to David after a wild, frightening night. He caught a short nap later in the day and welcomed the feeling of motion when they lifted off in the darkness.

The next sun after Tisok was murdered, Udoro was back in her Riaghe home, exhausted. She was comforted by her second- and third-mothers, both of whom had seen loss at the hands of the Violets. By the end of the day, she felt well enough to venture out looking for Kutah. She found him at dusk, with Tefin, on their hill. Kutah held her as she talked until the Night Glow rose in the east, the stars bright in the clear sky above them.

"He was a good male, Kutah. He had someone he loved waiting for him, too."

"Yes, Tefin told me the whole story. We should always remember Tisok."

Udoro waved away his comment. "I will remember Enote. Her pain has plunged deep into my soul. I don't know how to heal the gash the Violets have left in me."

Kutah stroked her gently to both calm and reassure her. "I will always be here for you. We will walk this hard path together, as long as it takes."

She stiffened. "You can't say that. You don't know that. If the Violets catch you tomorrow, I'll be in Enote's place. Don't promise me what you can't deliver."

Kutah released her. "What you say is true. But, as long as I take breath, I will be here for you. We can't know what's coming, but whatever it is, I will always be devoted to you. That much I know I can promise."

She leaned back into him, and they remained on the hill until the Night Glow was high in the sky. They escaped the rapidly cooling air, spending the rest of the night at Kutah's.

In the morning, they shared their meal in silence.

Finally, Kutah asked her, "What happens now?"

Udoro set down her utensil. "I will receive a new list and make a new selection."

"How long?"

"A six-day, at least."

Kutah looked at her hopefully. "And meantime?"

Udoro touched his hand. "Meantime, I will be right here with you."

Kutah's face reflected his sadness and frustration. "I cannot do this many more times, Udoro. It was hard enough to see you leave the first time. I cannot do this over and over again."

Kutah finished his meal and left to prepare for his next trip to the Violet landing field. Elder Wocos had much to tell him and many warnings to give.

Intrepid
Zeta Doradus (b)
Monday, March 4, 2080, 0820 UTC

The time had come for *Intrepid* to 'arrive' at Zeta Doradus and begin the process of removing the Preeminent from the planet. *Cobra* had detected the arrival of a small Preeminent ship the previous sol, presumably carrying Asoon and Ateah. That same day David, Gabrielle, and Greg had flown out to the fifth planet of the system and re-boarded *Intrepid*.

Once back in orbit at Zeta Doradus (b), *Intrepid* established VHF communications with Asoon, and the time and place were set. David flew *Cobra*'s Recon Shuttle down, carrying only the academics, Joanne Henderson and Liwanu Harry. He landed near the headquarters building on the northeast side of the landing field, just a few meters from the Preeminent shuttle.

They didn't really expect trouble, but at Joanne's direction, the three officers wore sidearms.

"We mean business, not trouble," she explained as they drew weapons from the Marines' magazine. David surprised them as he drew out his personal weapon from the lockup. If he needed to shoot anything, he'd prefer the weapon that dropped the First.

"Is that what I think it is?" Joanne asked.

"Yes."

"Taking it for symbolic effect?" Liwanu asked.

David smiled. "You know, Lieutenant, I had not thought of that. I just wanted my own weapon. But, now that you mention it, that idea might come in handy. I'll keep it in mind."

Stepping out on the surface ninety minutes later, they were greeted by Asoon, Ateah, the Preeminent Governor, and his Speaker. 'Greeted' was a highly questionable description. The PG didn't want them there, and he made no effort to hide his opinion.

"So, here are the Vermin who have come to steal my planet?" Asoon translated.

David turned to Asoon. "The Governor is aware of his instructions, correct?"

"Yes, Rmah Teo Segt has been very clear." There was a sharp exchange between Asoon and the PG.

"Asoon?" Joanne inquired.

She looked at the PG and spoke briefly. The PG again spoke quickly, his hand gripped in fists. "The Governor insists I translate your questions or instructions to him and reply only with his words."

David looked at Joanne, then back to Asoon. "But you're not actually going to do that, right? He can't possibly know the difference."

The Governor moved closer to Asoon and spoke again. "He asks what we are saying and why you and I are not talking to him."

"Just tell him you're explaining his instructions and how dense we are at not understanding. He'll like that."

Asoon looked at David for just a second before turning back to the PG and speaking for several seconds. The PG seemed to grunt as she turned back to David.

"The Governor says he is surprised we should have lost to such a dim-witted race."

David smiled. "Perfect. Now what?"

"The Governor has selected a nearby village for you to make contact. His Speaker will make the announcement and handle translations for us."

Gabrielle spoke up. "And what of Ateah? Did we not bring her here for just this purpose?"

"The Governor insists. But, Ateah will be along."

David stepped aside, touching Joanne's arm as he moved several meters away.

"Lieutenant?" she asked.

"I don't like it, Captain. We should stick to *our* plan, not his. God only knows what she's going to say."

Gabrielle, overhearing David, came closer. "Yes, but we have Ateah as a backup. She knows why we're here and has some hint about the PG."

As they were talking, the PG raised his voice and pointed to Asoon and then at Joanne.

"The Governor is impatient, Vermin, and will not permit any further waste of his time."

David suppressed a smile. "Is that verbatim, Asoon?"

"It is."

David glanced at Joanne, who stepped back towards the group. "OK, then, we'll do it his way, for now."

It was less than a kilometer's walk to the village the PG had selected. He wanted to bring six Combatants along to guard them, but Joanne stepped in and refused the escort. They argued for several minutes, the Governor making clear that he was mostly concerned for his own safety, but Joanne would not be moved. Asoon finally reminded the PG that he had been ordered to comply. If the humans did not want the Combatants, they must stay back.

The PG replied with a long, loud string of syllables Asoon refused to translate.

"They would be, as you would say, derogatory obscenities."

David could not hide his amusement, and a smirk escaped his face, an expression he hoped the PG would not recognize. He shook his head and said, "OK, well, same to him. And, as the captain said, let's get moving."

Niocli Village
Zeta Doradus (b)
Monday, March 4, 2080, 1045 UTC

As they turned the last bend in the road to the village, they could see movement ahead, Zeds were moving back and forth, and they could hear the sounds of doors slamming. A small group gathered across the road, standing behind a lone individual. David noticed that the taller Zeds appeared to hang back, with the shorter ones standing towards the front. As they came closer, the one he assumed was the leader walked forward. That action struck David as courageous, and he took that as a positive sign. They halted about two meters apart.

The PG's Speaker began: *"We would speak to the leader of this settlement."*

David saw the Zed make a small, quick fist as he responded, *"I am Elder Niocli Totet."*

There was an exchange between the PG's Speaker and Asoon. She turned to David, "This is the leader of the village. He is known as an 'Elder.' Shall I translate his name?"

"No, I would probably butcher it if I tried to say it. Inform the Elder that we are here to arrange their release from the rule of the Preeminent."

Asoon and the PG's Speaker went back-and-forth for a minute when finally, the PG Speaker addressed the Elder.

"These Vermin are here to release you from our protection."

The Elder, no fool, turned to the Speaker. *"And why would they want to release us?"*

Asoon turned to David. "He questions your intentions."

"Intentions? What intentions? We're just here to announce their release." David thought for a moment, "Wait, does he think we're going to somehow replace you?"

"I don't know."

"Tell him again, we are here to release them from your rule and set them free."

"I will try."

She spoke again to the PG's Speaker, who translated it: *"The Vermin have come to force us to leave you unprotected, and you will not provide goods to us anymore. You will be alone."*

The Elder thought for a few seconds and then responded, *"I am unconvinced who these new aliens are, and whether I should believe either you or them. How can we trust them when they walk with these Violets who kill us?"*

"They remain unconvinced," Asoon said, from the PG's Speaker's translation.

"I don't get it." Joanne said, looking at David.

"I didn't expect this kind of resistance, Captain. I thought they'd be very happy to be rid of the Preeminent."

Joanne looked at the PG, then the Zeds. She shook her head and said, "Fine. Tell the Elder we will return again, but to please consider what it is we're saying. And that it is not the Preeminents' choice. They will be freed."

The PG's Speaker translated this as *"The Vermin will come back to demand your agreement."*

The Elder looked at the Speaker, waved his hand as if to brush her away, and turned to walk back to the village. The PG's Speaker spoke to their backs, then turned to Asoon and spoke in her own language.

"It is time to return to the spaceport," Asoon reported.

As they turned to walk away, Ateah touched Asoon's arm and held her back. They waited for the humans and the PG's Speaker to move out of ear-shot and then began a rapid, whispered exchange. David glanced back over his shoulder twice, trying to get an idea of what was happening without calling attention to it.

"Don't look back again, Powell," Joanne said quietly.

"Yes, ma'am. " David took three more steps before he spoke again. "Gotta wonder what they're talking about."

"Somehow, I don't think Ateah agrees with madam speaker's translations." Greg offered.

Gabrielle agreed. "They didn't seem very happy to see us, did they?"

David glanced over at Greg. "Can you understand any of it?"

Greg shook his head. "Some. I just don't have enough vocabulary memorized to follow it all. The sounds are hard to interpret. It sounds a lot like one of the tonal languages back home, like Vietnamese, but the shadings are far more subtle."

Joanne spoke quietly, not breaking stride. "Can you say anything about their attitude? You know, are the words angry or fearful or whatever?"

"Some. I felt the Speaker was projecting an angry, demanding tone, but we'll have to hear what Ateah thinks."

It was less than a half-hour later when they arrived back at the parked shuttles at the Preeminent spaceport. The Governor entered his headquarters without looking back, without even breaking stride. It was as if the humans weren't even there. The PG's Speaker turned around for the first time, and David thought he caught a look of surprise as she realized that Asoon and Ateah were walking far behind.

"Asoon and Ateah, why have you not remained with the group as directed?"

"There was no such direction. You may have had that expectation, but that is not our concern."

"What have you been discussing?"

"That is also not your concern. We are pursuing our task as the Science Directorate has ordered. You need know nothing more."

"The Governor will demand to know what it is you have been talking about."

Ateah spoke for the first time, her voice defiant. *"The Governor can demand whatever he likes, we are not under his command, and we are under no obligation to consent. Tell him that, Speaker, tell him that in very clear language."*

"Do we make ourselves plain, Speaker?" Asoon said.

"The Governor will be displeased."

Ateah and Asoon made no answer, and the PG's Speaker finally turned to enter the headquarters building.

The humans stood to one side while this spirited argument was going on, waiting to hear from Asoon what it was all about. After the PG's Speaker left, Asoon and Ateah came to them.

"David, Ateah reports that the Governor's speaker distorted your words."

"What?"

"Yes, Ateah says she was making them believe you were worse than us, that they would be cut off from our 'protection.'"

"Some protection," Joanne said quietly.

"Yes, Captain Henderson, it has been quite bad for them under this Governor."

"What else did she say? You talked after we got back here."

"We made clear our task here, and she indicated that the Governor will be unhappy if it succeeds."

"So, her loyalty is to the Governor, not to you or the SD?" Gabrielle asked.

"That is clear, yes," Asoon responded. Ateah again touched Asoon's arm, and there was a conversation between them.

When they were done, Asoon answered the unasked question. "Ateah asked me to describe our conversation. I have done that."

Joanne looked at Asoon. "So, has Ateah's assessment of our intentions changed? Does she now see what we're really here to do?"

"She finds the Governor's behavior most dishonorable. This offends her greatly, and the contrast between the behavior of the Governor and his Speaker, and yours, is striking. She is surprised at this, but the result is that she now has a firm belief that you are doing the right thing, as you would say, and she is fully committed to helping you."

David nodded. "That's very good news, Asoon." He turned to Joanne. "So, what do we do?"

Joanne looked at the shuttle, then glanced up towards where *Cobra* was likely orbiting. "I want to cons —, uh, I want to think this over, talk to my officers, and determine where we go from here."

"How long will you need?"

"Let's meet again at the next sunrise."

"As you say, Captain." Asoon bowed slightly as she and Ateah re-entered the small, by Preeminent standards, ship that had brought them. In there, they would be safe from any retribution by the PG.

After stepping back into the Recon shuttle and securing the hatch, Joanne opened a laser comm link to *Cobra* and put Evans on the display screen. She summarized what had occurred so far, including Ateah's assessment of the PG's Speaker's translations.

Evans nodded. "Well, it's obvious then that the PG is trying to obstruct us as much as possible."

David spoke. "The Zeds are skeptical, sir, suspicious even, and they've got good reason."

"But we can't talk to them without a Speaker, right? So, we're stuck being associated with the Preem."

"So, it seems," Gabrielle answered.

Joanne looked up at Evans' image on the screen, "Rich, can you get a message to Rmah? Tell him we need him to light a fire under the PG? Get him to cooperate?"

"Yeah, sure I can. There's just one problem."

"What?"

"I'm not here, remember?"

"You just got here, OK?"

"Hmm. Not sure Rmah or Glur is going to buy that."

"Then I'll send it from *Intrepid*. *Resnik* is still there, right?"

"Yes, although Elias keeps whining in the back-channel about being stuck in orbit. He says it's way too much like shore duty for his taste."

"OK then, I'll send *Resnik* a message for Glur that the PG is actively obstructing the process."

"Good enough."

David looked up. "But, what do we do next sunrise? Asoon is going to expect some kind of plan."

"When is that?" Joanne asked.

"0525 tomorrow. It's close to noon local already," David answered.

"Noon?"

"Yes, ma'am, local noon is just around 1230."

She looked back at the screen. "Rich?"

"We are charged with the liberation of this planet. We are not subject to the whims of the PG."

"So, go on without his support?"

Evans nodded. "Yes, and without his Speaker, too."

David smiled. "That, sir, is going to royally piss him off."

David thought he saw a smile appear and quickly disappear on Evans' face. "We don't care."

Joanne stood up. "OK, Rich, that's what we'll do, thanks. I'll check in with you later, OK?" She closed out the transmission. "OK, it's going to be a long day, folks. Get some rest. Next sunrise, we go back to that village with our own Speakers and tell them what is really going on."

It was shortly after 1600, late afternoon local time, when the shuttle shook from an explosion nearby.

Kutah's Observation Post
Zeta Doradus (b)
Monday, March 4, 2080, 1610 UTC

Kutah and Tefin watched with amazement as the flashes came one-two-three-four in rapid succession at the Violet's loading dock. Kutah had been watching through his telescope and was blinded for a few seconds. The blast wave passed over them as a rolling thunderous roar, louder even than any storm either of them had ever seen. When they looked back, the wagons were on fire, as were some of the Violets that had been unloading the deleelinosh shipment. Kutah put the telescope back up to his good eye and watched as they flailed and struggled before becoming still as the smoke rose from their bodies.

Tefin grabbed his shoulder. "Footsteps! They're coming!"

Kutah followed him back through the underbrush, their haste leaving more noise behind than they should have.

"I saw a flash over here when the bomb went off!" Combatant 58467 said to his companion as they raced across the field. "Someone was here!"

As they approached the edge of the forest, 58467 heard the noise of something moving in the brush. He lifted his weapon and fired at the sound. 59554 fired as well, their plasma bolts sending blasts of noise through the dense forest. In the distance they saw two figures running away.

Kutah ran as fast as he could, his legs sometimes tripping against small bushes and low branches of trees. Tefin followed his lead, running diagonally away from the Violets' hot death.

58467 fired twice into the trees, then zeroed in on the trailing figure and fired three times in quick succession. He was rewarded with a scream of pain.

Kutah heard Tefin's cry. He stopped, then ducked down and crawled back to his friend. There was no mistaking the stench of burnt flesh. Tefin was breathing hard, but he was still alive.

"Arm!" he said to Kutah.

"They can't see us down here. Can you crawl?"

"Yes."

"Then crawl. We need to get another hundred meters away."

Back at the edge of the forest, 59554 fired twice in the same area, then turned to his superior. "What do we do now?"

"We report that the natives were watching from here. I hate spies, so I am glad you hit one."

"You think it's dead?"

"I don't care. Let it suffer and die, or live with the burns. The more pain it's in, the better."

The two Combatants turned towards their headquarters, eager to report their success to the Governor.

As Kutah and Tefin stumbled into their village, Elder Wocos was waiting. He sent Tefin to the healers. His wound was serious, but he would live. Kutah recounted for Wocos the attack, four explosions, and fire all around, then the Violets suddenly coming for them.

"Bad luck, Kutah," he said.

"I don't know how they could have seen us. They came so fast right after the explosions!"

"Enough about that. I have other news. There is another alien species present."

"There are *other* aliens here?"

"Yes. I spoke earlier with Elder Niocli Totet. They called him out and spoke to him." Wocos paused to take a breath and a drink of water. "The grey liar was there with them and two other greys and a Violet."

"Strange."

"Yes. These new aliens are taller than us, but not so much as the Violets. Their faces are flatter and their skin lighter. They have something growing out of their heads that Elder Totet doesn't understand."

"But, are they on our side or the Violets'?"

"It is confusing, but they say they are here to remove the Violets, but they walk with the liars and Violets. I do not trust them."

"But if these others are here to remove the Violets, have they become weak somehow? We have wondered for some time what has happened to the ships that used to come here."

"They said they will return. We will see if they do after tonight."

"The attack was violent, Elder. Many Violets suffered painful deaths. They will be angered."

"Yes, they will. But I need you to focus on the new aliens. Get back to your place in the morning. Try to see if they have a ship and what they are doing. I don't trust them, but if they are here to remove the Violets, that *could* be good."

"Only could?"

"If they are here to replace the Violets, they might be far worse."

Kutah left Wocos to check on Tefin. The healers had cleaned and wrapped the burns on his arm and back and given him an herb drink to quiet him down. Tefin was sleeping now, and safe, so Kutah made his way home and found Udoro waiting for him.

Kutah sat with her on their hill, and he repeated all that he had reported to the Elder.

"So," he finally asked her, "have you made a new choice?"

"Yes, a Saognu up north. I must leave in three suns."

"Three suns."

"We can spend those together if you like."

"I would like, but I must be back at the Violets' landing field before sunrise. I have no time tonight." He stood and bid her goodbye, then returned to his home for a short rest.

Tomorrow would be a long day on his belly.

Preeminent Spaceport
Zeta Doradus (b)
Monday, March 4, 2080, 1700 UTC

Joanne stood outside the Recon Shuttle, watching the fires rage a kilometer away. David ran out of the shuttle and handed her the electronic field glasses. With that magnification, she could see the agony of the Combatants who had been unloading the wagons. She felt no love for the Preeminent, ruthless conquerors that they were, but she also believed that no one deserved to die that way.

She handed the glasses back to David. "Did the Combatants burn like this the first time the Zeds attacked?"

After a moment of watching, David took the glasses down from his eyes. "No. They must have added something else, something flammable that sprayed on them."

"They're not making our job any easier, are they?"

As they were watching, Asoon came around the edge of her ship, with the Governor beside her.

"The Governor would speak to you."

Joanne didn't move. "Very well, let him speak."

"You see what they have done, these vicious natives?"

"I see it, yes. Your retributions are bearing fruit. There is an old saying on Earth, that you harvest what you plant."

"I will make them regret this impudence!"

Joanne didn't miss a beat. "You will not."

The Governor moved closer to Joanne, and David placed his hand on his sidearm. "I will beat them down until they scream. I will take a hundred for each Preeminent death."

Joanne stood very still, unmoved, and unintimidated by the PG's size and proximity as he towered over her, his disgusting hot breath in her face.

"You will not. You will remain in your headquarters."

Hearing the PG's angry voice, Liwanu moved smoothly outside, taking a position on Joanne's left flank, his weapon drawn but down at his side. David, already standing on Joanne's right, glanced over at Liwanu and placed his hand on his weapon as well.

Asoon saw this and turned to the Governor. *"If you take another step towards her, they will kill you."*

The PG's head snapped around at her words. *"Kill me? They wouldn't dare."*

"They would, and without hesitation. Two of those who shot the Revered First are standing before you. They will not miss, and you will not survive."

"What are you telling him, Asoon?" Joanne asked.

"I see your weapons. I know you are ready. I have warned him not to approach you any closer or he will die."

Liwanu smiled. "Good advice."

Joanne never looked away from the Governor. "Yes, it is. Now, remind him that he lost the war. That we are here on our own authority as well as that of the Science Directorate. He can cooperate, or he can just sit in his headquarters and pout. I don't care which. But if he interferes, he might well die along with many of his Combatants."

There was a sharp exchange between Asoon and the Governor.

"He says you are as impudent as the natives. He says he is the Preeminent, not you, and he will decide what happens to the natives. He believes it, Commander. He's not, what is the word...*bluffing*."

"Asoon, I can't say this any clearer. He must not strike at the natives. I will level this building with him in it if he does. You have seen what we can do from orbit, Asoon. Tell him."

Asoon and the Governor had another hard exchange.

"He says you are not the only power that can strike from afar. But he will comply. For now."

"A wise choice. Tell him we will be watching, and we can prevent him with force if necessary. Make sure he understands."

85

"Yes, Captain."

Back inside the Recon Shuttle, Joanne called Rich Evans again and briefed him on the exchange with the Governor.

"I assume you're watching this place?" she asked.

"Yes, best as we can with this weather. The planet is warming up, and clouds are moving inland from the ocean from time to time. That's probably only going to get worse as the season progresses."

Joanne shifted in her chair as she thought about what to do next. "Should we get some more Marines down here to maintain a watch? If they start marching off to some village, I can't really do much to stop them."

David spoke up. "We don't want to provoke them, either, ma'am. We have at least a day. If we can make contact with the Zeds, maybe we can head off any more attacks."

"I'm skeptical of that," Greg offered. "They see us with the Preem, and we are just an extension of them. I'm not sure I would trust us, either."

"We have to try," David repeated.

As they were considering what to say to the Zeds, Jack Ballard appeared behind Evans.

"There's been some SLIP activity. Three short messages from the PG's headquarters."

Joanne sat upright. "He's calling for help. That's going to be trouble."

"Let's not be hasty," David said, "They're at least four days away."

"And we don't want to tip our hand that we're detecting their message traffic," Jack added. "We can't react like we know what's happening."

"I need to get back up to *Intrepid*. If there's going to be a fight, I need to be there."

David looked at Joanne. "The Preeminent are going to wonder why you suddenly disappeared. They're going to suspect something."

"Make something up, Powell, or don't. What we do is not for them to question."

"Yes, ma'am."

David thought for a few seconds. "In the morning, we'll just take Asoon and Ateah and go."

Joanne looked at him. "You're just going to head off and see where the Zeds take you?"

"More or less, yes. But I think we should go somewhere else. I'd like to go to that town we were watching before, it's one village removed from the spaceport and a little bigger. We'll go there and make our pitch."

Evans could be seen shaking his head on the video. "You are one trusting son-of-a-bitch, Powell."

"Yes, sir, no question, but we need to get inside Zed society somehow. We need to get past their initial resistance and get them to see the truth."

Joanne looked around the shuttle. "What about the rest of you? Ready to set off into the jungle with him?"

Liwanu nodded, then said, "It's not like we're defenseless. We'll take our weapons, and the NetLink in the shuttle will know where we are and provide whatever comms we need."

"Supplies?" Evans asked.

"There's a stock of MREs in the back for just this kind of exploration. It's enough for several days, at least."

"What do you think, Captain Henderson?"

"I think I need to get a shuttle down here to take me out of this insane asylum."

Intrepid's shuttle arrived less than an hour later and left almost immediately. At sunrise, Asoon and Ateah arrived as expected, with the Governor's Speaker. David dismissed the PG's Speaker, despite her insistence that she must translate for them. Once she was gone, he explained his plan to Asoon and Ateah.

"This, um, adventure, might take several days. You can ride there with us in the shuttle."

The Speakers had a brief conversation.

"We will accompany you, but Ateah fears the wrath of the Governor."

"No need to worry. You know our word is good, and we will protect her. But I have other questions."

"Yes?"

"We have food for our own needs that we will bring along. Do you need to obtain supplies from your vessel before we set out?"

"Ateah and I will be fine. We can go some time without food, so long as we have water available."

"OK, then, let's go."

Asoon recalled the uncomfortable human seats from her last short trip in one of their small ships. They were not designed for the sizable and sensitive tail stump of her species. She warned Ateah to sit lightly, and lean slightly to one side, to minimize the discomfort. They were both extraordinarily happy when the shuttle's movement stopped, and the tall male with the weapon opened the hatch.

CHAPTER 5

Riaghe Village
Zeta Doradus (b)
Tuesday, March 5, 2080, 0615 UTC (A half-hour past sunrise)

Kutah was about to set out to find a new watch post when a large object came out of the sky and settled on the road just south of town. It was unlike the Violets' ships, smaller, darker, and more angular. A large door opened on the side, and six aliens came out: two grey liars and four of the new aliens Wocos had described. As they started walking towards him, he called out an alarm, and the townspeople began to gather.

Elder Wocos slipped through the growing crowd, stepping forward to meet the new aliens. He looked carefully at them as they approached. The two gray liars were a familiar type to him, but the other aliens were very different. One was shorter with an obviously different shape in the torso. The other three were taller, much taller even than a female of his own race. All four wore oddly decorated clothes, covered in splotches of dirt and grass colors. Two of the taller ones carried something metallic at their side. *A weapon?* he wondered. As they got closer, he understood what Elder Totet had meant about something growing out of their heads. It was thick, fibrous, and each was of a slightly different color. The shorter one's hair was longer, and one of the tall ones had very little at all showing underneath his, or her, cap, which matched the clothing's decorations. It was all very confusing, and Wocos could scarcely take it all in before they stopped a few meters away from him.

Ateah addressed Wocos. *"These are humans,"* she said, speaking the word phonetically, *"and they have come to liberate you from our rule."*

"Free us? Why would they do this?"

Asoon explained to the humans what had been said. "He is skeptical. He asks why you would free them."

"Tell him the truth," David directed Asoon. "Tell him we have defeated you in a large conflict, and we now require that you set them free."

After hearing Ateah's translation, Wocos looked at Ateah with surprise. *"We have seen nothing of this conflict."*

David thought for a moment after the translation came through. What the Zed said was true, he could not have any knowledge of the war. "Tell him it was fought above the planets, yours and ours. Tell him again we are here to release them from Preeminent rule."

Elder Wocos was a man of his time and technology. He knew the Violets could fly their machines back to their home planet, wherever that was. And now, clearly, so could these 'Vooman' as the grey liar had called them. But war in space was something he struggled to comprehend. War itself was an unfamiliar concept to him, but the Preeminent were excellent teachers. In his society, differences were rare and dealt with quietly between clans. There was too much at stake, too many years of life left for all, for any kind of violent conflict to arise.

He looked at Ateah. *"Why would you free us? You Violets killed twenty just a few suns ago."*

"He is unconvinced. He refers to the governor's retaliation. And, he uses an insulting slang term for us."

"Slang?" David asked.

"Best translation, from what Ateah says, is 'Violets' because of the Combatant's purple color. They call us 'Gray Liars.'"

"Surprisingly accurate for an insult, don't you think?" Liwanu commented

Wocos watched this exchange then said to David, *"You come with them, you are no different than them. Why would you not be liars like they are?"*

David and Gabrielle discussed the Elder's response. She turned to the Elder.

"We come with the grey liars — tell Ateah to use their term, Asoon — because that is the only way we can speak to you. We don't speak your language, and you don't speak ours."

"Also," David added, "tell him the Speakers with us do not lie. Tell him I know that is hard for him to accept, but it is the truth."

Elder Wocos had to admit to himself, somewhat reluctantly, that this made a certain amount of sense. If, that is, they were truthful in what they said. He decided to test them.

"You are lying!" Wocos said and turned away from David and the others.

Kutah stood in Wocos path. *"Why would they lie? What do they have to gain?"*

Wocos, impatient, answered, *"It doesn't matter. We will push you Violets off soon."*

David, hearing the translation, called out, "Wait!"

Wocos turned back to him without waiting for a translation.

David looked at Asoon. "Be sure they get this right. Be sure Ateah understands completely what I am saying."

"Yes, David."

"Tell him to not attack the Violets again. Tell him they are still powerful. We are here to take the Violets away without bloodshed on either side."

Asoon answered, "What the Elder just said implies that it is too late for that."

"Something is going to happen, and it's not good," Gabrielle commented.

Liwanu nodded. "The PG will slaughter them, and we might not be able to prevent it."

The Elder watched the conversation, then spoke to Ateah.

"He asks what you are saying. Shall I tell him?"

"Sure."

Wocos listened carefully to this new grey liar. It didn't speak quite as well as the last one, but he detected no deception in it. From another, its words would have sounded like a threat. These words seemed more like a warning.

As he turned his back once more, Udoro came forward and said, *"Bring them to the green, let us talk more. Perhaps they tell the truth."*

Wocos thought for a moment. Udoro was a female, and therefore entitled to some level of deference. But he was the Elder of the village, and the decision rested with him, even though he was just a male.

"As you say. Udoro, we will let them talk more.

Wocos turned to the grey liar. *"Follow me, and we will talk more about this freedom you claim to offer."*

Preeminent Spaceport
Zeta Doradus (b)
Tuesday, March 5, 2080, 0815 UTC

Niat Seo Pagg had been the Governor at System 952 for almost three revs. He hated the place, its unbearable frigid winters, and its sweltering summers. The natives worked hard enough, just barely hard enough, from the spring thaw to the freeze-over before winter. But sometimes their excuses for missed deliveries were unconvincing, and so a few would have to be dispatched as an example to the rest. It didn't harm production that much, and Niat believed they would be far lazier if he didn't slap them around from time to time.

He had spent the entire war with the Vermin here at System 952, safe enough but in a duty devoid of honor or conquest. Now, the war was over, and according to the messages from Home and what the disgusting Vermin on his planet claimed, he had lost a war he never fought. As a result, he must now surrender his position.

It was a meal too bitter to swallow.

But Niat had another ploy in mind. He was a fervent believer in the Revered First and his species' singular place in the universe. The First had been defeated, yes, but that could not possibly be the end of it. There were still six warships nearby, commanded by like-minded, strong Preeminent ready to strike back at these despicable Vermin trespassers.

He had already summoned help, and three cruisers were headed his way.

91

They would find and destroy the Vermin ship overhead, but he had more immediate plans.

The Vermin had that very day the temerity to refuse his Speaker and proceed to a native town of their own choosing to propagate their lies. This sin, just a day after the natives had incinerated twenty-seven of his Combatants, was more than he could tolerate.

He summoned his deputy and ordered the assembly of a hundred Combatants to eliminate the Vermin and any natives they had contacted.

"But, Governor, you told me the Vermin female instructed you to refrain from striking out at the natives. Are you certain — "

"I am certain, Deputy, that I am Preeminent and she is not! Gather the force and get moving!"

Far above Niat's headquarters, in *Cobra*'s Operations Center, techs were sounding an alarm. Rich Evans came to the Center and watched the video from the surface for several minutes.

"They're gathering northwest of the headquarters."

"Yes, sir, it looks like a hundred, more or less. Hard to count while they're still milling around."

"Where is the Recon Shuttle, again?"

The tech zoomed the image back slightly, then pointed out the shuttle sitting next to the road one village to the north.

"OK, move back a little." There could be no question in Evans' mind. The Preeminent were getting ready to march on the shuttle.

He picked up the phone. "Get me Henderson,"

Joanne answered immediately.

Evans wasted no time on formalities. "Captain, are you watching the spaceport?"

"Yes. Looks like the PG is planning a little party for our folks."

"I'd like to, um, discourage that thought."

"OK, so...what?"

"How about a Lance detonation at five hundred meters between them and the road?"

"Sure. I'll get that done right now."

Niat ordered his deputy to take the hundred Combatants he had assembled and find and kill the Vermin. He ordered the Speakers to be detained and brought back to him, unharmed if possible. They would be dealt with later. The guards who walked the perimeter of the spaceport had seen the Vermin ship land, so there could be no question where his Combatants should march. They formed in formation five across and twenty long, weapons high and ready. The deputy gave the order to move. But before they had covered a hundred meters, there was a flash and a deafening explosion in the sky above and in front of them. Bits of metal rained down all around.

Niat, watching from his office on the highest level of the headquarters, recoiled in shock as the Lance exploded above his force without warning. But, he realized, it *was* a warning. The Vermin could easily have killed his Combatants but did not. *Of course,* he thought, *they're weak.* But he decided to recall the Combatants and await a more opportune time to eliminate the threat. Once the cruisers had destroyed the Vermin ship in orbit, he could deal with those on the surface at his pleasure.

Riaghe Village
Zeta Doradus (b)
Tuesday, March 5, 2080, 0830 UTC

David was in the process of explaining the terms that ended the war with the Preeminent when a loud explosion rolled up from the south.

He turned to Liwanu. "That was a Lance."

"You're sure?"

"Yeah. Call Henderson and see what's going on. Asoon, advise the Elder we need a few minutes to confer."

Liwanu stood up and walked a few dozen meters out of the circle. As he called *Intrepid*, he was aware of two Zeds watching him.

"What do you suppose it is?" Kutah asked Udoro. *"Male or female?"*

Udoro looked at David carefully. *"It's one of the tall ones, so I think female."*

"If they have male and female, that is!" Kutah said.

"How would they not? They must repro somehow."

"Yes, they must, but they might not be at all like us."

"Well, they don't look like egg-layers to me." Udoro looked back at Gabrielle. *"What about the shorter one with the lumps? What do you suppose that is?"*

"I don't know, but it looks different than any of the others. The strings on its head are longer and I think the voice is higher, too."

Udoro stared at Greg, who had not removed his sunglasses. *"What about the eye covers? They're not glass, exactly, but they are like glass."*

"Yes, it looks strange when the covers are on their eyes, as if they're hiding themselves."

"When they take them off, they look more normal. What do you suppose those are?"

"I don't know. Why would they need to hide their eyes?"

Liwanu was distracted by the conversation behind him but managed to get through to Henderson.

"Powell says he heard a Lance go off."

"Yes, he did. The PG was sending about a hundred Combatants after you. We thought he should reconsider."

"I see. How many did we kill?"

"None, I think. We did an air-burst well ahead of them."

Liwanu smiled. "A shot across the bow? How very Navy of you."

"Harry, you know, sometimes..."

"Yes, ma'am. Thanks for the info."

"How is it going, anyway?"

"There is much talking, Captain, but I am not sure there is much progress. We'll update you later."

"Fine. Tell Powell that Evans is sending Herrera back down after dark with her three Marines. We want you to have more security."

"Yes, ma'am, will do."

Liwanu turned to go back to the circle and was suddenly face to face with two Zeds, one a head taller than the other. They had been talking rapidly behind him and seemed surprised at his sudden course reversal. After a moment, they moved aside, their eyes glued on him, and Liwanu returned to the discussion.

Kutah leaned over to Udoro. *"Did you see the stuff on its head? What is that?"*
"It's much longer on the short one with the lumps."
"I think the same stuff is on their hands, but sparse. I have to check that out."
"Other than that, they're not so horrible looking, you know? Not ugly like the Violets."

"He says he must consult with his superiors," Asoon reported after a lengthy exchange between Ateah and the Elder.

"Was that all he said?" David asked.

"No, you are to return in two days. As they say, two suns."

"Ask Ateah if she thinks they understand what we're saying. Do they realize that you must leave and they will be free of your rule?"

Asoon and Ateah had a short conversation.

"Ateah believes they understand what you say, but she is doubtful that they believe. But she thinks it is a good sign that this Elder is going to take the question to his superior."

"Fine. Gabe? Greg? Follow me." David also pulled Liwanu off a few meters outside the circle. "Two suns, as he says. What do you think?"

Greg looked back at the Elder and then to David. "He's unconvinced, if we're to believe Ateah, but still talking. I agree that's good."

"So," Gabrielle asked, "you think we should come back as requested?"

"Yes," Greg answered.

"No," David said, surprising them all. He looked around at his three companions. "We aren't coming back because we aren't leaving. We can hang out in the Recon Shuttle here just as well as we could back at the spaceport."

"What about Asoon and Ateah?"

"They said they were ready for several days. Let's hope they meant it."

David returned to the circle and looked at Ateah. "Tell the Elder we are content to wait until he is ready to continue, but we will not be leaving." He waited for the double translation to complete, then pointed in the direction of the Recon Shuttle. "We will be right there. If they want to talk to us, we're here. Let's talk."

The Elder dismissed them, and they made their way out of the village.

As they arrived back at the Recon Shuttle, Liwanu Harry pulled David aside. "Evans is sending Herrera back down after nightfall. She's worried about security after what the PG tried to do."

"That's fine. How many?"

"Four, she said."

David looked at his NetComp. "OK. Sunset is 1421, so we have a few hours to wait."

Liwanu shook his head. "Yeah, I can't tell what time it is, let alone what day it is."

David smiled. "Don't you just love space exploration? First, we get a planet that spins half as fast as ours, now one that's like fifteen percent faster."

During the afternoon, David had several conversations with Rich Evans to clarify just what had happened with the Preeminent. He explained to Asoon and Ateah what the PG had tried to do and was satisfied with their surprise. They could not have known about it in advance. Evans told David he was dropping any pretense of absence and sending a message directly to Glur Woe Segt, telling him to get his Governor in line, or Evans and Henderson would do it for him.

Shortly after sunset, *Intrepid*'s shuttle landed next to the Recon Shuttle, and Herrera and her crew came out with their full recon gear. They brought additional weapons and ammo for Powell and Liwanu Harry and lightweight body armor for all.

Gunnery Sergeant Sabrina Herrera explored the road south and north of the recon shuttle for a few hundred meters. There was a bend to the south, right before it entered the next village. That turn would have to be watched. She set up a guard position just north of the bend, and another right by the shuttle, covering the north approach. She doubted the Zeds would present much of a threat, but they should still be watched. On the other hand, the south approach seemed dangerously close, and if the Preeminent decided to come to get them, she wasn't sure they could be stopped.

Kutah was watching, of course, dispatched by Elder Wocos to keep his eye on the new Voomans. He was surprised when just after dark, another ship landed, and more of them came out. It was hard to see how many, but they carried something long and metallic that reminded Kutah of the Violets' weapons. These Voomans might appear friendly, but Kutah saw that they could be dangerous, too.

Wocos' other spy came back to report that the Violets had started to advance to the road, but there had been an explosion in the sky that made them turn around. He didn't understand it, but bits of metal had rained down right afterward, so it had to be some kind of device.

Wocos told Kutah to go back to the Violets' landing field in the morning and see what they were doing. He told Kutah the Vooman needed no observer. Wocos would be watching them himself.

Recon Shuttle
Zeta Doradus (b)
Tuesday. March 6, 2080, 1130 UTC

Shortly after their second sunset on the surface of the rapidly spinning planet, David joined Gabrielle and Greg outside the shuttle, sitting around a small table with a lantern on it. Sergeant Herrera was again stalking around from south to north, making sure they were safe. She also checked on Asoon and Ateah, who had settled themselves on the opposite side of the shuttle for the night. Marine Lieutenant Liwanu Harry was inside the shuttle, looking at *Cobra*'s maps in preparation for what might come the next day.

They sat and talked quietly, sipping decaf, getting ready for another short night. Zeta Doradus would be back in the sky by 2030.

"David," Gabrielle asked, "what have you heard from Carol? The last time we talked like this, you were worried about her."

David nodded. "I had a good message from her yesterday. She's getting counseling at FleetPers, and Lieutenant Perez seems to be making progress. She said she felt better, had a better handle on what happened and how she felt about it."

"That sounds hopeful," Greg added.

"Yes, she's planning to go home to the family farm next week."

"Is that good?"

David looked up for a few seconds to think, then back at Greg. "I think it is, yes. The farm is home, of course, and her parents are incredibly supportive and understanding. Have to say I am more than a little jealous of that."

Liwanu Harry came out of the shuttle. "Excuse me, Lieutenant Powell? You're talking about Commander Hansen?"

"Yes. Come and sit down."

Harry took the empty seat between Gabrielle and David. "I just admire her so much, sir. So much courage in such a small package."

David smiled. "We're just talking, Liwanu. You can leave off the sirs and ma'ams and such."

"Yes, sir. I watched her all through that fight at Seeker Woods. No one could have asked her to do any more. You can ask Commander Hayden. She was there; she saw it, too."

David's curiosity was engaged. "You're close to Hayden, aren't you?"

Liwanu smiled. "I think she sees me as the little brother she never had."

The group laughed.

"Really?" David asked.

"Yes. She's very kind, and she appreciates what I did for Mister Price. That meant so much to her. I know she loved him very much. Since then, we've had some really good talks about grief and setting the past aside."

Gabrielle took a sip. "That sounds healthy."

"She told me something, long before the battle in the woods, something I've never forgotten. It was right after we got back to Beta Hydri. She said that she was trying, every day, to be as fully alive as she could. She said she couldn't change the past, so her goal, every day, was to make new yesterdays to look back on."

"Incredible," Greg said softly.

"Yes, she is."

"I agree," David said, "Which is why I sent Natalie to shake Carol up and get her out of the funk she was in."

Liwanu smiled. "They were quite the pair that day on Beta Hydri. Incredible, both of them."

"Oh?"

"Yeah, and oh my god, they could talk serious smack about the Preem! I am honestly not sure which of them killed more, and if together they may have killed more than my whole platoon!"

"That's hard to figure," David said.

"Not if you include the ones Commander Hansen fried inside the shuttle when she set off the tanks!"

David looked up from his coffee. "She what?"

"Yeah, right after they landed, she wasn't shooting at the ones on the ground.

She was shooting at the shuttle itself, and in a minute or two she'd popped both tanks and the damned thing started to burn. There must have been hundreds of them still inside."

Gabrielle looked over at David. "That lovely, soft-spoken wife of yours is one ruthless son-of-a-bitch, Powell."

David smiled. "Yes. Yes, she is. And I am so proud of her!" They laughed again at David's response.

Soon it was time to get some sleep, so they broke down the table and moved inside the Recon Shuttle. Liwanu parked himself on the steps, taking a turn on watch so that the others could get a little more rest. As he watched the stars turn and the bright band of light rising from the east, he thought of Natalie. He reflected on how their lives had crossed more than once and examined his feelings about her again. She was two ranks above him, seven or eight years older, and thirty-eight light-years away. He still looked on her as a grieving widow, someone still off-limits for an indeterminate length of time. A year and a half just didn't seem quite long enough for what he saw in Natalie's eyes as he repeated Ben's last words for her.

No, not nearly long enough.

South of Riaghe Village
Zeta Doradus (b)
Wednesday, March 6, 2080, 2030 UTC

"Lieutenant Powell? Someone is coming, sir."

David heard the Marine on picket duty call his name. He stepped out into a cool, cloudy morning to see the Elder, or who he thought was the Elder, approaching with another Zed. This one was short as well, for whatever that meant. As he turned to look for her, Asoon came around the far side of the Recon Shuttle, Ateah close behind.

Gabrielle made it out before the Elder stopped a few meters from them, Greg right behind her, still carrying his coffee cup.

The Elder looked at Ateah and spoke.

Asoon turned to David. "The Elder says this male is his superior. I think the best translation would be a member of the ruling council. Neither of us is sure how to translate the council's name."

"What else did he say?"

"The village Elder says he does not yet believe what you say. But he is willing to listen further. The council member wants to know more about the recent conflict."

"So, the short ones are the males? Did I hear that right?"

There was another long conversation between Asoon, Ateah, and the Elder.

"Yes, Elder Wocos informs us that the males of their species are shorter. Females are generally taller and larger since, as he says, they must produce offspring. He is curious if it is not the same for humans?"

David glanced at the diminutive Gabrielle, who was watching for his reaction with some amusement, then replied, "It varies, but no, it is not the same with us. Tell him that for us, size is often less important than ability."

"Nice save," Gabrielle said quietly as Sabrina Herrera came up behind her.

David smiled briefly at her, then refocused on the Zeds. "This is not the time for that discussion. What does he want to know?"

"He wishes to know why this conflict occurred and how it was ended."

"I see." David thought for a moment. "Asoon, tell Ateah I am aware that this may be painful for her. I understand her loyalties to her own society. But I must have a proper and accurate translation of what I am about to say."

They had a short conversation. "Ateah understands."

"OK, then." David began with the battle at Inoria, the rain of death and fire that destroyed most of the city, taking thousands of lives. He explained the loss of *Liberty* and most of her crew. He included that his own life-partner had barely survived and the pain she felt from it. He went on through his own battle and near-death aboard *Sigma*, the fights at Beta Hydri, and the final blockade and victory at Alpha Mensae. It took him about twenty minutes, with interruptions by the Zed for questions.

In the end, they asked him again what happened to the Preeminent leader.

David pointed at Liwanu then back at himself. "We shot him." David, keeping the answer simple, left off the rounds delivered by Natalie and Carol. The Zeds turned and walked about twenty meters away.

"Can this tale be true?" Wocos asked his GuildMember.

"We see machines that fly from star to star, Wocos. That they should fight out there seems only natural."

"For them, perhaps. I do not understand it all, the destruction, the death, the incredible waste."

"There would have been much more death here had we not given in to what the Violets wanted."

"Yes, I remember. It was wise of the Guild to agree."

"So, what of the Vooman's story?"

"If what the Vooman say is true, the Violets will leave on their own."

"And then what, Wocos? Do we serve the Vooman instead?"

"But, Guildmember, if the Vooman defeated the Violets, perhaps we can, too. Perhaps they are weak enough that a hard push will do it?"

"They are not too weak to kill six or thirty-six if they choose. They've proven that. There is a plan, Wocos, to force the Violets off. The Guild has been working for several snows to build weapons. The explosions at the landing field were just tests."

"Expensive tests. Many snows have been lost in their retaliation."

"True. I want to believe them, Wocos. I want to think that the Violets will be somehow taken away."

"But you are not yet convinced?"

"No. But if the Vooman are truthful, none will die, and we will be free of the Violets."

"So, is it worth the risk to take them to the Guild?"

"I don't fear the Vooman's weapons, Wocos. I fear their ideas and their possible treachery. What, after all, will they want from us?"

David watched the conversation carefully. The new Zed was doing most of the talking, the Elder listening. After a few minutes, they turned and walked back to the group standing outside the shuttle.

The council member turned to Ateah and spoke.

"He asks," Asoon began, "what will they owe you after we are gone? Ateah says he sounds skeptical. Based on her description, I think in English the best translation is a 'hidden agenda.' As if there is something more you're not telling them, something important you're hiding from them."

"I understand. We will ask nothing of them. We would be happy to have contact with them, share ideas, perhaps explore their culture to learn more about them. But they will owe us nothing."

There was a long conversation between the Speakers, then Ateah spoke to the council member.

As the Zeds paused in their conversation, Asoon looked at David. "They wonder how this could be? How can there not be a price to pay? Ateah thinks he believes we Speakers are lying to them."

David thought about his first commander, the single-minded Len Davis, and sweet Lisa Briggs, who he was sure had a massive crush on him, then all Carol had gone through, and was still going through. He could still see little Leah, who loved that bear-faced Tennessean Travis. The faces marched past him quickly, his eyes filling.

He fought off the emotion rising in him and looked at Asoon. "Too many friends of mine have already paid with their lives. We are here to collect what's already been bought."

Wocos heard the translation from the dull grey talker and looked carefully at the Vooman who had spoken. That male was clearly in charge. He could tell not just by his words but by the way the others looked at him. They watched him carefully for guidance. He and the GuildMember stepped back again.

"The leader, that male, was quite emotional, I think."
"Yes, Wocos, I had the same impression. I believe they are telling the truth."
"But you are not certain?"
"No. But I believe him well enough to take them to the full Guild."
"You would take Gray Liars to the Guild? They would then know where it is."
"We must, Wocos. As the Vooman said, we can't talk to them otherwise. We will have to risk it."

The Zeds turned back to Ateah and spoke at length. After the Speakers exchanged translations, Asoon said "They ask us to accompany them to meet with their ruling council."
"How far is it?"
"They say we must go with them, on foot. They will not allow you to fly the shuttle there."
"OK, so, how far?"
"It is two days on foot. From what Ateah says, it is somewhere in this same direction."
David turned to his companions. "A two-day hike into Zed-land. Thoughts?"
"It's more like four or five," Sabrina offered. "Up, back, and some time to haggle with their council."
"Yes, right. Still, anyone have any reservations?"
"We have provisions for that," Sabrina responded, "if we don't take everyone."
David looked around the group and saw only agreement. "OK, we'll need some time to pack up." He turned to Asoon. "Six days, Asoon. What will you and Ateah need to do that? Do you need to go back to the spaceport?"
"Can they give us some deleelinosh? Tomorrow, perhaps?"
"Some, what?"
"The ocean species they ship back to Home. If we could have some of that, it would make it possible."
"Tell Ateah to ask for what you need. Tell them we will not need anything beyond access to water. Any stream will do for us; we have filters that will make it safe."
"Would you share that with Ateah and me?"
"Of course. How much will you need?"
"In your measures, three or four liters a day should be fine in this climate."
"Fine. Ask them about the food."

Wocos listened with shock and surprise at the request. "They want deleelinosh, but it has to be dead for two days?"

"Awful to consider. It will smell. It will begin to slime over."

"They want two every other day. What should we tell them?"

"I'll send a messenger to the pens. If we have to kill some, we can. A few die naturally, anyway." He turned back to Ateah and said, "Yes, we will supply that for you."

"They agree to our needs," Asoon reported. "It will be two days before we can eat, but Ateah and I will be fine until then."

"Two days?"

Asoon looked at David. "We are, by human definition, reptiles. We do not cook our food but wait for it to tenderize naturally."

Liwanu broke the uncomfortable silence. "You mean wait for it to rot, right? Your food has to rot for a while before you can eat it?"

"A crude construction, but yes, that is accurate."

David smiled. "Now I understand why your planet smells like decomposition. It's just the food."

"Yes. Do not think less of us, David. It is just our physiology."

David shook his head. "We are all different, Asoon, and I am sure some of our methods are difficult for you to understand, too. No worries."

After a short discussion, and a consult with Rich Evans, they decided the party would include David, Greg, and Gabrielle, plus Sabrina Herrera to provide additional security. Liwanu would return to *Intrepid* to personally bring Henderson up to speed on what was happening. The rest of the Recon Marines would keep watch on the Preeminent and guard the shuttle.

FleetPers Counselor's Office
Ft. Eustis, VA
Thursday, March 7, 2080, 1000 EST (1500 UTC)

Carol steeled herself every day for another confrontation with Rick Court in FleetPers, but again today he was not in the office when she arrived. She took her seat in SLT Darin Perez's comfortable guest chair as he finished some notes on his workstation.

"So, how are you, Commander?" he asked as he stood and closed the door. "How is it with Commander Miller?"

Carol looked up as he walked around her and back to his desk. "I don't know if she's actually dialed it back or I'm just adjusting to it, but it seems better to me. More tolerable, anyhow."

"Good to hear. You're supposed to be on medical leave, but you're still working?"

"I wanted to finish a project. CINC took me out of the command school, so there's more time to work in Plans. Did you talk to her?"

"I didn't." He finished his notes and turned to her. "I considered it, but I did not want to bring any more attention to you."

Carol looked directly at Perez. "I thought these sessions were confidential."

"That's the other reason. But we can intercede where a commander or supervisor is the problem."

She nodded, then changed the subject. "I haven't seen Court in the office."

"Ah, yes, the great Lieutenant Court." Perez smiled for a second. "The day after you first were here, he came in limping and bruised, complaining that you had physically and verbally assaulted him."

"Oh?"

"It didn't take fifteen minutes on the phone with Security to get the full story. He's gone, Commander, and this time for good."

"I see."

"Court is a recurring issue for you, isn't he?"

"Yes." Carol paused, then took a deep breath and let out a long sigh. "Biggest mistake of my life. I still regret it a lot."

"How'd that happen, anyway? You hardly seem the bad-boy type."

Carol looked off in the distance, then back to Perez. "He was so young when he came to the U, and so wounded by his past. Rick opened up a little when I first talked to him, which I really liked. There was potential there, or so I thought. But eventually, he shut down as I tried to get him to see that he didn't have to be what his father said he was. He was hard to get along with, but I really thought I could help him. I was naive enough to think I could get through to whatever was deeper inside."

"Wait, who's the counselor here, again?"

Carol smiled grimly. "I was just trying to care about him, fix him, and before I realized it, I was far too invested in that to let go. I was determined to 'save' him. That was the mistake."

"And did you ever get through to that inner person deep inside Mister Court?"

"Oh, sure. But deep inside Rick, there's just more Rick. There's nothing else there that I could find."

"Somewhat harsh, wouldn't you say?"

"For anyone else, maybe. For him, that's just how it is."

Perez looked down at his notes, then back to Carol. "Enough about Court. You've talked a lot about Cornell over the last two weeks. You feel strongly about him, that is, about what happened to him."

Carol looked up at Perez and cleared her throat slightly. "Yes. He was the first person I led in combat."

"Right, in Inoria. Did *he* ever doubt you?"

"Never said so. But that loyalty was misplaced."

"I've read your after-action report, and Hayden's, and Harry's. In the Battle of Seeker Woods, he volunteered to go to the beach, correct? Take a message to Swenson?"

"Yes, but only because he believed in me."

"Well, why shouldn't he? You got him out of Inoria, right?"

"That was more Terri Michael than me,"

"You saved his life when the ship was disabled. That wasn't anyone else."

"It was not enough," Carol responded harshly. "I was supposed to get him home. Alive."

Again, she looked away, a sad expression on her face.

Perez heard the catch in Carol's throat, a hint of something coming forward. He let that simmer for a short while as he swiped through a few pages on his NetComp. "Tell me, Carol, have you ever read the Marines' report of the Seeker Woods battle? If we gave out medals, you'd be getting several."

Carol shook her head. "Not interested."

"Yes, I know, but you received praise from the highest practitioners of the military arts. What does that say to you?"

Her stomach began to tighten. "I don't know."

Perez tapped the NetComp. "The woman I see here — no, the *leader* I see here — did everything she could to win that engagement. She ran from one end of the line to the other. Under fire. She fought and fought and fought to keep the Preeminent attackers away from her people."

Carol could feel her eyes filling, a hard lump in her throat, and wished she could pull the tears back somehow, rein in the now-galloping emotions. She squirmed in her chair and grabbed a tissue off the desk as she turned away.

Darin Perez left her to experience it for a full minute. "Let it happen, Carol."

She shook her head. "Strong...gotta be strong. Can't make it in this business if you're weak."

"You can't make it if you're incapacitated, either."

She shot him an angry glance, then turned away and let go, the pain flowing out of her.

He let her cry for a few minutes, sitting next to her and giving her a few words of encouragement to experience the feelings she'd repeatedly been shoving deep down inside.

Finally, he sat back down in his chair. "It's an old cliche, Carol, but it's true: the enemy gets a vote, and not every engagement will end as we would like,"

"I tried so hard..." she said, starting to get herself back together.

"I know you did. Everyone involved knows how hard you tried and how much you cared about your crew. And by any reasonable measure, you succeeded. It's only by your own impossibly high standards that you have fallen short."

Carol laughed a little through her last tears. "I do seem quite the cartoon sometimes."

"Now, no more of that. No more negative thoughts. No more telling yourself, you're something you're not."

"OK," she sniffed, "I'll try."

Perez looked at her carefully as she dried her eyes and settled her emotions. "Have you talked to your folks? When was the last time you were home?"

"Not about this, no. I was back to the farm a few months ago, not long after the wedding. I was fine then."

"Yes, you had enough happy distractions that you could avoid thinking about this. Well, you're going now. You were given medical leave for a reason, Carol. I'm telling you to take it."

"I was thinking about it."

Perez was unmoved. "Commander Hansen, you will take that leave now, or I'll call CINC, and you can explain to him why you're not."

She smiled slightly and nodded, surrendering. "OK, Darin, you win."

"Go home, Carol, like we discussed last week. Go Home. Ride your horse. Hug your Mom. Not in that order. Call me when you think you're ready to come back."

Carol gave him the same weak salute she'd waved at Marcia Soto on *Antares'* bridge after she'd been wounded. "Yes, sir, mister counselor. Sir."

Darin smiled. "Better. I like your sarcastic side. It balances the goody-nice-girl side rather nicely."

Carol took a few minutes to gather herself, then left FleetPers and walked to Plans, knocking on Commander Miller's open door.

"Yes, Hansen, what is it?"

Carol sat down, then looked up at her boss. "I've been instructed to take my medical leave effective immediately, Commander."

Miller looked at her, but her expression lacked the scowl Carol had generally received. "I see. May I ask your plans?"

"Home. I've spent the last three weeks working with Lieutenant Perez, and it's time for a change of scenery."

"Very well. Let us know when you're able to return."

"Yes, ma'am."

Feeling dismissed, Carol stood to leave.

"Hansen?"

She turned back to Miller, who was looking down at her desk. She looked up and said, "You will let us know if there is anything we can do for you?"

Carol suppressed her surprise and answered, "Yes, Commander, I will."

"Very good." Miller paused a second. "Get some rest, Carol. Come back when you're ready."

"Yes. Commander."

Carol stopped at her workstation just long enough to clear off her desktop and make it ready for her return. She sent a few notes to herself and co-workers to mark the status of what she was working on. Then she sent David a SLIP. She knew he would surely be wondering how she was doing.

```
SLIP PERSONAL 208003071800UTC
TO: INTREPID/SLT DAVID POWELL
FROM: FLEETPLANS/LDCR CAROL HANSEN

I'VE COMPLETED ALMOST THREE WEEKS OF COUNSELING AND FEELING MUCH
MORE NORMAL. SOME THINGS - LIKE GRIEF AND GUILT - JUST CAN'T BE
AVOIDED FOREVER, I GUESS.

I DID THE BEST I COULD AND THAT IS GOING TO HAVE TO BE GOOD
ENOUGH, EVEN FOR ME. I HATE HOW THAT SOUNDS BUT THAT'S WHAT
PEREZ HAS HELPED ME SEE.

PEREZ SAYS I NEED A BREAK SO I AM GOING HOME FOR A WHILE. THERE
WILL BE MORE SESSIONS WITH HIM LATER.

I'LL SEND YOU ANOTHER MESSAGE IN A WEEK OR TWO.

HOPE ALL IS GOING WELL THERE.

LOVE ALWAYS

CAROL

END
```

Intrepid
In Orbit at Zeta Doradus (b)
Thursday, March 7, 2080, 2125 UTC

Joanne Henderson jumped as the alarms sounded from the Surveillance position.

"IR transients, Captain. Assess as enemy ships exiting FTL."

"Where are they?"

"About a hundred thousand kilometers outside our orbit. They look like Type IIIs."

The phone rang in her position. "Henderson."

"Our company is here," Evans said.

"Right on schedule. At least they're predictable."

"Indeed, they are. Let's wait a few hours and see what they do."

Another alarm went off on the Surveillance station, and Joanne set down the phone to see what it was.

"Intrusion detectors up on all three enemy ships, ma'am. And it's really strong, stronger than I've ever seen."

Joanne picked the phone back up. "You seeing the intrusion detectors?"

"Yes. They're looking for us."

"I think we should move orbits now, Rich, and keep moving every few hours. I don't know what they can see by cooperating the way they are, but we shouldn't make it too easy for them."

"Right. I'm thinking ellipticals, apogees twelve hours apart?"

Joanne nodded slightly to herself. "Yeah, works for me. Go ahead and maneuver. I'll follow when you're back around."

Cobra broke the communications link as it moved to drop into an elliptical orbit with a low perigee and high apogee right over the Zed's home. Joanne got down from her command chair and stood right behind the Surveillance position. The tech looked up nervously at his captain, then back down at his data display.

"They're splitting up, Captain," SLT Marco Gonzales pointed out the blips on the main display, slowly separating. Marco had been with her since she took over *Intrepid* what seemed like a lifetime ago. He knew what she wanted, knew what she needed.

Joanne leaned back against the raised command station, "Could they be trying to cooperate somehow? To combine each other's signals somehow to find us?"

"Yes, that's possible. They're all on exactly the same frequency. If they were each worried about themselves, I'd expect each one to be on a slightly different freq. We've seen that before."

Marco paused a second. "Or..."

"Or what?"

"Well, it's more of an 'and' than an 'or'."

"Marco? Can I get that in a slightly less cryptic form?"

"They could also be trying to catch us in front of the star. They are outside of us, relative to Zeta Doradus."

"Or against the planet?"

"Yes, different time of day, but yeah. That would be a problem, too."

"We keep coming back to this, Marco, every time we run into them."

"Yes, ma'am, we're pretty paranoid about it because that is the one thing we can't fix. The ship is as invisible as we know how to make it, but it still takes up space and will still block a star, sun, planet, or whatever. If we get cocky or careless, they'll see us."

Joanne nodded. "Keep on it, Marco. Get me an update on their positions in two hours. I want to be able to tip *Cobra* off when they come back around the planet."

"Yes, Captain."

On the Road
Zeta Doradus (b)
Thursday, March 8, 2080, 2230 UTC

David's NetLink vibrated slightly, announcing a new message. Gabrielle watched his face go from curiosity to surprise. The Zeds were walking several meters ahead. They had just cleared the first village and were now on a two-meter-wide, tree-covered dirt road. David recognized it as one of the 'old trails' Evans had shown him.

"So, what is it?"

David looked around, then turned back to her. "The PG's three friends are here."

"What does that mean for us?" she asked, keeping her voice neutral.

As Gabrielle was speaking, David heard Sabrina's NetLink, and they locked eyes for a second after she read it.

"Nothing. Henderson and Evans will handle them. The Marines back at the shuttle will need to stay alert."

"Should I go back?" Sabrina asked quietly. They were all trying very hard to not alarm the Zeds or the Speakers.

David shook his head. "Your Marines will be fine. I'd rather you stay with us, just in case."

"All I have is a .45. Not much firepower if we get into a shit with them."

He smiled over at her. "Oh, sergeant, don't lie to the naive young fleetie lieutenant. You've got at least one K-Bar concealed somewhere, right?"

Sabrina smiled. "Yeah, true, and a stiletto somewhere you're not likely to find it."

"To say nothing of the mace."

"Mace?"

"Inside your back belt. Cylindrical bulge that isn't, you know, you."

"Pretty perceptive for a fleetie, Lieutenant. What about you?"

"Besides my great-grandfather's .45, there's a K-bar on my right calf and a filet knife under my left arm."

"Nice."

"I really love these little insights, David," Gabrielle smirked, "Learning stuff I never knew I needed. Like just how ruthless you two might turn out to be."

"Oh?"

"Yes. And for the record, high-concentration pepper-spray, right pants pocket. Just in case you need it."

David had to smile. "I think, all in all, we're going to be fine."

As they finished their inventory of weaponry, the Zeds stopped and came back to them.

Asoon reported, "They would like to hear more of Earth. They are curious about you."

"Have you told them anything of Alpha Mensae?"

"We do not discuss Home with obsequient species."

"Asoon, do you know how that sounds to me? That sounds like an old Preeminent, not you."

"I understand, but such has been the policy, and the SD has said nothing new to change it."

David didn't respond, instead turning to Gabrielle. "You've learned a little about this culture. Do you think you could answer some questions for them?"

"Sure. Nothing too specific and nothing about weapons or military, I assume?"

"Right. Just beauty and diversity and how life is so wonderful there."

"OK, so, tell lies. Got it."

David shook his head. "No, not lies, just keep it positive."

"OK, will do."

"I should go with her," Greg said. "I've been head-down in this language for a few weeks now. I need to see if I can keep up with the conversation."

David nodded. "Done. If you can speak it, or even just understand it, we'll have a check on what's being said."

Gabrielle and Greg walked with the Zeds several meters ahead, the Speakers just behind, busily translating back and forth. They continued until the group arrived at the next village, Gabrielle talking in her animated, expressive way, her hands in constant motion. David could hear what she said, the questions coming back from the Zeds and her answers. They seemed quite curious about human physiology, male and female, food habits, living arrangements. Clearly, the Zeds were very different from either humans or the Preeminent.

As they approached the next town, David and Sabrina again locked eyes.

"Smoke," she said quietly. David nodded but didn't say anything else. It was a dense smell, not a campfire or cooking fire. It had an industrial intensity. As they came into the village proper, they could also hear the sound of hammers on iron.

"A forge," David said.

As they walked through the small town, perhaps a half-kilometer in diameter, iron pieces were everywhere, all kinds of shapes in various stages of completion. But the most frequent item David saw was a cylindrical object that looked to be a half-meter long or so. They were nearing the far edge of the town when Sabrina suddenly cried "Ouch!" and knelt down beside the path to take off her boot.

The entourage stopped while she took it off and shook it.

"Stone. Been feeling it for an hour!" she said smoothly. She put it back on, laced it up, and they continued their trek north.

After several minutes she looked over at David. "Gun barrels. No question about it."

David just nodded, not wanting to get into a larger conversation with the Speakers and the Zeds nearby. But clearly, this was trouble. If the Zeds were planning a major assault on the Preeminent, they would naturally strike back, and his job would become just that much more difficult.

The day was beginning to fade as they arrived in the next town. Asoon returned to David and Sabrina.

"This is the council member's town. We will be staying here for the night. He invites you four to stay in his home."

"What about you?" David asked.

"We are instructed to remain in the forest on the edge of the town. It is not far from his home."

"Can you tolerate that arrangement?"

"We can. The climate here is sufficient for us. We will be fine. He says he will provide a guard, and we will be safe there."

"That's a little alarming. Should I get you some security from *Intrepid*?"

"No. I think he is just cautious. They hate Speakers, David. They have good reason since Speakers are always bringing them bad news."

"You're sure about this?"

"Yes. We have accepted his offer of a guard, more for diplomatic reasons than any real need. We are females, but we can defend ourselves if necessary."

As they arrived at the GuildMember's home, David wondered just how close Asoon and Ateah would be. The round, multi-domed dwelling faced the center green of the town. The green itself was far more impressive in person than it had been in overhead imagery from *Cobra*. It was fifty meters in diameter, easily twice the size of anything they had previously observed. There were plantings of low shrubs around the perimeter that seemed to define the space. In the center of the green, a low, dense green plant grew that reminded David of the clover-ish ground cover on Big Blue. There were benches, shorter than the human version, at regular intervals throughout. No flowers, he noted. But then, there were not many flying insects here, either.

David led his small group out into the green, where they dropped their backpacks and sat in a small circle out of earshot of the Speakers.

"OK, Gabe, tell me about your conversation."

She smiled widely. "Oh my God! They wanted to know *everything!* By Terran definition, they're mammals. Sort of. They bear the young alive and produce milk but don't have hair. Hair, in fact, is a major mystery to them. None of the animals here have it, and they don't get what it is or what it's for, why mine is long, and Sabrina's is short. Um, let me think...oh, right. The genders are far more consistent here than at home. The idea that both Sabrina and I are female, while you and Greg are males, is hard for them to grasp. Sabrina is about as tall as you, David, while I'm almost as short as they are. That just confuses the hell out of them."

"Interesting. What else?"

"Their society is organized by extended families, what we might call a clan. There are eighteen of them, based on their maternal line."

"So, what clan you belong to is defined by who your mother is?" Sabrina asked.

"Yes, and it's very strict. They don't marry like we do, exactly, and I don't understand yet how it works with them, but it seems females must pick a mate outside their own clan. Maybe it's an inbreeding taboo of some kind? There's something I'm missing about all that, because the rest, while very different from us, all makes a kind of internal sense, you know? Not at all like us, but still a logical system."

"What did they ask about Earth?"

"They're curious about how far away it is, but I didn't know how to explain that. A light-year would be meaningless to them since they don't have the tech to understand the speed of light or what a year is. I tried to translate their days into ours, but I finally just said it takes us forty days to get here. That seemed to satisfy them."

"Good. What else?"

"I talked about the different kinds of people, races, countries, etc., back home, but I am not sure they grasped that. This is a small place with just one culture. I'm so tan from the desert that Sabrina and I don't look very different, even though we have very different ethnic backgrounds."

"That's good information," David said, turning to Sabrina. "So, were they gun barrels?"

"Yes, no question those iron pipes we saw are something like a musket barrel. I didn't have time to see if they were rifled or not, but I kinda doubt it."

"I wondered about those, too," Greg said.

David frowned. "There were easily hundreds of them, maybe more."

"Yeah," Sabrina answered, "and how many hundreds more are already complete? They're raising an army, Lieutenant."

"Agreed." He turned to Greg. "How goes the language?"

"Better. The structure is simpler than English — "

"What isn't?" Sabrina interrupted with a smile.

"True," Greg responded. "It's not as rigid as Seekerish, but I'm getting it. I could follow most of the conversation, but there are still big blanks in my vocabulary."

"Are Asoon and Ateah helping with that?"

"Yes. They're actually impressed that I can speak more than one other language. The Speakers' abilities are amazing, but they're limited to a single language other than their own. Strange."

Sabrina looked down at the ground. "Not sure I care about impressing a couple of Preems."

"Well," David answered, "on one level, I agree with you. But if they are positively inclined towards Greg, that works in our favor." He turned back to Greg. "Can you speak it?"

"Not yet. I tried a few words and got back something Ateah explained was laughter and derision. I apparently have a long way to go."

David couldn't help but smile at Greg's self-deprecating tone. "Fine. Stick with it. We're staying here tonight. The Speakers are being sent out into the woods outside town. I guess the Zeds don't want them in their houses."

"Understandable," Gabrielle responded.

"Right, but it puts me in a difficult position. Still, Asoon agreed to it, so I guess we'll be OK."

Asoon came out to the group on the green. "The council member asks your preference for evening meal and if there are any requirements for sleeping arrangements."

"Tell him we have our own food, and if it is acceptable, we would like to eat together right here. As for sleeping, we will need a private space to lay down, that's all." He tapped his backpack. "We have everything else we need."

After Asoon left, David pulled out his NetComp and opened the map *Cobra* had compiled, and laid the tablet on the ground. "We started here," he said, pointing, "then came through this town, where the forge was, and now we're here." He looked around to make sure everyone understood. "This town, here up north, is what *Cobra* thinks is the capital. I'm pretty sure that's where they're taking us."

"Any word about the PG's friends?" Sabrina asked.

"No. I expect *Intrepid* and *Cobra* will just avoid contact with them."

Greg looked worried. "Can they do that? Can they play hide-and-seek with three Preeminent cruisers?"

David shook his head. "No problem. *Cobra* could pull right up to one, and unless they were looking out the window, they'd never detect it. *Intrepid* is almost that good. My guess is Henderson and Evans will just keep moving around, adjusting their orbits so the cruisers can't get a solid track on them."

Asoon returned to say that it was acceptable for them to eat in the central green, and in fact, the Zeds would like to join them there.

"Can you stay to translate?"

"Yes, of course."

The Speakers sat just outside the circle of four humans and three Zeds, the GuildMember's female partner having joined for the meal. The Zeds ate with spoons, much like the human utensil, out of wide, shallow bowls containing a stew of grains and fish. It didn't smell very good to David, but then, they weren't asking him to try it, either. The humans ate a cold meal of dried meats, cheese, and crackers from their MREs. It wasn't great, but it was enough protein and calories to see them through the night.

The conversation centered around foods, what the humans ate at home, especially what varieties of grains or plants they consumed. The Zeds had just three edible plants, two root crops and one that sounded to David to be very similar to wheat. Everything they ate was combined and simmered until it reached a smooth consistency.

"Sounds too much like porridge," Gabrielle commented, ripping open a chocolate bar.

"It does, but if it works for them..." Sabrina answered with a shrug. "Food is just food. Fuel for whatever is next."

Gabrielle frowned. "Oh, Sabrina, when we get back, I have a whole list of places I'm taking you!"

As the Night Glow rose, they moved inside to a surprisingly bright and warm room. The Zeds pulled a curtain — or, at least, some kind of fabric — over the opening. Greg heard them say, 'this is all we have' and passed that to the others. It would be enough for the night as they pulled their sleeping bags from their backpacks and settled for the night.

Sabrina sat cross-legged with her back against the wall opposite the entry, her weapon in her lap. "I'll take the first shift."

"OK," David answered. "Wake me in three hours."

"Will do."

CHAPTER 6

GuildMember's Home
Zeta Doradus (b)
Friday. March 8, 2020, 1300 UTC

David's watch over his small command ended just before sunrise. His NetLink had vibrated quietly twice during the night. As his three companions began to stir, he picked up his NetComp.

"There's been a couple of updates from Evans. Like we thought, *Intrepid* and *Cobra* are moving their orbits around to deny the Preeminent a stationary target. At least one will be visible above us at all times; most of the time, both will be there."

He stopped to look back through the curtain. Seeing nothing, he continued. "There are three Type III's up there, looking for our ships with their intruder detectors. My guess is that they'll fail unless they happen to get lottery-type lucky."

"What about us?" Greg asked.

"Us? For us, nothing has changed. We continue as before. We need to get this central council to call off whatever they have planned. The shipment bombs were bad enough. If they stage a direct attack, it will be holy hell trying to stop the Preeminent from wiping them out, even with *Intrepid* here."

The star was just over the horizon as they returned to the town green to eat breakfast. The sky was clear and bright blue above. David detected just a hint of smoke in the slightly cool, moist air. *Cooking fires,* he decided.

The Zeds did not ask to join them for breakfast.

Asoon and Ateah arrived just as they were finishing. "Have you been provided food?" David asked.

"It has been promised for tonight."

"You are otherwise OK? Enough water?"

"Yes, we are fine."

David stood, wiping his hands with a disposable towel, and stuffing it in the waste bag on the side pocket of his backpack. He turned to Asoon, his face set with annoyance.

"Tell Ateah to inquire of the council member when you will be fed. Make it clear that I am the one asking, that I want to know when they will do what they said they would."

Asoon spoke to Ateah and then turned back to David. "Why are you so concerned about this?"

"You are no less my responsibility than Gabe or Greg. I must see that your needs are met and that you are safe."

Several Zeds gathered nearby, watching the humans eat, and staring at the Speakers as they were talking.

David looked over his shoulder at them, then back to Asoon. "Ask them what they would like to know."

After a short exchange, Asoon reported, "They want to know how soon you Vooman will get the ugly grey liars out of their town."

"Ouch. I'm sorry I asked. *Vooman?*"

"Yes, that is as close as they can get to 'human.' Ateah and I are not liars, but they can't know that, and we understand that this is a normal reaction from their point of view."

David had to smile. "For a latter-day dinosaur, Asoon, you're remarkably understanding."

There was a pause before Asoon responded, a pause filled with Greg trying very hard not to laugh and Gabrielle poking him to make him stop. "If I understood correctly, that was a compliment hidden somewhere in a humorous comment made at my expense?"

Even Sabrina smiled at that. "You know, Asoon, sometimes I'm not sure who is making fun of whom."

"I will take that as a compliment as well, thank you."

The Elder and council member finally appeared out of the council member's home, and the assembly soon moved north out of the town, onto a different, narrower old path. There was little conversation from the Zeds this morning as they walked a few meters ahead. They had not taken kindly to David's challenge about food for the Speakers. Ateah reported that they were offended that David would even question them about it. David ignored that and had her repeat to the Zeds that the Speakers' needs and safety were his responsibility, and it was his duty to inquire about them. The Zeds' attitudes didn't change. David was reasonably sure they were delaying the delivery as a tactic to punish the Speakers for being Preeminent. The whole place was a damn deleelinosh factory, after all. They could not possibly have any real problems providing for them. David saw it as petty and vindictive, and he didn't care for that one bit.

The next town again announced itself with the smell of industrial smoke, but this place was a glass works. As they walked through, they could look down, well, more like *around,* the narrow, curved lanes and see panes of window glass and other practical pieces like drinking glasses stacked outside the many small kilns.

It was almost noon when they approached the large town that David was sure was their destination. The Zeds stopped them just before they passed the first ring of houses.

"This is the center of our society," Asoon translated for David, "and here you will meet with the council."

David nodded. "Yes, we understand. "

"There has never been a Violet or Gray Liar in this town. We have kept its location hidden from them, and we cannot have them learn where it is. We require your commitment that these Gray Liars will not tell their masters about this place."

David made an immediate decision, one he hoped he would not regret. "Tell the council member I do not wish to insult him or his society, but I knew what this place was and where it was before I landed on the planet. I knew as soon as we left the Elder's village where we were going. I have no doubt the Preeminent already know these things as well."

There was a long silence after Ateah completed the translation. David looked over at Greg, who gave him a slight nod of confirmation. The translation had been correct, near as Greg could tell. The Zeds looked at each other and turned to walk into the town. David and the rest followed a few meters behind.

They were led to a large, open-sided structure in the center of the town green, which was even larger and more extravagantly planted than the one they had breakfast in that morning. The building reminded David of a picnic pavilion in a park back home, perhaps thirty meters in diameter. There was a crowd of Zeds there which seemed to organize itself as they approached. Eighteen pairs of seats were arranged in a circle, a meter or so between each pair. There were females present, too, which surprised David since up to now, he had dealt exclusively with males. Gabrielle had reported that this was a matriarchal society, and on reflection, David wondered why they had not dealt with more along the way. Who was really in charge here?

The council member who had brought them north turned to Ateah and spoke. Asoon then said, "This council member must now take his place with the sixth-mother of his clan."

"Sixth-mother?" Gabrielle asked.

Asoon and Ateah talked for a moment, then Asoon said, "That is the best translation of what he said."

"That's what I heard him say, too," Greg added. "It was as if she is the sixth mother in some line, like a sixth-great-grandmother. That part is still unclear to me."

The Elder again spoke to Ateah, and David thought he heard a different tone in his voice. "You are being honored here," Asoon said, "The council typically only meets in what you might call the spring of the year, after the winter snows have dissipated."

The four humans and two Preeminent remained outside the circle as Elder

Wocos entered to greet the female talking with his council member.

The Guild gathered for an unusual second time since the last snow. Elder Wocos spoke to the Vooman, telling them what an honor it was that the Guild would agree to hear him. The Vooman lacked many basic social graces, he thought, subtlety being most obviously absent. They were haughty, he decided, thoughtlessly arrogant in their bearing and speech. The leader's blunt comments about the location of their capital, something so private and critical to his society, were particularly hurtful. His GuildMember left him shortly after they arrived to join the sixth-mother of his clan in the Guild ring. Wocos did not know the full scope of what the Guild was planning, but if the Vooman were going to change any minds, this was their best chance. Wocos was not sure the Guild should change their plans, but reason dictated that the Guild should hear the Vooman out.

Wocos took this opportunity to speak with his clan's sixth-mother, a female chosen every six snows to lead her clan. She might literally be a sixth-mother, or even more, but the ceremonial title remained the same. She commended him on his work and that of his observers, and Wocos was pleasantly surprised that she would know his name, let alone the work he had done. That she would ask of Tefin's progress healing from his wounds was even more surprising. He would be sure to tell Tefin of her inquiry when he returned home. Tefin would be honored.

The GuildMaster also spoke to Wocos, instructing him to permit the Vooman inside but demand the Gray Liars remain outside the circle. Wocos explained that the greys were required for the Vooman to speak, but the leader was unmoved. *They cannot enter this space,* he said. *Let them speak from outside.*

Wocos came out to see the Vooman. The leader looked down at him with a strange look on his face. After two days of travel and talk, Wocos still could not comprehend the Vooman's expressions or voices. They were loud, that could not be missed, and that alone fed his impression of their arrogance. Their language seemed dull and flat to Wocos' ears, able to climb in volume but not in tonal sophistication. He wondered if that flat sound reflected their thinking, too.

The Elder turned to Ateah and spoke.

"They invite you to enter and speak, but Ateah and I must remain outside the council structure."

David looked at Asoon, then back to the Elder, speaking while looking him in his dark, round eyes.

"Tell him I am disappointed at his attitude, but we will respect their council's desires." After a moment, he added. "I require a few minutes to consult with my companions."

"What's on your mind?" Gabrielle asked after they had walked a few meters away from the council.

"Well, first off, do I confront them with what we know?"

"What do we know?" Greg asked.

"The gun barrels," Sabrina said flatly. "The hundreds and hundreds of gun barrels."

"Right," David said. "I can either hit them with that right off, or I can hold it back as a trump card for later."

"Wait," Gabrielle said immediately. "Keep it for when you need it. If we offend them in the first minute, they're not going to hear anything else you say. Listening to Wocos, I think they see themselves as honorable but frustrated by the constraints of the occupation. They are an old culture, with simple but rich traditions. Their reaction to your inquiry about the Speakers' food reflects that attitude. So, work to their belief in their own wisdom and hold the bitter facts for when you need them."

"OK, that makes sense to me."

"Second off?" Greg asked.

"My take on this whole mission is that we're announcing something that has already happened; we're just here to administer it. The PG, and the Preeminent in general, really have no choice. They are obligated to withdraw. They are just the beneficiaries of the Preeminent defeat."

"Yes, sounds right," Gabrielle answered.

"OK, here goes."

"One more thing, David?" Gabrielle asked.

"Yes?"

"Greg and I were talking about their language last night. It's nuanced, with complex tones and shades of meaning. The structure is simple, but the content is anything but. Try to explain this clearly, but, like I said before, with some degree of deference to their society."

"So, less McArthur and more Marshall?"

Gabrielle smiled. "I was actually thinking less Patton and more Lincoln, but, sure, Marshall will do."

David looked at her in surprise. "Patton? Really? *Patton?*"

As they turned to face the Zed assembly, Sabrina leaned into David's ear. "I kinda see you more as an Omar Bradley type myself."

"Oh, the dog-faced general? Thanks for the confidence builder." David took his sidearm from its holster under his left arm and handed it to Sabrina.

Sabrina smiled as she slipped it into her belt and looked over at the pavilion. "Time to wade ashore, sir. Do try to come back in one piece."

David stood in the middle of the thirty-six individuals that comprised the ruling council of the Zeds. The significance of the number was not lost on him: the square of the number of fingers on two Zed hands. It could not be a coincidence. He slowly turned a full circle, looking carefully at each pair of representatives.

"My name is David Powell, and I serve in my planet's space force, something we call the Fleet." He watched Asoon carefully, making sure he was not overwhelming her or Ateah before pausing for translation. "We have just fought a war with the race you call the Violets. We know them as the Preeminent, which is the name they acknowledge."

Several sets of eyes swept from him to the Speakers, then to Gabrielle standing next to them, and back.

"We have defeated the Preeminent in this conflict. The terms that ended the war require the Preeminent to withdraw from all conquered worlds."

There was a low buzz as the implications of his statement became clear.

"Yes, there are other worlds, not that different from your own, that the Preeminent have subjugated and must now set free. I want to emphasize this point: your freedom from the Violets has already been granted. They must leave. They *will* leave."

He paused for a moment to re-gather his thoughts and allow the translators to catch up.

"We are here to announce this to you and to observe the process and ensure its proper completion. It is not something that requires any action by you. It's done."

After this, David said simply, "I welcome any questions you may have."

Ateah completed the translation, but no one spoke. David looked around carefully, making two complete circuits of the council members. The faces revealed no emotion to David. Each was neutral, best as he could tell, just looking back at him. Interpreting any alien's facial expression was hard for humans, he knew, but he thought there should be *some* little message there, telling him how well they were hearing him.

There was only silence. Finally, David turned and moved outside the pavilion. He turned immediately to Greg. "What of the translation?"

Greg shrugged. "It seemed fine to me. I didn't detect any spin or attitude that she might be adding to your words."

"What of the tone?" he asked Gabrielle.

"In English, it was fine."

Greg nodded. "I agree."

As they stood talking, Elder Wocos came to them.

"The council will consider what you have said. You may retire to the other side of the green to await their decision."

David looked at the Elder for a second, then just said, "Very well."

"I have a question for the Elder," Gabrielle said to Asoon.

"Yes, he asks, what is your question?"

Gabrielle looked at Greg, then David, then said, "This is the ruling council of your society. But I see no signs of any aging on the members. What happens to the older members of your society? Do they die off naturally? Are they culled somehow? I am very curious about this."

The Elder responded with pointed questions to Ateah, which were followed by quick conversations between Ateah and Asoon. Finally, the Elder spoke again.

"He does not understand your question. The oldest members of the society are here. He says the leader of the council has seen more than ten thousand first snows. The second, eight thousand. He is confused why you would think they would remove the most valuable individuals from their society. It makes no sense to him."

"Wait," Greg said. "Ask him how many snows he has seen himself."

"Ten thousand snows, if Ateah's understanding is correct."

The party of six moved silently away from the pavilion, finding a bench conveniently placed under a tree about fifty meters from the council pavilion.

David laid down on the green and covered his eyes with his cap, trying to force the stress out of his neck and gut with deliberate breathing and conscious relaxation. After several minutes, it still wasn't working. There was just so much that could still go wrong.

"Ten thousand years?" Gabrielle asked herself aloud.

"It's more like thirteen thousand." David's voice came from under his hat. "Their year is about thirty-five percent longer than ours."

"How could this be?" Greg asked.

"Good genes, I guess. I kinda wish we had Doctor Scranton with us. She'd have an answer."

"Scranton?" Sabrina asked.

"She ran the op on the wreck at the *Sigma* battle site. She was the first to figure out the Preeminent were actually Terran."

Sabrina looked down at David from the bench where she sat watching the council pavilion. "So, do we need to get this to Commander Evans?"

"Not right away. We'll call him after we hear from the Zeds."

Sabrina watched the discussion from a distance, different individuals standing, speaking, walking around, then sitting as the next speaker took their turn. From time to time, the crowd standing outside would turn and look at the humans or the Speakers seated on their own bench nearby. It was strange to watch a group so obviously talking about her companions and herself. She felt like she, and they, were somehow on trial.

Zed Capital
Zeta Doradus (b)
Friday, March 8, 2080, 1920 UTC

"Something is happening," Sabrina said quietly. David sat up and replaced his hat on his head. As he looked at the pavilion, the Zeds were moving around as if greeting one another. Elder Wocos and his council member emerged and walked in their direction. David called over the Speakers, anxious to hear what the Zeds had decided.

"You are to return to the council to hear their decision," Asoon translated. They picked up their gear and moved back outside the pavilion. David again left his sidearm with Sabrina and went inside to the center of the council circle.

The Zed leader spoke to David, and he turned to Asoon for the translation.

"The council says that they don't know you or why you are here. They say they will push we Preeminent off the planet themselves."

David looked up at Gabrielle, who nodded.

"Tell him we have seen the weapons they are making. We've seen the hollow steel tubes they are building. It will not be enough. The Violets will fight back." He paused again for translation. "Even if you win, which I doubt, hundreds will die." He thought about what Wocos had said about their lifespan, "How many millions of first snows will be lost then? How many will not live to see their next snow? This is folly! You must not do this!"

The leader again spoke to him, and David began to understand what Zed anger looked like.

Asoon paused a moment after Ateah finished translating. "I will leave out the pejoratives. He remains in disbelief."

David turned to her. "Pejoratives?"

"Crude, ignorant, arrogant; things like that. Haughty, even."

"Arrogant? Make this clear, Asoon. I am *begging* them to wait. *Begging them.* The Violets will leave soon if they simply leave them alone. If the Violets are attacked, they will naturally feel entitled to protect themselves."

He waited a moment for the translation. The pauses annoyed him, but there was no other way to communicate.

David went on. "You have called me crude and arrogant. I am very sure I am not so refined as you who have lived five-hundred times as long. If that offends you, I apologize, as that was not my intent. I understand your desire for freedom, to be released from the rule of the Violets. But new violence will make that situation worse, not better."

The translation took a few more seconds to complete, and after a moment the leader again stood to address David.

"No, he says, they have suffered enough. The Violets are weak, and now is the time to act." David's shoulders sank as the leader resumed speaking. "However, in case you are telling the truth, they will give you six days to remove the Violets. If they are not gone by that time, they will be forced out."

"I do not know if this is enough time, but I will do everything in my power to see that it is done."

The leader had no further response, so David left the assembly and walked well into the center of the green. Asoon came with them.

"Ateah believes they are lying to you."

"What?"

"She detected notes of deception in the leader's speech. She cannot be certain, but she does not think they will wait the six days."

"Greg?"

"Ateah is far more expert than I. I didn't hear what she did, but I see no reason to question her conclusion."

"Shit. I thought we'd have to hold the Preeminent back. I thought the Zeds would welcome someone here to take the chains off their necks, but no. They want to make more trouble for themselves. For people who live thousands of years, if we're to believe that, they don't seem to value their lives as much we do!"

They walked away from the council pavilion, and began to check their shoes, shoulder their packs, and mentally prepare for the long walk back to the Recon Shuttle.

"Damn," David said quietly, mostly to himself. "Damn, damn, damn a race that sees wisdom in mindless pigheadedness."

He took one last look at the council pavilion, even turned as if to go back and make another argument, then let his shoulders fall and turned back to head down the old dirt path. Gabrielle fell in silently beside him, with Sabrina and Greg behind with the Speakers.

.

Zed Capital
Zeta Doradus (b)
Friday, March 8, 2080, 2031 UTC

They were only a few hundred meters down the path south when David's NetLink went off. It was Evans.

"The Zeds fired on the Preem this morning. They killed four pickets who were walking the perimeter. The marines at the Recon Shuttle heard it."

"I guess the guns we saw work."

"I guess so, yeah. The PG has already marched into the village where the attack came from. I don't know how many he killed. This cloud cover is a giant pain in the ass."

David looked to the south, and indeed, while it was bright sunshine where he was, there was a solid, low cloud deck a few kilometers away.

"Well, sir, I have more bad news for you. The Zeds are planning a large-scale attack on the Preeminent. I begged them to delay it, and they gave me six days to get them off the planet."

"Not much time."

"No, and Ateah thinks they're lying about that. She thinks they won't wait."

"I've already sent Rmah a message to get his PG under control. He's coming, but who knows when he'll get here."

"It might be too late for that, sir."

There was a pause as Evans thought over his options. "I'm coming down. I'll pick you up first and drop you at the Recon Shuttle. Let's get everyone back up here and figure out what we do next."

A half-hour later, *Cobra*'s shuttle landed on the wide capital green. The six travelers climbed in, and it lifted off, having been on the ground less than two minutes. A few minutes later, it landed at the Recon Shuttle, dropping David and his party. The Speakers rode back to the Preeminent spaceport with Evans and Jack Ballard. David flew the Recon Shuttle up to *Cobra*.

As soon as they were in the ShuttleLock, XO Elaine DeLeon shifted *Cobra*'s orbit as a precaution. The Recon Shuttle was pretty stealthy, but not as much as *Cobra* itself. Even a small maneuver would defeat the Preeminents' attempts to track them, efforts which had not abated since they arrived.

At the same time, Rich Evans was talking to the PG outside his headquarters, Asoon doing the translation.

"You *must* cease these retaliations on the natives. You no longer have any right to do that."

"I am the governor here, Vermin, not you. And while I am governor, my rule on these obsequients will not be questioned."

"Segt sent you a message ordering you to obey our instructions."

"How would you know that? Who told you?"

"No one had to tell me. I told Segt to send it. Do you still not understand your position here?"

"*You* will understand, Vermin. You will understand soon enough."

"What, those three ships you have up there stumbling around in the dark like blind children? I could destroy them any time I choose. They're helpless up there. It's frankly embarrassing for you just how bad they are."

The PG ignored the insult. "Segt is not in charge here. I am, and I will protect my Combatants as I see fit. They attacked us, in case you have forgotten!"

"It would have been better if they had not killed your Combatants, I realize. We did not know of that, or we would have stopped it."

"Why should I believe you?"

"Because what I say is true. Rmah Segt is coming to take over, so I suggest you behave yourself until he arrives. He may forgive this retaliation, but I don't think the natives will."

"I care nothing for them. They are worse than you."

"And I don't care what you think. You're obligated to obey orders."

"The First would never have tolerated this."

Evans looked at Asoon for several seconds before replying. "The First is dead. We killed him. Don't forget either of those facts."

Asoon stared back at Evans as if waiting for him to change his mind. When he didn't, she did the translation, and the PG turned and walked back into his headquarters.

Asoon remained outside. "I would have advised against that challenge, Commander. It threatens him. He may not react as you expect. He is not human. He is a Preeminent, bred from his egg to conquer."

Evans shook his head. "He will need to adapt, Asoon, or he will die. I will not permit any more attacks on the Zeds, no matter what they do. You may pass that along to him with my compliments."

"Yes, I will."

"Emphasize that if he wishes to return home alive, he will do well to listen."

Evans flew the shuttle back up to *Cobra*, discussing the results of his conversation with Jack Ballard.

Ballard shook his head. "He's going to do what his instincts tell him, Commander. Our warnings are not going to deter him."

"Maybe not, but if they don't, he'll learn the price of disobedience."

David was waiting as they exited the ShuttleLock.

GuildMember's Home
Zeta Doradus (b)
Friday, March 8, 2080, 2255 UTC

Elder Wocos and his GuildMember walked from the capital back to the GuildMember's town before dark.

"Might we be misjudging the Vooman? Might they be telling the truth?"

"No, Riaghe Wocos, I think not. The Guild heard him out twice, and they are

125

unanimously unimpressed. He is like a child, Wocos, not even fifty snows, I believe."

"It must be different with them. They were surprised that the GuildMaster had lived ten thousand snows. I think their lifespan is limited and very, very short."

"Why do you say that?"

"The small female asked about what she called 'aging,' as if they become somehow less functional as they get older."

"We see this in lesser species, but not in ourselves."

"Yes, the Gift prevents it."

"Correct. We do not speak of it often, Wocos, but the Gift is a wondrous thing."

They walked in silence for a while.

"Still, what the Vooman say is logical," Wocos said. "If they won this conflict as they claim, they might well demand the Violets relinquish their slaves."

"Being logical does not make something true. The Guild has spoken, and we will abide by its decision."

Wocos thought for a moment of continuing the discussion but decided there was little point to it. "Yes, GuildMember," he responded.

Wocos declined the offer of a bed for the night and continued towards his small hometown in the darkness. There were few travelers on the path that late at night, most of his kind more inclined to remain comfortable in their warm, safe homes with an even warmer companion. His own partner had been with him three hundred snows, and in that time, they had not grown tired of each other's company. She was wise; her three repro licenses had taught her much about caring for others and finding a way to make every day pleasant and productive. Her absences had been hard for Wocos, and his selection to repro in yet a different clan was difficult as well. He had gone and done as the society required, fathered two males, and returned once they were adults. He looked back on that time with mixed emotions. He cared for his children, but the female was not as kind or flexible as he would have preferred. As the mother, her word carried more weight than his, and he had limited ability to do for his sons as he would have liked.

The Night Glow was past the zenith as he arrived home, peeking down through breaks in the overcast. He went straight to his bed and was asleep soon after.

Riaghe Village
Zeta Doradus (b)
Saturday, March 9, 2080, 0830 UTC

Elder Wocos awoke before sunrise to Kutah and Tefin's voices outside his home. He dressed quickly and came out to see what they were upset about.

"Did you hear what happened? Did you hear what your guards did?" Kutah challenged him.

"I know the Violets struck the Niocli village and killed fifty."

"They did that because the guards you assigned to us panicked and killed four Violets."

"What?"

"We were watching the landing field from the new position, like usual. The guards you sent waited back about twenty meters, hidden in the trees. The Violets patrol the edge of the field regularly. They always have. When they're coming, we just crawl back a meter or two and let them pass. They don't even know we're there." Kutah stopped to catch his breath, his anger rising again as he relived the previous morning. "Along came four of them, which is unusual, but we've seen that before. It doesn't change anything. We just let them pass."

Tefin touched his friend on the arm and took over. "When the Violets were right in front of us, the guards stood up and fired their new weapons. Three of the Violets went down, and the other started shooting back."

Wocos' face reflected sudden stress, and Kutah thought he was beginning to understand just what a disaster he had unleashed. "What did you do?"

We kept ourselves hidden," Kutah answered, "Finally, the guards killed the last Violet. Two of the guards were killed before the other two could finish him off."

"We dragged them out of the forest and brought them back," Tefin added.

"This is very unfortunate," Wocos said sadly.

"*Unfortunate?*" Kutah yelled. "*They could have gotten all of us killed!* I told them to remain where they were unless I instructed them otherwise. I had no desire to surrender my snows to their incompetence. Watching, Elder Wocos, watching means patience. It means quiet. One does not call attention to yourself."

"Yes, I see."

"I am not convinced that you do, Elder Wocos. Fifty are now dead, plus the two guards. All for four Violets. If we keep that up, we will all be dead and they will have to farm the deleelinosh themselves."

Wocos could not mistake the fire in Riaghe Kutah's eyes. Or, Tefin's. He had sent the four young guards with their new weapons to ensure Kutah's safety, but their impulsiveness had cost many lives.

127

"I regret that this happened, Kutah. Your safety was my only concern. There will be no more guards."

"Good. You should have listened to me from the beginning. You are older than I, Elder Wocos, but I am the one who does the watching. I am the one who knows the Violets best. Next time you will listen to me."

Kutah and Tefin left the Elder and went to Tefin's home. Udoro was still there, preparing to leave in a few suns to meet her repro partner.

"Are you going to the landing field?" she asked.

"Not today. I went back late yesterday, and they had doubled the patrols and were using lights to look under the shrubs at the edge of the forest. "

"What will you do?"

"Early tomorrow, I will go back and see what they are doing from a distance, then Tefin and I will decide how we can watch them."

"I am afraid," Udoro said quietly.

"You should be. If the Vooman could not stop the Violets' retribution yesterday, what else can they not do?"

"They say they're here to force the Violets to leave."

"And yet," Kutah snarled, "they did not stop them."

"They are just people, like us," Udoro said. "We cannot expect them to do the impossible."

"Perhaps," Kutah said reluctantly. "But if they defeated the Violets as they say they have, we should not have so many bodies to dispose of."

Udoro touched Kutah gently. "I am sorry for what happened. I see how it angers you."

"Yes."

"I would spend these last few suns with you if you are willing."

The thought of simple days and nights with Udoro was like a drug for Kutah. It was what he most desired and what he knew he would soon surrender to her repro license. He was torn on both sides, he thought.

"Yes, that would be welcome. I am not going today, so we can spend the day walking the meadows. Like we used to."

"And the night?"

"The night will follow its own course."

Kutah left home ready for the respite Udoro offered. He would not go to the landing field today, and, he thought to himself, perhaps not tomorrow, either. *Let the Vooman keep watch on the Violets.*

Intrepid
In Orbit at Zeta Doradus (b)
Saturday, March 9, 2080, 1055 UTC

"This asshole is not going to bend," Evans said to Joanne Henderson over the laser link. "He is a true believer."

"What about this last SLIP message?"

"We caught it after the retaliation raid yesterday, Zed time. There were three responses, and based on the timing, he's calling in the rest of what he has at DSX."

Joanne tapped her stylus on her NetComp as she thought about her options. "I could go smoke it, but I expect there will be no one there."

"Yes, I agree. I think we need to keep you and your Marines right here."

"Fine, but he has to pay the price for his bad behavior, don't you think?"

"What did you have in mind?"

"We disabled their ships during the blockade without killing anyone. How about I shove a Bludgeon up someone's ass and let them know we mean business. When is Rmah supposed to arrive?"

"A few days. He was unclear in his last message when he was leaving."

"OK, I'll pick one out and remind them who's really in charge here."

"Fine. Meantime we'll keep an eye on the PG."

"Good."

Joanne stepped down and walked to the Surveillance station. *Intrepid* had just come back from perigee, so she had several hours to work out an attack before her ship dove behind the planet again.

"Where are they, Marco?"

Marco Gonzales pulled up a three-dimensional tactical display for her. "Here, here, and here," he pointed to the display.

"James?" she called to her Weapons Officer, who rose from his station and walked across the Bridge to where she was standing.

"Yes, Captain?"

"See this one, the furthest from us?"

"Yes, ma'am."

"I want a Bludgeon in his drive."

Jim Kirkland nodded. "Yes, Captain, we can do that. You're looking to disable, like the blockade?"

"Exactly. One more thing. I want to drop the weapon with at least an hour delay, with indirect routing. I don't want them to know where it came from."

"Sure, Captain, we'll get that done."

The Bludgeon dropped off *Intrepid*'s port rotary fifteen minutes later. It took a winding path that included a pass within a thousand meters of a different Preeminent ship, then exploded fifty meters off the drive end of the selected Type III.

Joanne had to smile at Kirkland's initiative and sense of humor. The SLIP detector lit up after the strike, which confirmed that her message was getting through.

Riaghe Village
Zeta Doradus (b)
Saturday, March 9, 2080, 1100 UTC

Udoro woke early. Leaving Kutah to sleep, she walked to their hill just behind his home and watched the sunrise over the village and the rolling meadows beyond that went on as far as the ocean. She had struggled all night with what Kutah had told her. The Guild had ordered that they fight the Violets and drive them off the planet, ignoring what the Vooman had told them. Kutah told her the Guild did not believe the Vooman, and even if what they said was partially true, what would replace the Violets? Their haughty attitude seemed to say the Vooman could be even worse, what with their habit of giving directions and making demands that the Guild refused to obey.

She had also listened to Kutah and Tefin describe their skirmish with the Violet patrol. They'd killed the four but lost two of their own, and then fifty more in the retribution attack on the Nicoli village. Fifty for four? Kutah was right that this could not be the way to freedom.

The Guild believed differently. As Kutah reported it, the Guild had been building weapons for several snows and was now ready to send hundreds of males to remove the Violets. Even Elder Wocos, the leader of their village and a male of thousands of snows, had not known what the Guild was planning until the day before. He was old and wise, but the Guild was dominated by Originals, the first of her kind to receive the Gift. They valued time lived and accumulated wisdom over what life might be ahead, and so to send a few hundred younger males into this battle was a risk they were willing to take. *Not much will be lost,* Wocos had told Kutah, *the core of the society will be intact.*

Kutah would be one of those to strike, and Udoro could not bear to see him as she had seen the two guards the previous sun; their features burnt to an ugly, horrid shape, their deaths bringing no advantage, nothing learned or gained from it. All their snows to come wasted, lost in a moment of impulse when faced with their enemy.

She slid down the small hill, her destination clear and nearby. She found Elder Wocos as he was emerging after his morning meal.

"Elder Wocos, I would speak to you."

"Yes, Udoro, what is on your mind?"

"You must stop this madness."

"Madness?"

"This battle you plan to send Kutah and Tefin into."

"Udoro, I don't know — "

"Do not lie to a female, Elder Wocos. You should know better."

Wocos took a half step back from her. She stood a full head taller than he, and she was strong, even for a female.

"Say what you have to say, female."

"Why are we doing this? Why would you waste all these males for no reason?"

"No reason? *No* reason? Did you not hear what they did just last sun?"

"I did. And I know they did that because *you* sent armed males with Kutah. They lost control, and now fifty more are dead. There were females killed in that village, Wocos, and more of that will happen if you continue."

"They are weak now. The Vooman have wounded them gravely, but they are not yet subdued, and they are still here. We are stronger now."

"How are we stronger now than when they came fifty snows ago? How?"

"We are prepared for their violence, we know their methods, and we have weapons that can reach them. We never had these before. The time has come to make this place unlivable for them."

"You are foolish, Wocos. Your thinking is more childish than a newborn unable to reason or speak. You will kill those I love. You may kill all of us in the end, when the Violets make this place unlivable for *us*."

Udoro turned and left him, returning to Kutah's home, and Kutah. She decided she would not go into repro, not yet. She would tell her chosen male that he must wait until this time of crisis is over. She also knew that he might perish in the coming conflict, and she would prefer not to know and then grieve for another like Weiknu Tisok. It also occurred to her that she could lose her snows, too. It was a painful, terrible thought that invaded her mind. It must not happen. *It must not be allowed!*

She kept Kutah with her well into mid-morning, then left for her own home to consult with her mothers and send a message to Niahwo Gisap that he would have to wait a while longer.

She hoped he would understand.

The Preeminent Space Port
Zeta Doradus (b)
Saturday, March 9, 2080, 1320 UTC

The morning found the Governor in his office, looking out on the Spaceport and stewing over the illicit actions of the Vermin and the locals. The rapid spin of this damnable planet only added to his annoyance at their behavior. They were both so insolent, so lacking in proper deference to him and his kind. He was a *Preeminent!* But for the Vermin lurking overhead, too cowardly to show themselves, he would quickly curb these new native crimes against him and restore order.

He could only maintain his sleep cycle for a few rotations, then he required an extra day to recover. The never-ending cycle of too little sleep and then over-sleep made this assignment a long line of dreary days filled with fatigue.

His assistant came rushing in. "Sir Governor, one of the cruisers has been struck by a Vermin weapon!"

He stood and looked out his window to the north. "How badly is it damaged?"

"They struck the propulsion system. No one was injured, but the vessel is now stuck in high orbit."

The Governor remembered the reports of attacks on the tribute ships arriving at his home planet. A grotesquely effective blockade that kept critical supplies in orbit but killed no one.

He turned back to his assistant. "Just like their tactics at Home."

"Yes, Governor, I thought the same myself."

He left the window and took his large seat, his face fixed and severe. "More help is coming, and when they arrive, we will find and punish the Vermin, beat down these disgusting natives, and take back our natural place in the universe."

The assistant, frightened, shrunk back from the vehemence of the Governor's speech. "Yes, Governor."

When the Governor said nothing more, the assistant left his superior and returned to his own small office nearby. He had read the messages from Rmah Teo Segt. He knew what the authorities at Home were telling the Governor: *Follow the humans' instructions. We are obligated to vacate the planet and return control to the natural inhabitants. Cooperate fully.*

But the Governor was doing none of these things. Despite his misgivings, the assistant could not communicate with Home himself without the Governor's knowledge. He was, after all, an assistant, a mere functionary, and not someone in authority. If questioned later, he would tell the truth. That was his only option. For now, he would perform his duties as instructed and await developments.

Intrepid
In Orbit at Zeta Doradus (b)
Saturday, March 9, 2080, 1655

"Oh, great." Marco Gonzales said quietly to himself as the Surveillance Station lit up with alarms.

His tech confirmed his suspicion. "Yes, sir. Three more."

Marco turned to Joanne Henderson, studying the maps of the Zed society at her command station. "Hail, hail, the gang's all here, Captain."

Joanne nodded. "Nav!" she called. "Let's move a few degrees east and drop a hundred klicks or so. Wherever they think we are, let's not be there."

Larry Covington had to smile a little at Henderson's command. "Yes, ma'am; vacating where we am and headin' where we ain't."

He moved the ship two and a half degrees east and seventy-five kilometers closer to the surface. Not enough to affect their view of the Zeds, but enough to ruin any tracking the Preeminent might be doing. Despite their stealth, Larry knew there were ways to be seen if your opponent just happened to catch a break.

Joanne's phone rang. It was Evans.

"Well, we have them all here now, Captain."

"As much as it tempts me, Rich, I can't shoot them for no reason."

"Yes, that would be something of an inconvenience for Rmah. Has Anderson been briefing you on the movement we're seeing?"

"No." Joanne sat up in her chair, suddenly alerted to another issue with her Intelligence officer.

"It's still preliminary, so he might be waiting for more confirmation. But, whatever, we are seeing nighttime movement of Zeds towards the Preeminent spaceport. It started in the villages farthest to the north and south, just a few dozen out later than usual. But last night, it grew to a hundred or more individuals all moving one village closer to the port."

"So, building up for an attack?"

"That's what I suspect. Powell's report of his meeting with the central council supports the idea of an impending assault."

"Which would be suicidal."

"Yes, I think so, too."

"Can you tell if the Preeminent are aware of this?"

"There's no SLIP traffic and nothing new on their voice frequencies. But, no guarantees there since we still can't understand their language."

"I will get Kamaria and Liwanu thinking about how to intervene if we have to. We can't let this get out of hand."

"Good. I will keep you posted on anything new."

Joanne hung up and left her Command station, heading back towards the Intel

Section as she debated whether to kick Anderson's ass.
Again.

CHAPTER 7

Riaghe Village
Zeta Doradus (b)
Sunday. March 10, 2080, 1240 UTC (Early Evening Local Time)

Kutah and Tefin sat on the ground next to the path outside Tefin's home, looking cautiously at the weapons they were to carry against the Violets. The iron barrel was heavy and hard to hold steady, so the fabricators had added a pair of legs near the muzzle end, each with a small flat plate on the bottom to take most of the weight. At the back was a hinged portion that folded down for loading. Tefin picked up one of the rough paper-wrapped projectiles they had been given and tried placing it in the hinged block at the back of the barrel as Kutah watched.

"That's backward!" Kutah told him. "The ball has to be on the top, so it comes out the barrel!"

Tefin shook the cartridge back out of the loading block and replaced it correctly. To fire the weapon, they would then close and latch the hinge, then slap the small round plate at the rear of the loading block. A plunger would be driven in to create a spark, and the weapon would fire.

Tefin took the cartridge back out, then closed the hinged block and set up the angled leg near the back, which they were told should be pressed into the ground to absorb the recoil.

"It takes a long time," Tefin said sadly. "The Violets shoot much faster! And, when will we be able to practice with these?"

Kutah waved off his comment. There would be no practice. "We cannot allow the Violets to know what is coming, Tefin. We will learn quick enough when we strike them."

"There are Niesci camped just outside the village," Tefin said quietly. Niesci were never seen this far south. Their skills with glass and pottery were legendary, and everyone used their products, but they rarely left their own town.

"Yes," Kutah answered, "and there are Saognu on the other side of the path. More are coming, I think."

Kutah was sure the Saognu, masters of iron and the forge, had constructed the weapons they held. Their skills were a mystery to Kutah, how could they take certain rocks and soils and turn them into metal? He had been far enough north just once to smell the hard scent of the forges, and it had frightened him.

When Udoro arrived home, she was not pleased. "This is too dangerous. We should listen to the Vooman and let them take the Violets away!"

Kutah looked up at her with resignation on his face. "You already made that argument with the Elder and were unsuccessful. We think the same, but we are obligated to obey the Guild. You know this."

"I will go to the Vooman myself. I will tell them!"

"Don't," Kutah said. "We must abide. Besides, I don't know of any Vooman around here right now. They have all gone back to their spaceships."

Udoro pushed aside Kutah's weapon and sat cross-legged in front of him, her face almost touching his. "Do not do this. Don't throw away your snows. Don't throw away all my snows with you, either."

Kutah smiled weakly. "You argue with the foot when it is the mind that walks, Udoro. I must do as the Guild requires." Kutah disassembled his weapon and prepared it to be carried over his shoulder. As he put it away and walked to his hill for the sunset, he could hear the Niesci moving quietly through the village. They would be camping tonight just outside the Reupna village a few kilometers to the south. It could not be long now, Kutah thought. He could see that they carried supplies for only a few days.

Udoro came out as she heard the males moving south, and as she stood there watching, she could see Kutah on the hill behind his home. She thought to join him there, but her anger and frustration drove her back inside. She started an argument with Tefin, but he was as unmoved as Kutah, and she quickly relented. If she could get to the Vooman, they would do something. They preached a peaceful exit for the Violets, and as much as Udoro hated the invaders, she would prefer they left unharmed than risk any of her loved ones.

She retired to bed early that night, just as the Night Glow was rising, trying to run from her fears in sleep. They followed her into her dreams.

Cobra
In Orbit at Zeta Doradus (b)
Tuesday, March 12, 2080, 1100 UTC

Jack Ballard stood in the Operations Center, staring at the large display on the aft wall. The dark infra-red image he studied matched both his dark surroundings and his darkening mood. It was deceptively quiet around him, the six techs currently on watch working together through small headphones and microphones that allowed fast and accurate communications with little volume. Jack heard their intermittent technical chatter as another bit of background noise, not much different than the cooling air moving through the equipment. The techs worked their stations, monitoring and tracking VHF, UHF, infra-red (IR), and visual data feeds from both the space around the ship and the planet below: Where were the Preeminent ships? What was happening at the spaceport? Could the Preeminent ships have detected them? These were the questions the six experts were working on, all without help or even much supervision from Jack.

It wasn't that he was disinterested in their work, far from it. But at the moment, he had a far bigger problem on his hands. The star had risen an hour and a half earlier where the Zeds lived, and Jack had called David Powell to join him in reviewing the IR surveillance data Jack had been watching for several sols. He'd kept David loosely in the loop on what he was seeing, but the picture was now coming into sharper focus and what Jack saw now alarmed him.

He had the IR tech replay in fast mode the recordings of the last three nights.

"Here's the first night," he said, pointing to an area on the monitor. David saw the light green dots that represented individual Zeds moving at a walking pace. The time-stamp showed him this was happening late at night, after local midnight when there was usually no traffic on the old paths. As Jack zoomed the image out, David could see that there were Zeds moving from village to village, a flow of individuals moving north and south, but actually all in one direction: towards the Preeminent Spaceport. Jack fast-forwarded to the next two nights, the dots becoming more numerous as they approached the villages adjacent to the Preeminent.

There could only be one interpretation.

Jack turned to David. "They lied to you."

David nodded sadly. "Indeed, they did, the sneaky bastards, not that I am surprised. Ateah said as much. They still think they can push the Preeminent off."

"They can't."

"Nope. And we can't let them try. We came here to sniff out a rebellion among the Preeminent, and instead, we're faced with suppressing an armed revolt by people about to be set free."

"Yeah, that about covers it. What now?" David and Jack already knew, well before it would happen, how this skirmish would end: the outnumbered and outgunned Zeds would die wholesale, likely without making a dent in the Preeminent force they planned to attack. It was beyond foolish, beyond suicidal. To David, it bordered on genocidal madness, but this time it was your own race you were killing. Incredible.

"Let's get Evans in here and figure that out. But, offhand, we need to get between them and stop this bullshit before it starts."

Commander Rich Evans sat backward on a chair in Center Console to hear their report. Jack stood at the large forward display screen to begin the briefing. "I went back a few sols, sir, and it started with just a few, perhaps a dozen, on the move the first night." He put up the same IR image he'd shown David. "This is from the extreme southern area." He played the rest of the images, showing Zeds walking north along the old paths, under tree cover but still visible in IR from *Cobra*. "The next night, it was a few more, and even more moving closer to the Preem spaceport."

Evans nodded his understanding. "Go ahead, Jack."

"Every night, more leave from the most distant villages, and they gradually pick up a few more in each village as they go. So, what starts as a dozen is upwards of fifty once they get down to the last villages that border the spaceport. Tonight, they've camped outside the last village away from the Preem."

Evans leaned back in his chair, arms crossed as he thought about the picture in front of him. "They're funneling down to, what, the four main access roads to the spaceport?"

"Yes, correct, sir. David and I estimate that there are between eighty and a hundred-twenty assembled to strike from each road."

"Well, David," Evans said, "clearly you were correct. They lied about the six sols, and they've decided to go ahead and attack and spoil our lovely peaceful exit for the Preem."

David smiled grimly. "It is amazing, sir, when a whole society decides it can't take 'yes' for an answer."

"The Preem have noticed, too," Jack said. "There were two shuttle trips down from the cruisers during the last sol."

David pointed to the IR image with the encamped Zeds. "They can't wait very long, sir. These villages near the spaceport can't support the added population for more than a day or two. Looking at the traffic on the paths last night, the last of the force looks to be in place tonight. I'd expect them to strike at dawn next sol."

Evans looked at the Zed clock on the main display. "Sunrise is thirteen-fifty-two tomorrow. That gives us, what, twenty-five hours? Get Gabe and Greg in here, and get Henderson on the line."

Intrepid and *Cobra*
In Orbit at Zeta Doradus (b)
Tuesday, March 12, 2080, 1630 UTC

Joanne went to her Intel section to hear the briefing from *Cobra*. Sitting with her Intel Officer Chuck Anderson, she watched Jack Ballard and David Powell explain what was happening on the surface. There could be little doubt what the Zeds had in mind and even less doubt how it would end: badly. The Zeds were deliberately and foolishly walking themselves into a bloodbath.

The briefing complete, she and Rich Evans debated what to do about the looming disaster on the surface. David shared his observations of the Zed weapons, which he believed to be single-shot muskets, and the numbers of the opposing forces. Joanne quickly agreed that the Zeds would suffer massive losses for very little chance of victory. Many would be dead, and they would be far worse off than before. The Preeminent would be enraged, and the deaths might extend far beyond the attackers. Direct intervention could be dangerous, but it was likely the only way to stop this battle from happening. They could not just stand by and watch. They would have to act and act quickly.

Henderson called a meeting of her officers, and as they gathered, she watched them. She'd been working with almost this same assembly ever since she'd set foot on *Intrepid*. Most of them were excellent, and for the few exceptions she had to work around, or through, she had already made plans for their replacement. This sudden assignment to Zeta Doradus had put those plans on hold.

The one truly hard void in her wardroom was Ben Price. She'd been able to depend entirely on him, his intelligence, and his keen insights into what was happening around them. Anderson was marginally competent, but his cool, superior attitude was not supported by his performance.

The other missing face at the table was, of course, Natalie Hayden. Her replacement, a young warrant officer a year out of school, was just fine: hardworking, amiable, kind to his staff. She couldn't really have asked for more, save Natalie's return, and that was not likely to happen anytime soon, if ever.

Anderson started the briefing with the maps and counts of Zed and Preeminent forces *Cobra* had provided. Three more Preeminent shuttles had landed and quickly left during the previous night, so clearly, the PG was augmenting his own sizeable force with Combatants from the cruisers.

"Do we even know how many Preeminent are there?" Liwanu Harry asked.

Anderson shook his head. "No, Lieutenant, we do not. I would estimate between five hundred and a thousand based on your previous experience with Combatants dispatched from cruisers. We know the PG also has a couple hundred of his own, but even that's only an estimate."

"Against at most five hundred Zeds?" Kamaria Allen responded. She looked over at Liwanu. "The Zeds will get slaughtered, and I doubt they will even set foot on the spaceport itself."

"No doubt," he answered.

Joanne stood up and moved to the map. "We are going to stop this, and we are going to do it without bloodshed."

"How, exactly, ma'am?" Kamaria asked.

"By placing a superior force between them, one neither side can defeat. They'll both have to turn back." She indicated the northwest access road. "Powell and his team will take this road. They have been in that area before and Powell thinks he can convince the Zeds there to stop. Lieutenant Allen, you will take the northeast road. Lieutenant Harry, you will hold the two southern approaches. I think one squad per road should be enough. We're not looking for a firefight."

"How is this going to work, Captain?" Kamaria asked.

"Greg Cordero has recorded three words in Zed: *Stop, home, safe*. He says most anyone can pronounce these, so you'll memorize them and call them out when the Zeds approach."

"What about the Preem?" she asked.

"Evans will speak to the PG personally and instruct him to stay the hell out of it. But, in the end, *Intrepid* will be responsible for keeping the Preeminent in their barracks."

Liwanu Harry shook his head. "Pretty thin plans, ma'am. Feels awfully risky to put ourselves between two forces that seem itching for a fight."

"Short notice, Lieutenant Harry, short notice, so we improvise. Get your people ready for transport as soon as it's dark."

She looked around the table, seeing no questions, she dismissed them.

As their departure time approached, Recon Marine Sergeant Sabrina Herrera settled into the Recon Shuttle with David, Gabrielle, Greg, and her three best Marines. Evans would be taking the ship's other shuttle down to inform the PG what they were planning and instruct him to stand down.

And, to make clear to him that if he didn't, *Intrepid* would stand him down.

Sabrina was more impressed with Powell every day. Calm, respectful, and exceptionally smart but equally adept at not flaunting it. After six years in the service, she could not think of very many Marine officers she would have wanted to follow into this potential disaster as willingly as she was this fleetie lieutenant. Too bad, she thought briefly, that he was already married to the most famous woman in the Fleet. She shook her head slightly as she checked her SigSauer .45: full mag, nothing in the chamber, fingerprint safety on. She slid it back under her left armpit and snapped the holster closed. She then pulled her high-intensity flashlight from its pocket on her right thigh and checked the charge. Full. She declared herself ready as the last 'thump' signaled that they were free of the ShuttleLock and headed down to the surface.

After the shuttles were off, both ships maneuvered, and Joanne ordered a Lance detonated ten kilometers in front of each Preeminent ship. The meaning of her warning could not be missed. They did not react, and Joanne took that as 'message received.'

South of Reupna Village
Zeta Doradus (b)
Wednesday, March 13, 2080, 0910 UTC

It was well after dark when David set the Recon Shuttle down across the northwest road. It was the same packed-dirt path they had walked to begin their journey north to the Zed capital. After unloading as quietly as possible, Sabrina posted her Marines towards the village, the directions from which the Zeds would approach. She slipped her radio earpiece in and checked that she was on the loop with David, Liwanu Harry, and Kamaria Allen.

David spent a few minutes in the shuttle, reviewing the maps of the Zed's old roads, making one last check for alternative routes the Zeds might use to get into the Preeminent spaceport. There were a few that ran along the outskirts of the facility, but none that David thought could support the movement of any usable force into the port. The forests, or more specifically the low shrubs that covered much of the floor near the edges, were too thick for even male Zeds to cross quickly or in mass. They could crawl under them, but only slowly and not in large enough numbers to matter. Those facts, and where *Cobra*'s IR sensors still showed they had camped after the last sunset, confirmed for him that they would have to come this way. They really didn't have much choice.

It was approaching midnight when David picked up his 2K7X rifle and climbed the access ladder to the roof of the shuttle. He sat down to wait and watch for any approaching Combatants. As he waited, looking out into the quiet, inky night, he allowed himself a few minutes to think about Carol, hoping that her last upbeat message meant she was on the mend. She'd been so strong and steady all the way through the war, while still open and expressive of her feelings with him, that he was surprised it had now taken such a toll on her. He felt another hard shot of regret that he was not there with her when she needed him. But there was nothing to do about that now but get this mission over with and get back home.

The night was clear, warm, and humid, and it reminded David of midsummer campouts back home in Indiana. The stars were brighter here except where the glow from the system's debris disk partially drowned them out. Zeta Doradus (b) was not so quiet at night as Big Blue, but it was still far quieter than a summer night on Earth. Whatever insects were out there trolling for romance, they were far fewer and quieter than Indiana crickets.

The two small moons that circled the planet were elsewhere tonight, so the stars were vivid in the dark sky. As he looked around, he could see an anvil-shaped thunderhead lighting up the sky somewhere up north, too far away to be heard, but a sure sign that summer was coming.

After a while, Gabrielle clambered up to join him. She sat just a half-meter to his right, her legs dangling over the edge of the roof next to his.

"My Lord, it is beautiful out here," she said, looking up. "But I confess, David, that I am frightened. I think I am as scared about tomorrow as I've ever been."

"You hide it well."

"I am hiding it less well every minute. What's going to happen, David?"

David didn't look away from the stars. "You'd be safe in the shuttle."

She looked at him. "You aren't afraid?"

David shrugged slightly. "Of course, I'm concerned that we'll fail and the whole thing will turn into a giant furball we can't control." He turned and looked at Gabrielle. "But I think that's unlikely. In fact, I doubt that a single round will be fired."

He returned his eyes to the stars. "Asoon says the Zeds call it the 'Night Glow.' Better than the 'Milky Way,' I guess. Which is, by the way, right over there..."

Gabrielle followed his eyes up to the faint band of light in the dark sky. "Their name is poetic in its way, I guess."

"Yes, a beautiful name for an amorphous cloud of miscellaneous crap leftover from system formation."

"Somehow, David, I see in you a hopeless romantic wandering around somewhere inside a technocrat."

David laughed slightly. "And crying to get out?"

Gabrielle nodded; the motion barely perceptible in the darkness.

"I always considered myself a romantic first, with the technocrat locked somewhere inside. I let him out from time to time when his services are required."

"Like tomorrow?"

"Yeah, maybe. On the other hand, preventing a pointless war is something the romantic can really identify with. The technocrat just needs to figure out how to do it." David let another minute pass before he returned to her fears. "I really think this is going to work, Gabe. The Marines can easily keep the Zeds at bay, and *Intrepid* can hold the PG in his headquarters. But seriously, you can wait in the shuttle. You will be safe there."

Gabrielle shook her head. "I came here to see and to learn, and I can't do that hiding under a table."

"True enough. Perhaps everyone involved will learn something this morning. Something about trust and integrity, who has it and who doesn't."

"I see the technocrat has a philosopher to keep him company."

"My dear Doctor Este, you are just a little too perceptive. But keep all that to yourself, OK? I do have my rep as a brainiac to protect."

"It'll be our secret."

David grinned and nodded, "Fair enough."

He picked up his night-vision glasses and spent several minutes watching the road to the south. It was empty, for now. He silently prayed it would stay that way. If the Preeminent would just sit tight, he was sure he could stop the Zeds and send them home. But if the Preeminent came out, even as a show of force to defend themselves, someone would get scared and make a mistake, and the whole thing would spin hopelessly out of control.

Gabrielle laid back on the roof of the shuttle and closed her eyes. David kept an eye on her even as he watched the road in both directions.

It was an hour before star-rise, the sky in the east showing just a hint of the day to come when the radio snapped to life.

"Allen here. I can hear movement from the north."

A few minutes later, they heard Liwanu Harry's voice. "The Zeds are on the move on both roads. Expect contact shortly."

Motion from the Preeminent side caught David's attention, and he lifted his weapon to the ready.

Gabrielle snapped upright with alarm, suddenly frozen with fear. *Is this the moment it happens? Is this when we lose control?*

"You will not shoot *me*, human Powell," came a voice from a distance. "For then, you would be struck mute, a terrible fate for one so chatty."

David smiled and put his weapon away. "Hello, Asoon. Your sense of humor is getting better."

"Yes," she said as she approached the Recon Shuttle and looked up at him. "As I have said before, Scad believes my mind has been permanently altered by your language, and he doesn't always mean it as a compliment."

"I am delighted to see you."

Gabrielle wilted with relief; her sudden terror now gone. David looked at her as her shoulders slumped. He reached out and gently shook her.

"It'll all be fine, Gabe. We will all be fine."

She nodded slightly in what looked to David like reluctant, or maybe hopeful, agreement.

Asoon and Ateah came out of the shadows and walked around to the Zed-facing side of the shuttle.

"Evans told me where you were. They woke me up to translate for him with the Governor. It was not a pleasant conversation. The Governor does not believe you Vermin will protect him."

David crawled down off the shuttle. "I'm not. I'm protecting the Zeds from themselves."

"I think it best we do not tell the Governor that," Asoon said.

"Yes," David answered, "best we don't. What's he planning?"

"Evans told him to stay in his headquarters, but he is going to assemble a partial cohort in case you fail. He told me to tell you that he will abide by Evans' instructions as long as the natives don't threaten him. But, if they approach the spaceport, he will respond."

"Well, then let's make sure that doesn't happen."

"He is also furious at your behavior overhead."

"What happened?"

"Your ship detonated one of your weapons a small distance in front of each of the six ships in orbit. Your ship, and the weapons, were not detected until they went off. The commanders above are frightened and frustrated with their inability to locate your vessels."

David had to smile at Henderson's message: *Stay put. I can kill you whenever I want.*

"Good," he said to Asoon. "Let them be frightened. Those weapons were a warning, a message from Captain Henderson that she can kill them at will if they don't behave. Hopefully, they will."

"And live."

"Indeed. There is no need for any more death here."

South of Reupna Village
Zeta Doradus (b)
Wednesday, March 13, 2080, 1350 UTC (Just Before Sunrise)

At each roadblock, the Marines' primary weapons were their flashlights. The plan was simple, in principle. They would shine them at the Zeds, using the intense light to both ruin their night vision and hide the Marines' own positions as they yelled at them to go home. It was a simple idea, and easy to implement, as long as no one started shooting.

David thought he heard something just as Sabrina raised her right hand and drew her flashlight with her left. Her Marines set themselves on the opposite side of the road, one forward, one back a few meters. The distant figures she'd seen in her night vision glasses were moving closer, and as they reached the edge of the forest, her crew lit them up.

"Stop! Go home! Be safe!" Ateah called out to them.

David saw the Elder who had taken them north in the lead, now shading his eyes against the harsh, bluish light of the LED flashlights. David thought he recognized some of the others from that same village, but his ability to recognize one Zed from another was limited. He just hadn't had enough time to understand how to tell them apart in daylight, let alone at night.

"Stand aside!" Elder Wocos called. *"You have no place here!"*

After hearing the translation, David walked directly into the light, Asoon and Ateah right behind him. He admired their bravery, following him in so close. A confused or angry Zed might decide he had heard enough and take a shot.

"Go home, Elder Wocos. Go home and live. We came here to free you from the Violets, but now you have forced us to first save you from yourselves."

"You are children! What do you know? Move aside, and we will drive them off!"

"No, Elder. If I step aside, they will kill you all. You have seen for yourself what they have already done here. I have seen their handiwork on other worlds, and I am quite certain I know what I am talking about. What you're planning is pointless. Go home!"

David looked over at Greg, who nodded that the translation was getting his message through.

After Wocos' last exchange with the Vooman, Udoro had heard enough and pushed her way forward. "Now do you see, Elder? Now do you believe?"

"I know no more than — "

She angrily swiped his words aside. "Here they stand, Wocos! Here they stand to protect us. Do you not understand what they said? The Violets will kill us all if we persist!"

Kutah's voice came clear from the front line of attackers. "How stubborn can one Elder be, Wocos? You would lead us into darkness just when the light is at hand?"

Wocos took a step back, surprised at the vehemence of Kutah's accusation. "I would lead you to push the Violets off this planet and allow you to live without their yoke on your neck."

Udoro was not impressed with his argument. "But the Vooman have already defeated them, Wocos. They will leave regardless."

"How do we know this? The Vooman may be no better!"

Hearing Wocos' words from Asoon, David broke into the conversation. "Elder! Do not misunderstand. I will tell you again what I told your council: The Violets aren't turning this place over to us. They're leaving." He paused a moment to think, then said, "We didn't win your planet in the war, Wocos. We won your release."

Udoro took renewed strength from David's words. "See, Elder? They stand here between the Violets and us. They are here to free us, not to put themselves in the Violets' place!"

Ateah and Asoon kept the translation going for the humans. David had to smile at the female and male who spoke out against the Elder. No one could tell a young Zed from an old one, but these two clearly had a lot to lose, making him think they were probably young. At least, young for a Zed.

"Listen to your own people, Elder," David said. "Listen!"

As he said this, his earpiece came alive again. "Harry here, southern groups are turning back."

"Lieutenant Powell, this is Allen. Northeast group is also turning back. We had to point a few weapons at them, but they finally retreated."

"Elder Wocos," David said. "The other groups have turned back."

Kutah heard the grey liar say that they had been stopped at the other three roads, but it did not seem like a lie to him. If the others had been met by the Vooman like he had, they might well have retreated. Kutah had had enough of this madness. He walked to Wocos, dropped his weapon at his feet, then turned and stood with Udoro. Tefin watched his friend in admiration, then came forward, laid his weapon next to Kutah's, and stepped back.

Wocos looked down at the weapons at his feet; weapons he had not even known existed just a six-day ago. He thought for a long time about what he should do, who he should believe. Finally, he considered the futility of going up against the full power of the Violets alone.

"Very well. We cannot press forward alone."

A wave of relief passed through the crowd of males.

"Kutah!" he called out, "Go now to the GuildMember. Tell him what has happened and ask for his instructions."

"And what of us?" Tefin asked, defiant.

"For now," Wocos said to the assembly, "let us accept the realities before us and return home."

David watched with relief as their resolve wilted in a moment. The Elder turned and followed his people back up the road to the north. They had managed to stop the fight before it began. Now, they just needed to get the Preeminent forces off the planet before the Zeds tried something stupid again.

Udoro watched the males leave, turning back north, defeated by the Vooman. *No,* she thought, *not defeated. Rescued.* She fiercely desired to be with Kutah, hold him and show him the depth of her relief that he would live and that their days together would remain unnumbered. But Wocos had sent him north to find the GuildMember. She looked instead at the Vooman who seemed to be in charge. At least, he was the one who did most of the talking. She thought the Vooman were strange-looking, with their unshaded eyes and underdeveloped features. The protuberance in their faces was obviously for breathing, but it seemed an inconvenient and unlikely place. The small openings in her neck seemed so much more practical and inconspicuous. The variety in size and shape between their females and males was confusing, too. It made them unpredictable somehow, strange, and so very alien.

Watching them talk to Wocos, she now understood why there were two grey liars with them all the time. One spoke her language, the other the Vooman language. It was annoyingly slow, as the two liars would take some time before delivering their translations. She approached them cautiously. The grey liars saw her and spoke to the leader, and he turned back to her. He was much taller than she, and she found it very odd to look up at a male. It felt enormously unnatural. Even the smaller Vooman female was taller than herself, and Udoro considered herself tall, even for a female.

The male looked directly at her, his eyes uncovered, and for the first time, she noticed they were the color of pale spring leaves. They were so unlike her own deep, subtle colors. The small female standing next to him, the one with the long strings on her head, had the same eyes. The tall female with short strings on her head had dark eyes, almost the color of rich soil, but truly different from any color in nature she could recall. It was all very confusing for her.

"I would like to thank you, Vooman," she said quietly.

Elder Wocos, who had been waiting for everyone to turn back north, turned at the sound of her voice.

"Your thanks are accepted, brave female," the gray liar responded. "He says he should thank you as well. Your words helped move your Elder to understand."

"Does he have a name? I am Udoro." She heard the grays exchanging words in their own language, then to the Vooman, then back.

"He does. He is David. He sends greetings that he is happy to know your name."

"He has saved my Kutah, and I will remember him for a sensenary of snows." Asoon spoke without taking her eyes off the Zed female, Udoro.

"She says you have saved one named 'Kutah,' and she will remember you for a very long time."

After Asoon said this, Ateah spoke again to Udoro, then back to Asoon.

"The number she gave is more than a thousand snows."

David looked at the female, Udoro, and then to Asoon, but Gabrielle was a step ahead of him.

"Can you ask her, Asoon, as kindly as you can, if she means that number literally?"

The female's question sounded odd, even offensive, to Udoro. *Did she mean what she said?* Of course, she did!

"I do not lie, gray one. I have spoken truthfully."

The gray liar responded immediately. "Do not be offended, native. What you said was surprising to the humans, and they ask only to ensure that they have heard correctly."

"I meant what I said. Why is there a question?"

Greg looked at David. "Yes, she means it. She used a term which in their numbering system is thirty-six squared."

"What?" Gabrielle asked.

"Yeah, one thousand, two hundred and ninety-six."

"They live that long? Ask her if she might tell us how many snows she has seen."

Asoon delivered the translation. "She says she is still young. Ateah and I believe the number is seventy-eight snows."

"Seventy-eight?" David asked, incredulous. "She's over a hundred Terran years old?"

Wocos listened to the conversation between Udoro and the Vooman, but suddenly he realized what she was saying and stepped forward.

"Udoro, say no more! The Gift is not for them to understand. You have said too much already."

"I have said only the truth, Wocos. Do not reprove me for truth."

"Yes, but the Gift must be protected!"

Greg's ear had finally tuned itself to the Zed language. "David...he's telling her not to say anything more. There is something about this they must hide, no, that's wrong; *protect* is a better translation."

"You're catching on?"

"Yeah, starting to hear it more clearly. They use a word I understand, but I don't quite get the implication. Asoon, ask Ateah...they're using a word that's something like an award or a present. Can she explain it better?"

The other male Vooman had started talking, and Udoro thought he was asking the grays something. Wocos stood with her, watching the grays and the Vooman talk back and forth. Finally, the second gray looked at her.

"What is this Gift you speak of?"

Udoro opened her mouth to explain, but Wocos stopped her. "Go home, Udoro. I will tell them what they need to know."

"But — "

"No, Udoro," he repeated sadly. "Go home. Kutah will be back before sunset, and you can share your hill with him."

"Until I leave," she said sadly.

"Yes, until then. Go now."

"He's sending her away," Greg said quietly. "We've touched on something here. What do you think, Gabe?"

"I think she's over a hundred years old and thinks of herself as young. Can't get past that just yet."

David watched as Udoro departed and the Elder came closer. He stood for several seconds looking at David, then slowly examined each of them, finally stopping at Greg.

"You speak our language?"

Greg shook his head. "Tell him I understand, but I can't speak it well enough yet."

After hearing the translation, the Elder made a fist and dropped it.

"He understands what you said. Ateah says the fist is a sign of agreement or recognition of truth. I would say it is similar to how humans nod their head."

"Udoro has already said too much, but I will tell you of the Gift."

Gabrielle moved off the road and sat on the soft, low plant that covered the ground. She motioned to the Elder, inviting him to do the same. The Speakers also settled to the ground nearby. Sabrina sent her Marines to keep an eye on the Preeminent but knelt just behind David, still alert and in communications with the other ground units.

Gabrielle set her NetComp to record and laid it on the ground in front of her. She thought about explaining to Wocos what recording was but decided against it. It would take far too long.

"You Vooman have spoken the truth to us, even when we did not believe you, so I will tell you of our Gift."

Gabrielle nodded. "Yes, please go ahead. We are anxious to understand." Greg was typing furiously as the conversation began.

"We were brought to this place by The Shepherds many sensenary ago."

"I knew it!" David said. "This system is way too young for them to have evolved here. Does he know where they came from?"

"Asoon," Greg said, "please ask him to continue, and please let's just let him talk, OK?"

"We are born small and weak, like most living things, but once we reach our maturity, we do not deteriorate over time like other species."

Wocos stopped there, waiting for another interruption. When it didn't come, he continued.

"I have seen five sensenary of snows, Some cold, some less so, and the last sensenrum under the Violets. The forceful Udoro, as she told you, has seen just two sensenrum plus a senrum."

Greg stopped typing, doing the arithmetic in his head. "He's almost ten thousand years old."

There was a long silence as they considered this possibility

"And the Preeminent have been here like fifty years."

Sabrina broke the silence that followed. "But, if they're all still young, how are they not up to their asses in children?"

Gabrielle looked to Asoon. "Yes, it's an important question. If they remain young and presumably fertile, how do they not overpopulate themselves?"

Wocos thought for a moment that he should keep this information from them, but he had gone so far already that there seemed little sense in holding back now.

"The Shepherds who gave us the Gift also gave us the solution. We can only create and bear young when we have eaten a certain fruit that grows near the city of the Guild. We do not understand why this works, but we know from many sensenrum of snows that it is true. A sendatum after starting to consume it, males and females can create a child."

"What happens then?" Gabrielle asked.

"They remain together until their children, usually two or three, are grown. After that, they may stay together permanently, or separate, as they choose. Most go back to their homes and the love of their youth."

"Youth?" David commented. "They're young forever."

"So, they don't marry, really?" Sabrina asked.

"Not exactly, no," Greg answered. "They stay together long enough to raise children, then move on."

"Given how long they live, it works for them," David said.

Sabrina shook her head. "Still, it's strange. It would be like having your fifth-great-grandmother hanging around, looking more or less like you."

"For us, yeah, it would be strange. But this is how they've lived for a long time."

David turned to Gabrielle. "But their tech is maybe sixteenth century. Isn't it odd that they are so long-lived and haven't progressed any farther?"

"I will have to think about that one. It does seem odd."

"No idea?"

"Not offhand."

Wocos watched the conversation between the Vooman. *"Is there a question you would ask?"*

Ateah spoke to the Elder, and Greg responded. "I would not have asked that!"

David's head snapped up, alarmed. "What?"

"She asked him about the Shepherds. Who they were."

Asoon spoke without turning her eyes away. "I have to say, I wonder the same myself."

"The Guardians?" David asked.

"Yes."

"We do not know anything of the Shepherds, only that they were an old race that brought us here. There is no record of why or of their appearance. Even the date is uncertain. We have long records, histories of our people, but they begin twelve sensenary ago, long after the Shepherds had gone."

"And nothing of where you were taken from?"

"No."

"Pity," David said, finally. "But I doubt that they are Terran — the placement of the opening for breathing and the three fingers are all very different from anything back home. They're alien, for sure."

"Still, more than fifteen thousand years of written history?" Gabrielle asked.

"That's what he says, yes," Greg reported.

David's NetLink buzzed, and Elder Wocos looked at it with alarm. It was not a sound he was accustomed to hearing.

"Evans says Rmah will be here tomorrow. Asoon, ask the Elder if he could meet with us here tomorrow, say, noon?"

"A leader of our home world is coming. Would you meet with him and the humans here, at midday tomorrow?"

Wocos made a quick fist and released it. *"I will. I will send for my GuildMember to attend as well."*

Greg nodded. "He says yes, and he's bringing his council superior as well."

"Good," David said, standing up and brushing the dirt and small dry leaves from his uniform. "Tell him I know this person and that Wocos can trust him."

Wocos quickly waved his hand across himself after hearing the translation.

Greg smiled. "Uh, I think the Elder is calling bullshit on the trust thing."

David nodded. "Understandable. But Rmah will convince him. Let's go. I'm beat. What the hell time is it, anyway?"

"0945," Sabrina answered immediately.

"Damn. I could use a nap."

The Recon Shuttle was gone in minutes. Wocos watched it lift off the ground, pivot, and then rise into the sky and disappear. Had he been religious or a follower of mysticism, he might have thought it magic. Or, a miracle. But his people were rationalists, so it simply meant there were things in the universe they did not yet know.

Revolt at Zeta Doradus

CHAPTER 8

Intrepid
In Orbit at Zeta Doradus (b)
Thursday, March 13, 2080, 0645 UTC

Captain Joanne Henderson was asleep in her duty cabin when the Alert Status One siren began ringing throughout her ship. Jim Kirkland had the conn, and if he was that alarmed, there was damn well something to be alarmed about. She picked up the phone by her bunk.

"Conn!" she said, almost loud enough to be heard without the phone.

"Kirkland."

"What's going on?"

"A Type II just came out of FTL and looks to be headed to the planet."

"Light that sucker up, James. Get us moving towards it. I'll be there shortly."

"Will do."

As Joanne visited the toilet and pulled on a fresh uniform, *Intrepid* turned sharply to move towards the Type II, its radar pounding away. Joanne didn't care if the other six ships knew where she was at the moment. If the PG was planning to drop invasion troops, she would have to get in his way, and right now.

Within a few minutes, Surveillance Officer SLT Marco Gonzales reported that he had a good track on the Type II, and Weapons Officer Kirkland declared a firing solution. The port rotary moved out with twelve Bludgeons. Joanne was going to take no chances with this thing.

"The 180 signal is up on the Type II, Captain!" Marco called out. "I can hear voice on it, in English." His techs put the signal on a speaker.

"-son, this is Asoon on the surface. This vessel is carrying Rmah Teo Segt and is not a threat to you or to the natives."

Joanne rolled her eyes. "He could have warned us, right?" She turned to her Communications Officer. "Jessie, reply message received and thanks." She walked back to the command station and dropped into her chair. "Everyone secure from Alert Status One. Marco, secure the radar; James, retract the rotaries."

Larry Covington came to the command station. "Where do you want to go now, ma'am?"

Joanne leaned back in her chair, stretching and thinking about the good night's sleep she had just lost. "Oh, what the hell, somewhere back sorta where we were but not quite the same place, OK?"

"Yes, ma'am, I can do that."

Jessie came to the command station as Larry was leaving. "Follow-up from

153

Asoon, Captain. Seems Rmah plans to take the whole garrison and the crew of the disabled ship home with him. He needs the capacity of a Type II to do that. He apologizes for the lack of communications."

Joanne shrugged. "Whatever. At least we know we still know how to fight." She returned the Conn to Kirkland and headed back to her Duty Cabin just behind the Bridge. Maybe she could still get in a few hours' sleep.

Rmah Teo Segt arrived at the Preeminent Spaceport with his security detail just after sunrise. Within an hour, the Preeminent Governor was shackled and sitting in Rmah's shuttle next to his equally-shackled assistant. Before landing, Rmah had relieved the commanders of the six ships in orbit and ordered their deputy commanders to take over and return to Home. Except, of course, the one Joanne Henderson had disabled. That ship was in a high orbit, unlikely to decay for many decades. Rmah ordered it shut down and evacuated. They would deal with it later.

By the time Rmah was stepping out of the PG's headquarters, four of the five ships in orbit were already gone. With the PG under arrest, he took command of the garrison and ordered them to prepare to leave. There were no complaints; the Combatants hated Zeta Doradus, its climate, its natives, and the never-ending stream of fresh deleelinosh to be dumped, stored, and eventually loaded onto cargo ships. They were happy to be leaving.

Rich Evans and Joanne Henderson came down with David and his team to facilitate the meeting between Rmah and the Zeds. This time, the Recon Shuttle would stay behind, and they would use one of *Intrepid*'s regular shuttles, which had far more seats but far less technology.

Rmah arrived at the meeting place right on time, precisely at solar noon. The human contingent was already there: Evans, Henderson, Jack Ballard, David, Gabrielle, and Greg. Sabrina Herrera stood to the side with her three Marines, standing easy but ready should they be needed. Rmah's security detail of ten Combatants also remained at a respectful distance once they had escorted him to the site.

"It is good to see you again, Rmah," David said.

"Yes, Powell, good to see you as well."

The Zeds appeared out of the shade of the forest, two males walking forward, caution clear in their slow approach.

David indicated one of the Zeds. "This is Elder Wocos, leader of the village just north of here."

The introductions took time, both in translation and in the discussion of meanings among the translators. Greg corrected Ateah several times; her translations were occasionally carrying too negative a connotation. Greg felt the stress and fatigue of the recent days were beginning to wear on her.

Finally, Rmah was ready to begin. "I ask permission to speak to your council, Elder Wocos."

"Why would the Guild speak to a Violet? You have brought us nothing but pain and death!"

Rmah expected some resistance, and he believed the best way to address it was with the truth. "Yes, the actions here of our previous leaders are regrettable. But I come to offer a new relationship with you."

Wocos turned to the GuildMember. *"A new relationship? The Vooman said they would leave."*

"And we believed them!"

The Zeds abruptly turned and started to leave.

Greg looked up in alarm. "Asoon! Tell them to wait! Tell them there is more to hear!"

The GuildMember replied with anger. *"We were told the Violets would leave. This is what we want — nothing more than to be left alone."*

Rmah listened carefully to Ateah's explanation. "Tell them, yes, the Combatants are leaving today."

The Zeds hesitated, then returned. *"What then is this relationship you offer?"*

"Your deleelinosh are highly prized on our home planet. Under our rule, you have built a large industry to raise and deliver them to us."

"This is your offer? You wish to keep us bound to your demands?"

"No. We would prefer to come to an agreement, one with a reasonable timetable for deliveries and a fair price to be paid. It would be a simple agreement between equals."

"And what form would this payment take?"

"Commander Evans!" Gabrielle cried out after hearing the translation. "We can't allow this, this, *deal*, to disrupt their society. There must be limits on what the Preeminent gives them!"

Rmah turned to Gabrielle after hearing Asoon's translation. He hesitated a moment, thinking, then spoke to Asoon. "What is your concern? Within reason, I planned to give them anything they asked for."

Gabrielle shook her head vigorously. "These people are pre-industrial. They don't have much technology, nothing we would call modern, and I strongly advise against any kind of payment that would include technology they're not ready for."

"You believe it would be troublesome for their society?"

Gabrielle nodded. "I don't see how it couldn't be. They've lived the way they do for fifteen thousand years. Dirt roads. Stone houses. Hunting, fishing, and farming. We must preserve their society and not give them the seeds of its ruin."

"What are they saying?" the GuildMember asked Ateah.

Greg heard the question. "Asoon, Ateah should say that we are discussing the kinds of payment that would be most advantageous to them."

Asoon translated for Rmah, who agreed and instructed Ateah to repeat the message.

"Somehow, I doubt that's quite true," the GuildMember said quietly.

Hearing this, Ateah looked over at Greg, who shook his head. "Let them be a little skeptical. It's not a problem."

Returning to the subject, Rmah said, "We would hear your thoughts on that, Elder, and those of your council. We know we have a debt to repay, and we believe that continuing the deleelinosh trade would be a convenient and positive experience for both of us."

"He is unbelievably humble for a Violet," Wocos commented to his superior.

"I think the Vooman have humbled them." He turned to Rmah. *"I will take this proposal to the Guild. It will take at least two suns to assemble the full Guild to hear you."*

Rmah listened carefully. "We will meet here, then, in two suns?"

"Three would be more practical."

"Three it is, then," Rmah answered.

The GuildMember made a fist, then released it. *"How am I to send word if we are unable?"*

"The cargo facility will be lightly guarded, just my personal detail. You may send a messenger there, and Ateah will hear your message on my behalf."

"We will consult with the Guild and inform you as soon as possible."

David watched the Zeds walk away.

Rmah spoke to Asoon, who then turned to David. "Rmah hopes they will come back in three days, but he has doubts."

David nodded. "So do I. Tell Rmah it is important that he do as he said — the Combatants need to be gone today, as promised."

"Yes, he is committed to that."

"What about deliveries?"

"The caretaker of the deleelinosh says there have been none for three days. What he has in the tanks he can keep alive for another ten, perhaps."

"When is the next cargo ship due?"

"Two days, local time. We will send the shuttle up tonight with the garrison, so there will be space for the cargo ship to land."

"Three days, then. I hope you have success."

There was a quick conversation between Asoon and Rmah.

"Rmah asks that you return for the meeting with the Zed council. He would value your advice."

David looked over at Evans, who nodded slightly. "OK, Asoon. Tell him we'll be here."

"He is most grateful, David. This is a new role for him, for all of us, and we need your help."

"Fine. We'll be here."

The Fleet personnel climbed back into *Cobra*'s shuttle and were off the surface quickly. David was looking forward to a couple days off with plentiful showers and moderate temperatures. He might even get a message from Carol.

Hansen Family Farm
Near Lancaster, Ohio
Thursday, March 14, 2080, 1645 EST (2145 UTC)

Spring was coming, Carol was sure of that. But it wasn't here just yet. She'd been back home six days, and she still felt herself stuck somewhere between here and Alpha Mensae, unable to move in either direction. Every day she got up, talked with her folks, walked the fields, or rode Capella down the road to the diner for a solitary lunch. Her parents had decided they would wait for Carol to come to them. Love and patience, they said to each other, would be the rule of the day. When she was ready, she'd reveal what was simmering deep inside.

"I just need some time," was all she said when she arrived.

Last night's snow was slowly melting under the near-equinox sun as she and her mother Laura rode Rigel and Capella around the perimeter of the farm. The air was cool, but the sun felt warm on their faces.

"So," Laura asked gently, "are we going to talk about why you're here? It's been almost a week already."

Carol looked down at the ground, putting off her response by pretending to be concerned about where Capella was stepping, then looked back at her mother.

"I'm just having a hard time with some of the things that happened during the war."

"Thank God for that."

Carol sat up straight. "What? What do you mean?"

"Carol, my dear darling daughter, we didn't raise you to be a heartless warrior princess. What you went through must have had some terrible effect on you."

Carol pulled Capella up short, her eyes suddenly filling. "Yes, it did. It's just, just, way harder to get past it than I thought it would be."

"You've always been strong. That's not what I'm talking about."

"So much death, so, so much, oh god, such a stench, Mom. Burnt flesh and

157

blood and you-can't-imagine what else."

"I live on a farm, Carol. I'm familiar — "

"No, no, you're really not. I grew up on a farm, remember? A stillborn calf or a coyote attack is nothing like what we went through."

"OK, so tell me."

Carol looked down at Capella's mane, the words coming out stiff. "I don't really want to describe how a young man smells when he's taken a bolt of plasma to his chest, when he's barely twenty-one and staring up at me with eyes that will never see again. All because I sent him to deliver a message."

"I see."

"Or your best shipmate, so kind and funny and undemanding, is sliced wide open a meter away. He dies in seconds while you kneel there helpless, feeling his blood soaking through your pant leg. But, what the hell, he's dead, and you get to go on living,"

Laura waited a minute as the horses walked the path along the fence. "Does it feel somehow unfair to you?"

"Yes."

"Would you think the same, if you could, if it were Marty here telling me about how *you* died?"

"What?"

"Would you have wanted Marty to call it unfair that you were killed and he survived?"

Carol frowned, annoyed at the power of the question. "Well, no, I guess not. I would want him to just go on living his life."

"So, what makes you think he would want you to feel any differently?"

Carol looked away, then shook her head as she looked back at her mother. "It's just so damned random. Good people die when they shouldn't. Marty — Terri Michael — Cornell. Swenson. Marcia."

"And bad people...what? Should die first?"

Carol rode for several paces before answering. "I didn't see many 'bad' people on our side, I guess."

"I know. The Fleet is remarkable for its recruiting. They seem unusually good at weeding out the misfits."

Carol smiled grimly. "They took Rick."

Laura let out a small laugh. "Well, there's always an exception..."

"Yeah, he is that."

They rode a few more minutes in silence. Something was moving in her daughter, Laura could tell. She didn't know why it had taken so long, but with just a touch, she was opening up. It was enough for now.

"Listen, dear, we can talk with Dad tonight. I think he'll have some thoughts for you, too."

Carol just nodded, turning Capella down the next curve in the path.

That night, the warmth from the fireplace felt good on Carol's face as Ols rearranged the logs and tossed on another. Music was playing from the kitchen, a piano concerto streaming from Severance Hall in Cleveland. She sipped her drink, a well-fashioned old-fashioned her dad had mixed for her. She sat on the floor, leaning back against the sofa that her parents were sitting on. They were quiet for a while, just small talk until finally, Carol had to speak.

"The flechette, um, the *dart*, that killed Terri Michael is what hit me. That's how I got wounded. It blew right through her and into my leg. Her blood was everywhere, all over the floor, all over me."

"How awful," Ols said quietly.

"We had no clue, *no clue,* what those things were. There was a tech, a young surveillance tech, killed then, too. Had his brains splattered all over the forward displays." Carol paused to sip her drink. "I don't remember his name."

"Well, he wasn't in your section, right? You wouldn't have known him well?" Laura asked.

Carol stared at the fire. "I wrote a lovely letter home to his parents. You'd've been pleased."

Ols touched his daughter on the shoulder. "You have always tried to do the right things for the right reasons. A letter to comfort the parents of someone you didn't know is just another example. It was your duty...your...job...to write that letter. That you did it, and well, says a great deal about you."

Laura set down her drink. "We're so proud of you, Carol, but not for what you've achieved."

Carol considered that for a few seconds. "Why, then?"

Ols smiled. "For *how* you achieved it, and how much you love those around you and those who love you, too."

"I miss David." she sighed.

"Yes, I imagine you do," Laura responded. "I am sure he misses you, too."

"Yeah, but he's busy off saving another planet from the Preems, and here I sit wallowing in my blubbering." She shook her head slowly, feeling dissatisfied with herself, then wondering why she should be dissatisfied.

The conversation turned to more ordinary topics: the farm, the pregnant cow, the rotting fence posts that needed replacement. After a while, Carol finished her drink and went to her room, still just as she had left it when she went to SFU. She thought about that girl, that *child* who had happily leaped into a military world she admired but didn't fully understand. Carol compared the wholesome fresh face in the high school graduation picture on her dresser to the person she now saw in the mirror. Her face was thinner from the weight loss, that much she understood. But the stress and the pain she'd been through had also extracted their toll around the edges.

She looked down at the girl in the picture as if looking at someone else, a cousin maybe. "It's not the years, sweetheart; it's the mileage."

She put the picture down and got ready for bed, pulling the heavy quilted comforter up under her chin. It was cool in the room. It reminded her how she missed David's warmth next to her. She thought it funny how quickly she had come to depend on that, married only six months. But she knew she'd been right when she told Dan Smith back at Kapteyn Station that David 'is the other half of me.' She desperately missed him, not only his physical presence but also his constant, unwavering, complete belief in her. She had only recently thought of him in that way, and she wondered if that belief was what really brought her to him. She had always been smart, gifted even. She knew she was exceptional in that way. She could believe in her intellectual abilities, her instincts, and insights. But before David, she'd never believed in *herself,* her inner core, her essential character. David had given her that, and it was a gift beyond anything she could repay.

She closed her eyes, picturing him, his return, and how wonderful it would feel when he was again next to her.

Carol pulled her hoodie tighter around herself. It was cool out tonight, but the fire burned nicely in the little circle of trees not far from the farmhouse. She took a deep breath, the pleasant smell of burning wood filling her senses, a scent that brought back so many small, happy memories of her youth—campfires and cookouts were inexpensive luxuries on the farm. Even in lean years, firewood and time together were plentiful.

She looked up into the clear, clean night and was surprised by the stars. They were bright and steady, but there were no constellations — no Big Dipper, no Pleiades cluster, no Dolphin overhead. She was wondering about that as figures began to materialize out of the shadows in front of her. She thought it strange that she wasn't afraid, out here alone by the fire. She sensed that whatever those figures were, they radiated something good, something comforting. Something...loving.

Marty Baker was the first figure she could recognize, still young and with that same crooked smile. Terri Michael came behind him to take her natural place in the center of the steel Fleet-standard chairs across the fire from her. She hadn't noticed those before. James Cornell was followed by Leon Jackson, still the tallest, widest, and most handsome of the group. They sat easily, each looking at her without anger or accusation.

"We had to come, Carol," Terri Michael said. "We've seen all we can stand."

Marty spread his arms wide. "We signed up for this. We knew anything could happen, good or bad. We *knew.*"

"I told you that day on Alpha Mensae," Leon said with a smile, "That I would do it all over again. And I still would. I would gladly die again if it meant saving your life."

"But, Leon," Carol answered, "my life is not more valuable than yours." She looked at the group, "Or any of the rest of you."

"That's not the point, Carol," Jon Swenson said, suddenly seated next to Terri. "We did our duty, same as you. We did our jobs the same as you, as well and as long as we could."

Terri smiled gently. "But our deaths are not about you, Carol. We are the price paid to do what had to be done."

Marty nodded. "And we accept that. And we know, without you, there would be many more of us."

"You want to honor us?" Terri asked gently. "There is important work waiting for you out here. Go do it, best you can, as long as you can."

"But remember, Miss Carol," Leon said, "if I may call you that, the risks are still the same."

Jon somehow reached across and touched her shoulder, something he had done in life right before telling her something important. Especially when it meant she'd said or done something really dumb. "And you could just as easily be on the other side of this campfire."

Suddenly wide awake, but unable to move, Carol was frozen with excruciating fear. She tried to squeeze out a scream for help, but her voice refused. After a moment spent staring at the ceiling, she realized where she was and what was happening and closed her eyes to wait for the night terror to pass. Her brain gradually gave her back control of her limbs, and she rose to sit on the edge of the bed.

"Why," she asked the darkness, "why have you come now?" There was no answer, just the feeling of a presence in the room that persisted for several seconds before fading back into the night. An after-echo of the dream, she knew. She got up and went to the window that looked out towards the clump of trees that surrounded the fire pit. She thought she could see them still sitting there for a fleeting moment, but it was just shadows from the moonlight.

Carol was up early the next morning, the first time since coming home, and worked the chilly pre-dawn farm chores with Ols. They came into a warm house with one of Laura's enormous breakfasts waiting for them, and Carol ate like she hadn't in months, smiling and laughing about the animals and what she and Ols had done that morning.

Carol didn't say anything more, but her parents looked at each other with relief. She was back. She was herself again. Ols and Laura talked later in the day, wondering if they should ask her what had happened overnight, but decided it was best to accept the change and not raise any more questions. The shadow over her, whatever it was, was gone. They decided to rejoice in that fact and not fret too much about the hows and whys.

Two days later, Carol announced herself ready to go back to work. She called Darin Perez, then Catherine Miller, and was on a sub-car back to Ft. Eustis Sunday night.

The best way to love the lost, she decided, was to do what they did, and try to do it as well as they had. She had found the way out of the maze. There was light ahead, and the darkness was fading rapidly behind her.

Riaghe Village
Zeta Doradus (b)
Saturday, March 16, 2080, 0400 UTC (Local Sunrise)

The Guild met in the center of the Riaghe town, just one village removed from the Preeminent landing field, just as the star was rising. Kutah told them a Violet cargo ship had landed and taken the stored deleelinosh the previous night. The supervisor of the ocean creches where the deleelinosh were raised reported that while the fish were being maintained for the moment, nothing had been harvested or sent to the Violets for several suns. That could not go on indefinitely. They must either harvest or release large numbers back into the ocean before the pens became so overcrowded that the deleelinosh would perish.

When everyone was in place, the GuildMaster stood to speak. "We have discussed this proposal by the Violets several times as we have trekked south to confront them. Elder Wocos believes the Vooman support this arrangement but does not think they would impose such a thing on us."

The Guild, seated in a wide circle, murmured their understanding.

"But we are in agreement, are we not, on how we will proceed with these negotiations? We understand the risks of failure and of re-occupation by the Violets?"

The sixth-mother also rose. "I have consulted the mothers present, each and every clan. We agree with the males of the Guild that this is the correct decision. We must be free of them."

There was quiet after she spoke, a sign of respect and accord. Their decision made, the Guild rose and began the slow walk south.

David and the other humans stood off to the east side of the road, while Rmah, Asoon, and the rest of the Preeminents stood squarely in the center. The Zeds appeared on time, a large contingent with a male and female in the lead.

Rmah addressed them. "Thank you for returning. Have you considered what we proposed and what you might accept in payment?"

Greg's mouth dropped open as he listened to the Zed's response. Ateah paused before translating for Rmah.

"They wish no such arrangement. We are to leave and never return. The humans as well."

Rmah looked over at David, who said, "Ask them again, as humbly as you can, what it would take to establish this trade arrangement."

"What if they ask for something I can't give them?"

"We can manage that, Rmah. You need to get them to a point where they're willing to accept *anything*. At that point, some kind of agreement is at least possible."

After hearing Rmah's plea, the Zed remained unmoved.

"Leave. Your society survived without deleelinosh, and it will go on without it. We have no need of it, or you."

David listened, then spoke again to Rmah. "Remind them that you, Rmah, have kept your word. The Combatants are gone, the old governor is gone and will be punished for his actions."

They were not impressed.

"You practice honesty for convenience, for temporary advantage. We do not believe you will keep your promises in the future."

"Is there nothing?" Rmah asked them, "Nothing that would allow us to maintain a trading relationship? We are prepared to pay very well for this product!"

The answer was immediate. *"No. We desire nothing from you."*

Rmah looked at the speaker in frustration. He then turned to Ateah and spoke.

"We regret your decision, but we will respect it. Our rule here has been harsh, and we hoped to make some measure of amends for that by offering value for your product."

Rmah paused to think as the Zeds continued to stare at him. "I would like to return in the future, if you will allow it, to revisit this proposal."

The Zeds remained silent, and Rmah again looked at David for help.

"I don't know if this is a ploy, or they're just that adamant that you leave. Either way, I'd walk away. If it's just a tactic, they'll come to you. If they're serious, well, then there's really nothing more to be said. You'll have to go. So will we."

Evans spoke up for the first time. "This makes no sense. They already have all the industry built. They have people who know how to raise the fish, harvest, and deliver it. It is irrational to just abandon that trade for spite."

Asoon and Rmah had a quick conversation, then she turned to Evans. "What are you saying, RichEvans?"

"Powell is right. It is time to walk away. But don't leave, not right away. Give them a chance to see that you are honest in what you say and that they can make an agreement with you."

The GuildMaster watched the conversations between the Vooman and the Violet leader carefully. Even the grey liars were speaking. More, he thought, than necessary for mere translation. Two of the Vooman spoke to the Violet in what sounded like authoritative voices. What could it mean if the Vooman were advising the Violet, whom they claim to have defeated in an enormous conflict? Had they reconciled somehow? He could not understand anything that was said, and the gray liar that spoke his language offered nothing. But he thought he understood what was being expressed. The Violet did not know what to do. The Guild had stood firm, unmovable, and now the Violet had no response.
They had won.

Finally, Rmah spoke. "I will return to the cargo facility. I will remain there overnight and leave midday tomorrow. After that, you will not see us here again."
Rmah turned, barked orders to his detail and the Speakers, and began the walk back to the spaceport. David looked at the Zeds, half expecting them to call out, but they did not. He looked over at Evans, who just shrugged and inclined his head towards the shuttle. *Time to go.*

"That was anti-climactic," David said to Greg as they walked to the shuttle.
"I was so sure they'd make a deal," Greg said. "Evans is right — there is no good reason not to."
Gabrielle was less impressed. "Except they hate the Preem and can't wait to be rid of them."
David turned to look at the departing Zeds. "Yeah, well, there is that."

It was a quiet ride up to Cobra, each of them wondering if this stonewall was really the end of it. Not that it mattered to the humans, really, if a trade agreement could be struck or not. The Zed leader was right: The Preeminent had survived without deleelinosh, and surely could do so again. But, as David thought about it, here was a chance for the Zeds to turn the Preeminent occupation into an industry that could bring them something of real value. He didn't understand how people who had lived so long could fail to see that.
Except, as Gabrielle pointed out, they despised the occupiers and wanted nothing more to do with them. David understood that feeling, but he felt it was short-sighted.

Riaghe Village
Zeta Doradus (b)
Sunday, March 17, 2080, 0610 UTC (Late Afternoon Local Time)

Udoro and Kutah sat just outside the town green and listened as the Guild discussed their confrontation with the Violets and Vooman. They had been unmovable in their refusal to accept anything from the Violets, and the leader had agreed to depart the next sun. The Guild was pleased that their strategy had worked.

Now, they decided, it was time to move on to the next phase of the plan.

Kutah heard only bits of the conversation, his mind clouded by thoughts of his coming last night with Udoro. The fight with the Violets over, she would be leaving after sunrise to meet her repro partner. She would return perhaps twenty snows from now when her children were grown and set on their own paths. By custom, they would be Riaghe and live nearby, possibly in his own village or even on his own little path just off the green. In the meantime, they would live with another clan, neither hers nor her partner's.

Tonight would be his last with her for a very long time. He had seen just two sensenrum — seventy-two snows, the last sensenrum spent with her as they endured the rule of the Violets. Now, they were leaving, and so was Udoro.

The night was warm, so Kutah did not load the fireplace in his small home. They sat on the hill, admiring the stars, and talking about their times together until the Night Glow was almost overhead. Udoro gently stroked the back of his head, and it was time to move inside.

When Elder Wocos knocked on his door in the morning, Udoro was already gone, having crept away during the night. Kutah shook the grief from his mind and tried to listen to what the old male was saying.

"Kutah! Wake up! You must go to the Violet and tell him to come to the meeting place!"

It was hard to grasp what Wocos was saying initially, but Kutah set off as directed to inform the Violet leader of a new meeting.

Kutah had watched this place for many suns through his telescope. But he had never been so close to the Violets' main building before. It was massive, larger than anything his society could build, and, if possible, uglier than any structure he had ever imagined. It was a massive rectangle with thick, heavy walls. It radiated the power and malevolence he had come to expect from the Violets.

But as he approached this morning, Kutah was surprised at the guards' greeting. They pointed no weapon at him, and with hand gestures, they invited him to sit and wait. One guard went inside, and in a few minutes, Ateah and

Rmah came outside.

"The Guild would meet with you at the same place, at noon." he told them.

Rmah looked at this male skeptically. "They made their desires plain lastRot, did they not? There is something more they wish to discuss?"

"I am only a messenger. I do not know what they might have to say, only that you should come."

"I see. Tell them I will be there at noon."

Kutah listened to the translation, then left to report back to Elder Wocos.

As the star reached its zenith, its light filtered by a high, thin overcast, Rmah and his translator arrived at the meeting place. The natives came forward, the same male and female leading them. As they came to within five meters, they stopped, and the female began to speak.

"We are a simple people, Violet. We enjoyed our long lives here in peace until you came to rule over us. Many have died at your hand, so many no one can count the snows that have been lost, the children who will never be, the love that can never be shared. For this, you ask to make amends. There are no amends for your actions, and so it shall always be."

Rmah listened carefully. "I have expressed my regrets for our past actions. I cannot do any more."

"The Guild has decided, however, that there may be an advantage to us to continue the deleelinosh trade."

Rmah hesitated. Was this another tactic, or were they really ready to discuss terms?

"We have already shown our interest in this."

"We will permit one landing every six-day, no more. We will load the deleelinosh in the storage tanks and preserve them until your vessel arrives. No Violet may leave the landing area, and none may remain after the cargo is loaded."

"This is acceptable to me. However, we would prefer to maintain a small presence in the landing area."

The female would not budge. *"There will be no Violets on the surface. This is a test for you, leader, that you will keep your promises."*

"What kind of payment would you require for the product?"

"As I said at the outset, we are a simple people. We have no need for weapons or vessels to fly to other worlds. Your roads are unlike anything we have ever seen, hard and easy to traverse. We would ask to know how this was done."

Concrete? Rmah thought to himself. *All they want is concrete?*

"We can provide that." Rmah thought for a moment. "But so that you can produce it without our help, we may need to send experts, individuals who can show you where to find the required materials and how to prepare them."

The Zed group held a small discussion, then responded:

"Unarmed teachers as you describe may come for short periods. We also note the quality of your glass and metals. We would ask to improve our abilities in these areas as well."

Rmah found himself impressed with this council. They were asking to improve their lives but not overturn what had to be thousands of years of established culture.

"We will provide these. If the council permits, I may consult with the humans, who are more advanced than we are in some of these subjects."

Again, the group discussed this among themselves.

"This is acceptable. We have doubted the Vooman from the start, but they have proven to be honest and worthy of our trust. They have killed no one and prevented additional grief."

"When might the first shipment be ready?"

"Three suns from now. After that, you are to arrive every six-day."

"I will notify my superiors. I do not believe I can have a cargo ship here in three suns. With your permission, I will need to remain on the surface another sun to make these arrangements. Communication over such long distances takes time."

"We will permit you to remain two suns for this purpose. You are to present yourself here tomorrow to inform us of your plans."

Rmah was a scientist, a technocrat of sorts, but he found it still grated on his nerves to take orders from another species. He'd gotten used to the humans' direct manner, but this was much worse. He was being spoken to like a newhatch still wet from the egg.

"I will be here," he responded.

The natives turned and walked back north without another word. Rmah watched them go for a moment, then headed back to the headquarters to report to his maleParent that he had succeeded, and far beyond what he might have hoped. What the natives wanted was cheap for the benefit it would provide the SD, and the Home population in general. It was a major victory for them both, and he was sure Glur Woe Segt would reward him for it.

Late that afternoon, Kutah and Tefin relaxed on the hill, watching an approaching storm as it slowly covered the setting sun. Kutah's thoughts were of Udoro, where she was, and what she might be doing at that moment. He tried very hard, without much success, to not think about her time with another male. It was required, he knew, but still his heart burned.

Tefin missed his sister, too, but for him, life would go on as usual, except that there would be no more dangerous adventures spying on the Violets.

Their talk was interrupted when a voice from the road called Kutah's name.

"Kutah? Riaghe Kutah?"

The voice was unfamiliar, and from the accent, someone not of his clan. A southerner, perhaps.

Kutah turned from the sunset. "I am Kutah."

"Good afternoon, Riaghe Kutah. I am Giasso Hetah, and I bring you an invitation from Giasso Afoto to reproduce with her."

Kutah came down the small rise to stand across from Hetah. "And who is Afoto to you?"

Hetah handed over the writing, and Kutah read the fine script and expressive language of the invitation. He found himself wondering what Udoro had written to her candidates, if it was as emotional and intense as what he held in his hand.

"I am only a messenger, Riaghe Kutah. Your name is known all over the south. Giasso Afoto would be honored if you would accept."

Tefin came to stand next to him, reading the invitation over his shoulder. "It is most sincere, Kutah. Udoro has gone, so this is a good time for you."

Kutah looked at his friend, then refolded the invitation and handed it back to Hetah. "I decline."

Hetah could not hide his surprise. "Afoto is highly prized in our clan, Riaghe Kutah."

"If she is so highly prized, then there are many others who will accept her invitation. I decline."

Hetah placed the invitation back in his tunic. "I must ask, why do you reject her? She will want to know."

Kutah walked to the base of the hill as Hetah was speaking. He answered without turning around. "I decline, Giasso Hetah. My decision has nothing to do with Afoto. There is nothing more to be said."

Kutah turned and entered his home, closing the door loudly behind him.

Hetah looked at Tefin. "I do not understand."

Tefin looked at the closed door, then back at Hetah. "For Kutah, there is only one female, and she left him only yesterday to repro. Please assure Afoto that Kutah means her no offense. I am sure she will find an acceptable partner."

"Such as yourself, Riaghe Tefin? Your name is well known to us, too."

Tefin waved off the thought. "That would be for Afoto to decide, would it not? I am not one to simply take Kutah's place."

"But I perceive, if I may say, that Riaghe Tefin would not decline such an invitation?"

"We take these as they come, Hetah. You know that as well as I do. Should Afoto, or any other female, issue me an invitation I would, of course, consider it. I can say no more."

"I will carry Kutah's message, and yours, back to Giasso Afoto. She will be disappointed."

"I understand, Hetah. But, again, I beg her take no offense at Kutah's decision. He is grieving and cannot see past his own heartache. He could accept no invitation."

"Perhaps, her timing is inconvenient? Perhaps, she could try again later?"

Tefin looked again at Kutah's closed door. "That is for Afoto to decide. But if she were in my clan, I would advise her to look elsewhere."

"I appreciate your honestly, Tefin. I will convey your thoughts to Afoto."

After Hetah left, Tefin thought about knocking on Kutah's closed door but instead walked back up the hill to the fading sunset and approaching storm. His friend was suddenly different, his mind altered by the loss of Udoro. Tefin saw many solitary sunsets in his future, at least until Udoro returned and made Kutah whole again. He thought it foolish that Kutah would decline a repro out of grief. Or, was it spite? Either way, he could only decline so many times before the invitations would stop coming. Despite what he had said to Hetah, Tefin himself would never decline. He considered it part of his duty to the society, and twenty or more snows with a female partner would surely be better than those same snows alone.

As the clouds moved overhead, he could smell the rain in them. He stepped carefully down the slope and went home.

ISC Fleet HQ Plans Division
Ft. Eustis, VA
Monday, March 18, 2080, 0800 EST (1200 UTC)

Carol returned to work in FleetPlans feeling better about herself, with a clearer understanding of what had happened during the war. As she came into work that Monday, Commander Miller called her in.

"How are you feeling, Commander Hansen?" Carol was taken back by both the kindness in her voice and the respectful nature of her address. She had never heard that from Miller.

"I am better, ma'am. Ready to return to work."

"Good. You have a lot of work ahead of you."

"What, exactly, did you have in mind, ma'am?"

"After your call last week, CINC held a meeting Friday afternoon with the Dean of the Command School and me."

Carol felt a dread grip her stomach. Her performance at the Deep Space Command School had been, well, less than stellar. In fact, she'd been terrible. The nightmares and lack of sleep had seriously degraded her ability to concentrate. She had resigned herself to the likelihood that she would be tossed out on her ass, her career permanently scarred.

"Yes, ma'am?"

Miller smiled sightly. Carol hadn't ever seen her smile, and when she did, her face was transformed, becoming nearly human.

"You're going back to school, Carol, full-time until you catch up. Once you're up to date on your coursework, you'll come back to working here half time."

It took Carol a few seconds to form a reply. She was shocked that Miller would agree to such a thing.

"Thank you, Commander. I appreciate the second chance."

"Thank the Dean. It was his idea."

It was almost too much to accept. "And you, ma'am?"

"I was hoping he would suggest something so I would not have to. Better the school comes up with the idea instead of me telling the crusty old admiral how to run his ship."

"Thank you, Commander."

"Get going, Hansen. From what he said on Friday, it'll be a few weeks before we see you around here again."

Carol collected her NetComp and left Plans. But before heading over to the Command School, she stopped in FleetIntel and found Fiona Collins in her office.

"Hello, Carol! Welcome back."

"Thank you, Admiral. Do you have a moment?"

"Of course."

Carol dropped her coat and NetComp on an unused chair and sat down across from Fiona. "I'm worried about David. I haven't seen the daily intel summary since I've been on leave, but I thought you might be able to fill me in on how they're doing."

Fiona smiled as she lifted up her NetComp. "Actually, I just got an update from Evans."

"Really? Good news, I hope?"

"Yes, very good news, in fact. They headed off the battle between the Zeds and the Preeminent, and now the two sides have come to an agreement."

"Agreement? On what?"

"The Zeds are going to supply the fish the Preeminent have been taking, for a price. They're figuring out schedules and payment and whatever, but it looks good. Evans says the Zeds are hard bargainers."

"So, you think they'll be coming home soon?"

"Evans said something about remaining three days. If we assume that, I'd expect *Cobra* back here in about thirty days."

"That would be nice," Carol said wistfully.

"How are you, Hansen? I saw you're off the medical leave list."

"I was having a hard time with acceptance, but I think I understand things better now. I'm fine."

Fiona looked at her with sympathy. "But you miss Powell."

"Guilty."

Fiona looked at her for a second, then smiled. "Meet me at *The Drive*, nineteen hundred, last booth on the left. I'll buy."

Carol smiled and shook her head. "No alcohol for me, Admiral. I'm off that for a while."

"So, have a club soda or a ginger ale whatever. Just come out. I'll buy dinner, just this once."

Carol's first instinct was to say no, and remain at home alone, but in a moment, she changed her mind.

"Yes, Admiral, some company would be nice."

"For me, too. It's tough to find a good bar companion with Joanne gone. And once you get there, you'll have to forget I'm an admiral, OK?"

"Yes, ma'am, I'll sure try."

"Great! See you then, Carol."

Carol left Fiona's office and went on to the commissary for lunch. She'd been skipping too many meals before she went home, and Perez's recovery plan included getting back to more healthy habits. It was a push for her sometimes, but it came a little easier every day as her spirit returned.

She sat alone near the back of the cafeteria until two of the younger officers from Plans asked to join her. She could see the trepidation in their eyes as they asked, and she smiled and invited them to sit down. They had a pleasant conversation about the division and the projects they were working on. They relaxed as they talked, beginning to see Carol as a person and not the legend she had become for some. She saw in them the same feelings she herself had first experienced on *Liberty* when she sat with Nicolai Roskov and talked about Navigation. But now, she was the old veteran, and they were her new students, whether she wanted them or not.

She did.

The Drive Pub and Bistro
Just off Ft. Eustis, VA
Monday, March 18, 2080, 1900 EST

Carol found Fiona ensconced in her usual place: the last booth on the left in the bar. It was the same booth she had shared two years before with Joanne Henderson and Ben Price. As Carol approached, she set down her nearly empty Manhattan and smiled.

"Hello, Carol."

"Good evening, ma'am. Thanks for the invitation." Carol looked around as she sat down. "This is a really interesting place."

"Not been here before?"

Carol shook her head. The waiter arrived and she ordered a ginger ale with grenadine.

"Doctor's orders?" Fiona asked gently.

"No, ma'am, just my own discipline. I need to work some things out before I drink again."

"Enough of the formalities, Carol. It's just us in here."

"That'll be hard."

Fiona smiled. "Price had the same problem, but he got over it eventually."

"You were very close to him, weren't you?"

"Yes. Maybe too close, in a way."

"Oh?"

"Nothing romantic, no, nothing like that, but I just came to love his character, his intelligence, and how he carried it." Fiona took another sip, then leaned into the table. "Some people, you can just tell they know they're smart, and they like to show it off. He always offered whatever he had with a grin or a joke, and you never felt like he thought himself any better than anyone else."

The waiter brought Carol's drink and a fresh Manhattan for Fiona. They put off ordering dinner for the moment.

Carol took a sip and then refocused on Fiona. "I think I only spoke to him once or twice, but I recall thinking how nice he was and how natural it seemed for him. Some people can be nice when necessary, but it's not really who they are."

"Ben Price was a good person, Carol, all the way to his core. I saw it. "

"Captain Henderson took him with her to *Intrepid*, right?"

"In here, she's Joanne. But yes, she wanted him for the Intel position."

"Was there an issue with the previous intel officer?"

"Not really. She just wanted her own person. Not many people know what a mess *Intrepid* was after picket duty, and she wanted to have at least one person she could have absolute trust in, especially with a war on."

"Understandable. So, that's how he met Natalie."

As Fiona's eyes filled, she shook her head, trying to control the emotion rushing forth. "Yes, as they used to tell it, they found romance in the ass end of a Sentinel."

They laughed briefly before Carol turned serious again. "If I could ask, how does Cap —, uh, Joanne, feel about that? Obviously, they were close, too."

"She grieves him just like the rest of us. It's maybe a little harder for her than me, but aside from Ben, Natalie is the real casualty of that event."

Carol sipped her drink. "I first met her on Beta Hydri. Such a warrior! It was almost fun fighting next to her."

"Yes, and I think she's dealing with her grief in the same way: head-on. She's getting on with her life after Ben, but not denying or trying to avoid the pain."

"I admire her so much."

Fiona looked directly at Carol. "Well, I've heard her say the same about you."

Carol frowned. "Not sure I'm really up to that."

Fiona leaned forward on her elbows, her drink in her hands. "I want to say something, Carol, and I want you to hear me out."

"OK. But I thought this was a social occasion."

"It is. But first, I want you to know it's not your fault, Carol."

Carol stared at her for several seconds before speaking. "I'm sorry?"

"It's not on you that everything didn't work out like you wanted. They did the best they could. You did the best you could. You lived, they died. That's just how it is in war."

Carol's posture stiffened. "Doesn't feel that way to me. I could have —"

"What?" Fiona interrupted. "What, exactly, could you have done?"

Carol, surprised at her own willingness to open up to Fiona, paused to look off into the distance, somewhere beyond Randy Forstmann's close-up picture of Pluto hanging on the wall behind the bar.

"I'm not sure. Something."

Fiona shook her head. "No. There was nothing you could have done differently. That's something good commanders struggle to accept—that despite your best efforts, you couldn't save everyone."

Carol looked at the door. "I'm not sure this was a good idea."

Fiona smiled. "Hear me out, Carol." When Carol looked back at her, she continued. "Seems to me you hate the fact that everything didn't work out as perfectly as you'd hoped. And you're disappointed in yourself for that."

"I have never thought of myself as perfect."

"Yes, of course not, but that helplessness, the lack of control even when in command, it haunts you. I've known Connor Davenport for a long time, and I can tell you it certainly haunts him."

After a moment, Carol responded, "I had not thought of it that way."

Fiona nodded again. "At some point, circumstances and the actions of others are beyond our abilities to control or counter. When that happens, people die. It's just that simple."

"I have to ask, why are we having this conversation? I thought this was just a couple of drinks and dinner. I didn't expect an inquisition."

Fiona thought for a moment, twirling her glass in her hands. "Because you are as bright as they say. You have the potential to be not just a good ship's captain, but a great one. It would not surprise me to see you as Ops or CINC someday. And I will not have that talent diminished because you're not as perfect as you would like to be. Do the best you can, Carol, and trust that your best will be enough."

Her words echoed back to what Alex had said to her right after Terri Michael was killed, and she was thrust into the command chair: *"You do what you always do, Carol. You do the best you can, which is better than most."* She'd not believed it then, but maybe there was something in what Alex had said. Maybe.

Carol shook her head. "Were I to accept that, it would feel like an insufferable conceit to me. David has always said, even back at the U, that overconfidence was just another name for death."

"Humility is a virtue, to be sure, but not when it keeps you from acting when you should act. We should all have a healthy internal skeptic keeping ourselves honest, to be sure, but that honesty must be objective and not self-limiting. Your performance on *Antares* and *Sigma* was stellar. There is nothing you did in either of those commands that I would have done differently, except one."

"Alpha Mensae."

"Yes, I would not have gone to the surface with the Marines. Your first loyalty must be to your ship and crew."

Carol shifted in her seat and nodded. "CINC agrees. He yelled at me for fifteen minutes."

Fiona nodded. "And yet, he sent you to command school and gave you a career-track assignment in Plans. He's seen plenty of well-intentioned but impulsive choices by his officers, especially the young ones. You'll know better next time."

"I was there at the start. I knew this would be the end, and I wanted to see it through."

"Completely understandable."

Carol paused, then looked across to meet Fiona's eyes. "But I should have stayed with my ship."

"These are the sacrifices we have to make as leaders. We can't always do that which we would like or would give us some kind of personal satisfaction."

"Yes, I see that now. Still, the ship was in good hands."

"That's not enough. It should have been in *your* hands."

Carol nodded reluctantly. "Yes, ma'am."

"Enough of this for now. Whatever happens, we must take whatever lesson is there to be learned, then set the rest aside and keep going. We must always keep going and do better the next time."

Carol looked away, swallowed hard, then looked back to Fiona. "Will there be a next time?"

Fiona smiled quickly, inclining her head slightly. "Oh, yes, there will. I expect after Plans you'll get an XO tour under the right captain, then, yes, there'll be another ship for you."

Carol nodded slightly, looking into her glass. "That would be nice. It's good to be here, near my family and David, but I would not want to stay ashore forever."

"Actually, I think that will be a healthy challenge. But forgive me for ambushing you. I just wanted to tell you how I felt."

"Yes, ma —, um, Fiona. I'm not used to being confronted like this."

"I believe in you, Carol. So does CINC. You won't let us down." She turned to look for the waiter. "But right now, I'm famished."

Cobra
En Route Earth
Thursday, March 21, 2080, 0800 UTC

Her mission completed at Zeta Doradus, Joanne Henderson turned *Intrepid* for home. She hoped for a quiet transit with no side-trips or detours. Her crew had been deployed more than any other ship in recent months, and she wanted to get them some rest and time at home.

Similarly, as soon as *Cobra* slipped into FTL, Rich Evans ordered three rest days for the surface team. Their sleep schedules had been badly mangled by the short days and nights on Zeta Doradus (b), and he wanted to give them time to recover. Even on *Cobra*, the fastest vessel in the Fleet, it would be a long ride home, and there would be plenty of time for debriefs and discussions.

This morning they sat well-rested around Center Console, Evans in the center operations position, David, Jack, Greg, and Gabrielle around the outside. It was early, just after breakfast, and each of them carried in an oversized mug of their preferred caffeine delivery beverage.

"First off," Evans began, "do we accept this immortality claim? Are they really as old as they say?"

"I think they are," Gabrielle answered immediately, "but this isn't some metaphysical immortality. They can die — the Preem killed hundreds. But, other than some accident, they don't age at all."

"So, no physical deterioration over time? How is that possible?"

"Genetic engineering," David answered. "They've been, um, modified, such that their DNA doesn't lose its activity over time."

Jack Ballard nodded his agreement. "I've been digging through the medical references on board. The current theories of aging all involve some kind of damage accumulating in DNA until at some point the cell can't replicate itself and the line dies off. If the Zeds have been modified in some way to prevent this damage, they would be essentially immortal."

"Amazing," Gabrielle said quietly. "But what about their reproduction? They're sterile until they eat some kind of fruit? Did I hear that right?"

"Yes, that's what they told David. It's an interesting adjustment," Jack said.

"If they're young and functional forever, imagine the number of children any given couple could produce. Even at one every decade, in ten thousand years, that's a thousand offspring. Who, of course, then start having babies of their own, and, wow...You know, I should do the math on this..."

"Don't bother," David said, smiling. "It's gonna be a massively unsupportable number."

Evans laughed. "Yes, it would be. So, they were also modified, to use David's term, to only be fertile when a specific nutrient is present? That's more amazing than immortality if you ask me."

David looked over at Commander Evans. "These 'Shepherds,' as the Zeds call them, must have been a much older, much more advanced species. I mean, genetic engineering at this level of detail? That's stuff we're not yet able to do in higher forms. And then, there's the whole terraforming thing."

"Terraforming?" Gabrielle asked.

"Yeah, the Zeds can't be from Zeta Doradus. It's far, far too young for that. I mean, it's less than a billion years old. It shouldn't even have slime molds, let alone higher forms. Even the plants and other animals *must* have been imported."

"Likely from the same place, wouldn't you think?" Jack asked.

"It would make sense."

David was suddenly head-down on his NetComp, typing and swiping furiously.

"Powell?" Evans asked.

"Fifteen thousand years, sir. They said they'd been there fifteen thousand years." He spoke again, still pounding the NetComp. "A supernova might simmer for a thousand, right? Before it goes off?"

"You're taxing my memory of astrophysics."

Jack moved to look over David's shoulder. "No, sir, that's close."

Gabrielle looked up from her notes. "That number is not quite right, David. They said they had fifteen thousand years of recorded history."

"Oh, OK, right, I remember that now," David said without looking up.

"Kepler?" Jack asked David.

"Yeah. Timing's right, anyway."

"Gentlemen?" Evans asked, more amused than annoyed by their mind-meld approach to research.

"Supernova 1604, sir. Seen by Kepler in that year and later named for him. It was fourteen thousand light-years away, so it would have actually occurred about, um, twelve-thousand four-hundred years BCE. Add a thousand or two for the prodromal phase, and you're hitting pretty close to the right number."

"But, and this I do remember, supernovae like that one are from binaries where the stars get too close. The white dwarf starts eating the outer layers of the companion, and it doesn't really end well."

"Yes, sir, correct. But even that phase would take time, a long time from our perspective, and if there was a habitable planet in the system, there might well be time for a higher race to locate and rescue a culture like the Zeds."

Evans whistled quietly as he did arithmetic in his head. "Fourteen thousand light-years. That's twenty-five *years*, *years*, even in this ship."

Gabrielle smiled. "Plenty of time for a little genetic manipulation, don't you think?"

David shrugged. "Maybe."

Jack returned to his chair. "But it's more complicated than that, right? You have to know where to take them, and since Zeta Doradus is so young, you have to terraform the place before they get there."

"Which has to take hundreds, maybe thousands of years," David responded.

"More, probably," Jack said. "The logistics alone are mind-boggling."

There was a long moment of silence before Gabrielle spoke. "If we accept all this," she said, "then there is a massively advanced race out there somewhere."

Evans nodded. "Yes, one who specializes in saving endangered species. Am I the only one who equates the Zed's Shepherds with the Preeminent's Guardians?"

"No, sir," Jack answered, " I've been thinking the same thing. But, the Preem have been on Alpha Mensae for something like a hundred thousand years."

"Longer, I think," Evans answered. "But if there is a race like we're saying, that much time doesn't seem to be a problem."

"I'm somehow a lot more nervous now than I was at breakfast," Gabrielle said. "Who are they and what might they want?" The group rewarded her with a laugh.

Evans nodded. "I'm nervous, too, Doctor Este. I would not want to encounter such a race in deep space. I don't know what I would do."

"Don't worry. Commander," David added. "They'll know."

Jack looked over at Evans. "Besides, Commander, if they don't want to be found, we'll never find them or any evidence of them. The only way we'll ever encounter them is if they want us to."

The debrief broke up, each participant moving on to write their own reports for Fleet. They would meet again tomorrow to share their findings and exchange feedback, and suggest corrections. Evans loved these sessions, watching such intelligent people working hard to make each other smarter.

After everyone else had left, David remained alone in the Operations Center, taking some time to consider the star chart on the large aft-wall display. He'd joined the Fleet at least partly for adventure, to see the places few people would ever see. He was fine protecting the supply and trade routes that were opening up around the nearby stars, but for David, that was just a necessary sideshow to what he really wanted to do. He wanted to explore, to learn, to understand. But now, there was something he realized for the first time he might not be able to understand.

The Fleet had not, in any real sense, been ready for war. They'd been lucky, David thought, to come up against an opponent as arrogant and tactically unsophisticated as the Preeminent. If they had encountered a species even half as experienced as themselves, it would have been a much longer and bloodier conflict. They might well have lost.

He wondered as he stared at the stars where this ancient mystery race might be from and, more critically, where they might be right now. They knew about Earth, so it seemed inconceivable that they would not know about humanity. For a reason he couldn't quite identify, that thought threatened him even more than it did Gabrielle.

He left the Operations Center to prepare his report, too, carrying with him an uncomfortable and unfamiliar feeling that somehow, he was being watched.

ISC Fleet Shuttle Landing Facility
Ft. Eustis, VA
Sunday. April 14, 2080, 1145 EDT (1645 UTC)

Carol was up early. Actually, she had slept very little. The anticipation of David's return kept her mind spinning most of the night. As she got up to dress, she was reminded of the day, now almost two years ago, when he had returned from star base Tranquility II after saving what was left of *Sigma* and her crew. That day, she reminded herself that she was all in with David, that there would be no hesitations, no half-measures. She was going to let him know everything she was feeling, and she wasn't going to let go until he understood. She'd dressed for the part, too, carefully picking what she thought brought out her best features.

Today, though, tight polo shirts and shorts were out. It was cool this morning, so she'd do the best she could with a pair of jeans and whatever else she could find that still fit. Carol was pretty sure David would not care what she wore as long as she was wearing it.

Several times she checked the Fleet status on her NetComp. Yes, *Cobra* was back in orbit. Yes, the first shuttle, which David promised to be on, was due at the Shuttle Facility just before noon.

She did her makeup last, a little more than usual, following what Lori Rodgers had done for her a few weeks before. She couldn't bear walking all the way to the old airfield and back, so she took out her phone and rented an ASV. It arrived in plenty of time, and she quickly sat inside and dictated her destination.

It felt like she had waited an eternity before the long, dark shape of the shuttle materialized out of the slowly breaking overcast and settled silently to the ground. She was ready as David stepped off the last stair, suddenly wrapping her arms around him, her face pressed into his. They stood there for a long moment, rocking slowly back and forth until she let up just a little.

Which was good, because with her grip on him, David was about to pass out. "Haven't we played this scene before?" he asked quietly.

"Yes," she said through tears. "And I never want to play it again."

They walked to the ASV and let it take them home.

Later they sat lazily on their patio, enjoying an unusually warm, sunny afternoon. It was a small thing, nothing like the expansive deck at Ron Harris' place, but it was quiet and comfortable. Carol poured their drinks and sat down next to him on the love-seat glider they had bought right after the wedding.

"You seem yourself again," David said.

Carol sighed, closing her eyes as she let out a deep breath. "Yes, I am, but this self is a little different than the girl you left behind."

"How so?"

Carol leaned back, eyes still closed and face raised to the sky. "This one knows she can only do so much. This one knows that sometimes, as Fiona said to me, you can do everything right, and it still won't work out."

David took a long sip of his Scotch, then set it down. "So now it's *Fiona*?"

Carol sipped her drink and looked at David. "Only in the bar. She really helped me, but wow, she can be blunt when she wants to be. This version of me also knows there is a lot more work to do. I'm still seeing Perez twice a week."

"Good." David saw a chance to change the subject, and in doing so, take the pressure off Carol. "Rmah passed the Zeds' test. Sneaky smart folks, those ten-thousand-year-olds."

Carol brightened. "That is just too crazy! You think they're actually that old?"

"No reason to doubt it. Some are more like thirteen thousand. But their society deals with it in such a strange way...I mean...how do they manage to raise children with one partner, then leave and go back to someone else? The whole idea is just so foreign to me."

"You mean, like, alien?"

David laughed. "Uh, yeah, I guess so."

Carol thought about that for a moment, then looked over at David as they rocked gently back and forth. "Would you spend ten thousand years with me?"

"Yes."

"What, no question? No hesitation?"

David raised an eyebrow. "No. We are one, you and I. A human singularity. We've always known that, somehow, and nothing will ever change it."

She reached over and took his hand, entwining her fingers in his. "I do love you, Powell, I do."

David's eyes began to flow as she leaned over to kiss him, and the words he wanted to say stuck in his throat as he pulled her closer. He was home. She was there, safe, and back to herself. The moment was perfect, and he just wanted it to last for the rest of his life.

He ignored the buzz of his NetLink.

Revolt at Zeta Doradus

Appendix: Dramatis Personae

Name	Rank	Description
Ann Cooper	SLT	Deputy Chief, Fleet Intel
Asoon Too Lini		Preeminent Speaker of English
Ateah Gi Seba		Preeminent Speaker of 'Zed' language.
Carol Hansen	SLT	Our Heroine
Catherine Miller	CDR	New Chief of Fleet Plans. She was the Weapons Officer on *Dunkirk* during the war.
Chuck Anderson	SLT	Intel Officer on *Intrepid* after Ben Price's death
Connor Davenport	ADM	Fleet Commander (aka CINC)
David Powell	SLT	Our Hero
Denise Long	WO4	Inoria survivor, Reactor Officer on *Antares*
Eaagher Fita		Leader of the Seeker survivors
Elias Peña	CDR	*Resnick's* captain.
Fiona Collins	CPT	Chief of Fleet Intel
Frances Wilson		Senior Intel Analyst
Gabrielle Este		Archeologist. She was instrumental in understanding the Seeker culture at Beta Hydri.

Name	Rank	Description
Glur Woe Segt		Preeminent Principal Scientist, de facto leader of the Preeminent Society after the death of the Revered First.
Greg Cordero		Linguist who broke the Seeker language.
Jack Ballard	SLT	Chief Intel Officer, *Cobra*
Joanne Henderson	CPT	*Intrepid's* Captain
Liwanu Harry	1LT	Marine Officer, head of the detachment aboard *Intrepid.*
Natalie Hayden	SLT	Weapons Maintenance Officer on *Intrepid.* Along with Liwanu Harry, she and Carol led the Battle of Seeker Woods in S*ilver Victory.*
Patricia Cook	RADM	Chief of Fleet Operations
Peg White	CDR	XO of Sigma, which Carol commanded at the end of the Preeminent war.
Riaghe Kutah		Young Zed who Riaghe Wocos recruited to spy on the 'Violets.'
Riaghe Tefin		Kutah's best friend and Udoro's brother.
Riaghe Udoro		Kutah's love-match, Riaghe Tefin's sister.
Riaghe Wocos		Elder of the Riaghe village that Kutah and the rest live in.
Rich Evans	CDR	*Cobra's* captain.
Rick Court	LT	Carol's nasty ex-boyfriend from her days at Space Fleet University. Joanne Henderson

Name	Rank	Description
		fired him for incompetence when she took over Intrepid.
Rmah Teo Segt		Glur's maleChild, student, and co-conspirator
Sabrina Herrera	GSgt	Leader of the Recon Marine detachment on *Cobra*.
Scad Nee Wok		Preeminent Ship Commander. MalePair of Asoon Too Lini.

AFTERWORD

First off, I want to emphasize that Carol's PTSD experience is *fictional* and far from typical. Her symptoms are both exaggerated and simplified, and the timeline is compressed for dramatic purposes. Many people suffer from PTSD for years, often undiagnosed, and it can be debilitating for them and enormously frustrating for their families. That said, there is a lesson, I think, in a high-functioning individual like Carol, who seems to endure a harrowing experience just fine, only to later find themselves in serious trouble.

Again, I would not want anyone to think I have approached this issue superficially or without due consideration for real people trying to manage real disease. We should support their difficult paths and offer more than an expression of sympathy for their suffering when we can.

For the idea of a physiological immortality, I have to give a nod to my 90's evil pleasure, *Highlander*, both the movie and the series. This was my regular Saturday night the-kids-are-in-bed indulgence for several years. I must also acknowledge a very interesting but little-known movie, *The Man From Earth*, which explores some of this same territory on a much more limited basis. It is excellent science fiction, told without a single special effect. I must warn you that there are religious issues raised towards the end of the movie that many will find offensive. I did. But, like John Galt's long rant against religion near the end of *Atlas Shrugged*, I can set that aside and appreciate the quality of the larger work.

As always, my thanks to my beta readers: Chris, Dina, Erica, Jan, Kurt, Nancy, and Steve, plus my wife Carey and daughter Becky. As usual, they have saved me from some seriously red-faced embarrassment.

My editor Kim Karshner, again, kept me in line. I appreciate her expertise and understanding of these characters and this universe.

And, of course, I thank *you* for taking the time to read *Revolt at Zeta Doradus*. Please leave a review on Goodreads, Amazon, or wherever you purchased it. I enjoyed writing it and am already looking at ISC Fleet novel #5. Look for that sometime in 2022.

2022? Really? 2022? *Can I possibly be that old?*

Yep, I am.